Thyra

A Romance of the Polar Pit

Robert Ames Bennet

Thyra: A Romance of the Polar Pit

Copyright © 2012 by Indo-European Publishing

Contact:
IndoEuropeanPublishing@gmail.com

The present edition is a reproduction of 1901 publication of this work, produced in the current edition with completely new, easy to read format by Indo-European Publishing.

For an authentic reading experience, the Spelling, punctuation, and capitalization have been retained from the original text.

Cover Design by Indo-European Design Team

ISBN: 978-1-60444-612-8

IndoEuropean
Publishing.com
Los Angeles, CA, USA

Chapter I
From Above

Ice—ice on every side, north and south, east and west, as far the eye can see—not the broad, level floes of the Arctic Circle, with here and there a majestic berg towering skyward like some gigantic crystal cathedral, but a vast stretch of ponderous floe-bergs, ridged with jagged hummocks, their broken surface covered with snow, fast turning to slush under the blaze of the six months' sun. Here and there a narrow blue lane winds through the frozen wilderness, widening in places, closing in places, as the fragments of the great pack, separated by the spring break-up, drift south across the Polar Basin.

Such was the icy waste that had been our sole landscape for full eight months. In the fall of 1896, confident of success, we had started out across the Polar pack from our base camp on the north of Franz Josef Land. Never had a dash for the Pole been more carefully planned. Our equipment was as near perfect as money and experience could make it, and every member of our party was a trained athlete, thoroughly inured to Arctic travel. Lieutenant Balderston and his trusty negro sergeant, Black, each stood over six feet two, clear measure, while I myself could claim the negro's great girth and an inch more of height. As to Thord Borson, the Icelander, he was a veritable giant, seven and a half feet tall, and broad in proportion.

It was perhaps due as much to Thord's gigantic strength as to our good luck with the dogs that we covered a round three hundred miles of "northing" before the cold and darkness compelled us to go into winter quarters. We were fortunate, as well, in laying in a stock of bear meat sufficient to supply both ourselves and the dogs until spring.

The dreary months of twilight had passed with disheartening slowness, but the returning sun found us still cheerful and full of hope. Our one desire was to push on to the Pole. We had little doubt of reaching it. We need only duplicate our fall journey. But Fortune, never so fickle as in the Arctics, at last ceased to smile on us. Many of the dogs grew mad and died of that strange Arctic disease mistakenly called hydrophobia, and we had no more than started on from the winter camp when Balderston severely sprained his left ankle. As he could not walk, he was lashed to one of the sleds, and we struggled on as best we could across the terrible surface of the pack.

But the weather, too, turned against us. For weeks we had to lie under shelter while the spring storms raged over the frozen waste. Balderston's ankle improved very slowly; one after another the dogs continued to sicken and die; the floe-bergs became smaller in area, the hummocks higher more jagged, the drifts deeper. Still we struggled on, with dogged persistency, resolved to reach the Pole, or die.

Then at last came disaster, sudden and hopeless. After hardships and toil such as one cannot look back upon without a shudder, we had added another fifty miles to our northing. Almost spent, with only half a dozen dogs left, we yet faced the north, unshaken our purpose. But time had sped swiftly during our toilsome march. The spring had slipped by almost unnoted, and even while we vowed our firm resolve to continue onwards the end came.

In the spring break-up we were roused from sleep by a terrific crashing, and crawled out of our bags only in time to save ourselves as the floe beneath split open. We sprang safely away from the crevasse which yawned down into the icy-blue water, and Thord dragged with him the gun-sled. But the bulk of our outfit was engulfed and ground to powder as the walls of the crevasse crashed together under the shifting pressure of the pack.

The wreck of course compelled us to abandon all hope of attaining the Pole. The one object now was to regain Franz Josef Land alive. It was a problem—almost a hopeless one. We were out on the disintegrated pack, over three hundred and fifty miles from known land, without a boat to cross the lanes between the drifting floes, without food to last a fortnight.

But in the passing weeks, though our progress southward was almost imperceptible, no one starved. With the break-up of the pack, life returned to the frozen sea. The guns and ammunition saved by Thord stood us in good stead. After we had eaten the last scrap of dog meat, and were gnawing the bones, Balderston managed to shoot a bear. Long before that was devoured, another bear was killed, and, after it, two full-grown walruses. Then we rested easy. With food in abundance, we had only to await rescue by some venturesome whaler, when the drift had carried us down near Nova Zembla.

The 15th of June found us in the best of health, thanks to the fresh meat and frequent baths in the snow-water pools. For the sake of exercise we had spent much of our time in athletic contests, and each took turn-about in maintaining a constant patrol around the floe, on the lookout for game and a possible ship. But perfect as was our health, we were no longer the cheery, hopeful men who had fought their way northward against all the fearful odds of Polar travel. The bitterness of our failure had affected even Balderston, and we sadly missed his gay humour. Nor was our diet of raw flesh calculated to allay the irritation natural to men in our position.

Yet up to this time we had had no quarrels, none of those bickerings which occur so frequently in such parties, even during good fortune. I cannot remember a single harsh word spoken throughout all those eight months, and this notwithstanding Thord Borson's fiery temper. But on that June day the Icelander's patience at last stretched to the breaking point. Sergeant Black had come in from his four-hour watch, and halted before Thord, who sat staring morosely at the nearest hummock. Not noticing the latter's ill humour, Black saluted and held out the rifle, his face drawn up in the grin that the bullet-scar across his cheek made so grotesque.

"Yoah gahd, sah," he said, and he let the rifle slide down through his hand. In falling the weapon's stock glanced on a point of ice and struck sharply against Thord's foot. In an instant the giant was up, his eyes ablaze, his fiery hair and beard bristling, and his fist clenched to strike the astonished negro.

"Curse you!" he roared. "What do you mean by that, you black idiot?—You grinning dog!—Drop that gun, damn you, else I'll break your cursed neck."

"What's that?" cried Balderston, and we sprang up in amazement. We saw the Icelander striding forward, his gigantic frame quivering with fury, while the negro retreated before him, frightened and perplexed, but with the rifle at his shoulder. At the moment, his back struck against a hummock, and in sudden desperation, he sighted straight at the giant's heart.

"Halt!" he commanded. "One moah step, an' I shoot!"

"Thord!" I yelled, and together Balderston and I rushed forward to intervene. The giant turned at my cry, but we would have been too late. Seeing us coming, he swung about to rush upon Black. It meant death either to himself or to the negro—perhaps to both. For the moment, Thord was a madman—a Berserkir. But even as his great body bent forward to spring, the sergeant flung aside the rifle and pointed with both arms over the Icelander's head.

"Oh Lawd!—look!" he yelled. "A balloom!—a balloom!"

Around spun Balderston and I, and around spun Thord, sobered at the very height of his rage. Even as we turned a shadow

3

fell upon and our upraised eyes were met by a gigantic sphere, drifting majestically over the floe, not a hundred feet above us.

"A balloon!—it is a balloon!" shouted I, and we craned our necks in our efforts to catch a glimpse of the aeronauts. But not a sign of life could we see. No hand waved to us from the car, no curious face stared down to meet our upturned gaze.

"They're asleep!" roared Thord. "Signal them. Where's the guns?—_Ahoy, there! Ahoy_!"

The Icelander's hail could have been heard a mile; but the balloon drifted on without a word or sign from the car. The blood surged back into Thord's face and his eyes blazed with reawakened fury.

"Shoot! shoot!" he roared. "Riddle the scoundrels in their car!"

"No, no! Look at the guide-ropes. Capture her!" cried Balderston, and he dashed towards the three lines which trailed down from the balloon and far out on the floe behind.

"We can't stop her!" I protested. Nevertheless, I ran with the others, and together we seized the nearest line.

"She'll drag us over into the sea. We can't stop her," I repeated.

"Not by pulling," replied Thord; "but take a bend around a hummock—"

"There's the very one we want," cried Balderston. "Forward now, with a rush, and pass the slack about that ice-cake."

"Forward!" we shouted together, and in half a minute we had the line coiled twice around a block of ice that would have anchored a battleship.

"Good!" growled Thord, as we stood clinging to the line behind the coil. "We have her fast! I hope the shock will spill them."

"They'll at least wake up. See her sway!" I exclaimed. "Hold fast, all!"

"Fast she am, sah!" shouted Black, and we stared, panting and excited, up the tautened line to our monster prize. So swiftly had all occurred that we had lacked time for wonder; but now, scarce able to believe our good fortune, we could only stand open-mouthed and gaze in speechless fascination at the huge sphere, which tugged and swayed at the end of the line like a noosed bird striving to escape.

Presently another wonder came upon us. After all our shouting and the sudden stoppage of the balloon, there was yet no cry or signal from the car. If there were any aeronauts aboard, they must either be dead, or in urgent need of aid. The thought aroused me.

4

"What can a balloon be doing here?" I gasped.

"The car is empty, or I'm a liar," exclaimed Thord. "I'll bet the balloon broke loose before the party got aboard."

"Empty or not, we'll pull her down and see," replied Balderston.

"Ay; that's the word," assented the Icelander, and with a deft sailor hitch, he made fast the line. Then he turned frankly to Black and extended a huge fist—"I was mad just now, sergeant. Shake?"

The negro grinned his ghastliest, as he hastened to grip the proffered hand.

"All right, Mistah Thod,—all right. An' now, we'll haul in de captibe balloom."

"If we can," I added.

"We can, if there is no one aboard to cut her loose or shoot us," said Balderston.

"I don't expect that; but our weight may not be enough. It's a whale of a balloon."

"Our weight?—Why, John, we scale up over a thousand pounds between the four of us. If that's not enough, I can shin up one of the lines and open a valve."

"Ay; don't worry, doctor. We'll have her down, one way or another. Lend a hand, Black, with the sled. It'll be well to take our guns aboard whatever we do with the airship."

"Or she with us!—But it's a good idea, Thord, if we ever do get aboard."

"Come on, then. I'm not dying to linger on this cursed floe."

So the sled was loaded with the remains of our equipment, and we tramped across the floe, through the slush and over the hummocks, to a spot directly beneath the sway of the balloon. At a word from Balderston, Black knotted the rueraddies into a sling for the sled. Then, all together, we grasped one of the slack guide-ropes and began dragging it down, hand over hand.

"This is play," laughed Thord, as the coils of line piled up beneath our feet. But Balderston shook his head.

"Only wait a bit," he replied. "She's pulling harder already. I may have to climb for it yet."

"Not if we can help it," said I. "To lose gas, would mean a greater loss of ballast when we ascend."

"And probably the only ballast aboard is food and equipment," remarked Thord.

"Haul away, and save your breath," said Balderston.

The advice was well given, for with every yard of line we took in, our task became more difficult. As if this was not enough, we had to contend with the unsteady jerking of the line as the balloon swayed in the breeze. By the time three-fourths of the line had passed through our hands, even Thord longed for a rest. It was now that Balderston's sled sling came in good play. The line being hitched to it, we stepped upon the sled, and our weight, with that of the ammunition, served to anchor down the balloon.

Panting and exhausted, but full of joy, we stretched our aching arms and gazed up at our captive. The bevelled bottom of the wicker car swung less than thirty feet overhead, so that we could plainly see how it was splintered all along one edge, as though by some violent shock.

"Hello! Looks like our air-cart had been in a smash-up," remarked Thord.

"Rather!—Stand steady! I'm going aboard," replied Balderston, and up the line he went like a sailor. In a little while he was above the rim of the car; his hands grasped the bearing-ring, and he drew himself up into the little swinging gallery above the car. We waited impatiently for several minutes before his head reappeared over the bearing-ring.

"Empty house!" he shouted. "I've been in the car—down through a man-hole. But there's no one aboard. One of the valves is partly open, or she would never have sunk so low."

"Luckily for us. Now what do you say, boys,—shall we go for the Pole again?"

"Yes! For the Pole! We'll make the Pole yet. Hurrah for Doctor Godfrey!" roared Thord.

"De Pole!—de Pole! Jes' wait, honey; wese a-comin' dah!" sang Black, and he cut a pigeon-wing on top of the sled.

"Get a move on you, then," laughed Balderston, as he flung over a rope ladder.

"We're ready, Frank, you may bet," I replied.

But how about the sled?"

"One of you come up to help hoist. Two had better stay there to hold things steady. We don't want the car to swing around against a hummock and knock us out."

"That's true," I replied, and at a sign from me, Black climbed the ladder, with all five rifles and the two shotguns slung on his back. He was soon beside his lieutenant, and the two together speedily hoisted up every package of ammunition and the scant remainder of our equipment. Then, while Thord and I stood on the lower rungs of the ladder, Balderston swung himself up among the suspension ropes of the car and began ripping into the great canvas bags which held the stores. Soon he came upon a quantity of heavy

6

articles such as he thought we could best spare, and he cast out enough to raise Thord and myself five or six yards clear of the floe.

"All right. Come aboard," he called, and we scrambled hurriedly up the swaying ladder. With a shout, we clambered in over the bearing-ring and stood beside Black on the little platform, staring up at the great sphere of varnished silk and the confusing network of rope and cord. Neither Thord nor I had ever before been in a balloon, and we felt like fish out of water. Fortunately, however, both Balderston and Black had seen no little service in the army captive balloon manoeuvres, and were therefore better acquainted with aeronautics. Balderston was almost wild with delight. The moment we climbed aboard he cast over enough ballast to lift us fully thirty yards above the floe.

"All's well, boys!" he shouted. "It's a fair northerly breeze. We've only to let go and start on for the Pole!"

"Good-bye to the floe! We won't miss it! Let her go, Black," I cried.

"Done, sah!" shouted the sergeant, and he cast loose the anchor line.

"Hurrah!" cried Thord. The balloon had bounded forward like a hound from the leash. But our joy was short-lived. Checked by the weight of the two remaining lines, the balloon careened dizzily and swooped down into the very midst of the hummock crests.

Thord, with a sailor's quickness, leaped to the guide-rope bar, whirling an ice-axe, while Balderston up above slashed the lashings of a storage bag. Neither was an instant too quick. The car was dashing straight against the green crest of a hummock. I braced myselffor the shock. In another instant I expected to find myself whirling down upon the floe. Already I could hear the clash of the collision—when, in the snap of a finger, the ice crag dove beneath us and vanished. After it flashed the bag cut loose by Balderston. I saw the horizon begin to rise and widen, and the floes below us seemed to be falling into an immense basin. Even as I looked, the illusive sinkage became more swift, and I caught a glimpse of a slender object that whipped down through the air below the car. Then I understood. Thord had cut loose the second guide-rope before Black could interfere. We were ascending like a rocket.

Up, up, up we shot, balloon and car revolving like a bauble on a twisted string. We no longer gazed down on the falling ice world. We could only cling fast to the ropes and long for the whirling ascent to cease.

At last the seeming downward rush of air slackened, and the car revolved more slowly. But when, dizzy and gasping, we turned

7

our eyes to the barometers hanging on the suspension ropes, the indicators already pointed to an altitude of five thousand feet.

"Where is the valve-cord?" I cried. "Quick, Frank, open an escape valve!"

"No, no," he replied. "The ascent has stopped. Wait—what wind have we?"

"North!" bellowed Thord. "We fly due north, in the heart of a gale! See, the floes are sweeping beneath us like driving clouds."

"Fast express for the Pole!" shouted Balderston, and he swung down to join in the general handshake.

Chapter II
The Hyperborean

After the first whirling and swaying of our ascent, the balloon became perfectly steady, and swept along in the super-terrestrial hurricane like a bubble on a placid stream. We had only to close our eyes to imagine ourselves motionless on solid earth and in a dead calm. Relatively speaking, this last was indeed true; for swift as was the air-current in which we floated, it bore the balloon along with equal swiftness, so that to us there was not enough breeze perceptible to flicker a match flame. Yet, gazing down ward from our lofty height, we could see ourselves driving along at arrowy speed above that terrible ice pack whose hummocks and crevasses had put us to so much vain toil and hardship.

The thought of thus attaining in a few short hours what we had failed to win by months of strenuous exertions, keyed our spirits up to the highest pitch. Careless alike of cold, of hunger and of thirst, we stood immovable on the little platform, our eyes fixed steadfastly to the north. Mile after mile, the great ice-pack below glided away to the southward, while before us new stretches of the glittering waste rolled up above the distant horizon.

Hours passed—still we soared over the vast ice-world, cold and rugged and desolate as a lunar landscape. The winding lanes of blue water had long since disappeared, and nothing was visible to our straining eyes but the huge vault of heaven above us, and below, the illimitable fields of palaeocrystic floe-bergs.

Hunger at last roused the sergeant to action. He slipped down through the man-hole into the car, and in rummaging about, discovered an arrangement for swinging a little stove below the car's bottom. Presently the rest of us were drawn from our fascinated watch by a delicious aroma that wafted up around the car.

"Coffee!" cried Balderston, and all three of us sniffed the odour with an eagerness sharpened by months of abstinence.

"Black is cooking!" I exclaimed. "Think of eating civilised food again!"

"It makes my mouth water," said Thord. "Hurrah for the sergeant!"

"Ay; for at last he is doing something, while we stand here like fools," replied Balderston. "There must be instruments aboard, John, and it's high time we began taking observations."

"True enough," said I, and our idleness gave place to hurried action. As was to be expected, we found the balloon well provided with nautical instruments, and together we sought hastily to determine our latitude, our hearts beating with feverish anxiety.

"Half a degree beyond Nansen's farthest!"—we could scarcely credit our own words. Yet there was the calculation in black and white, plain before our eyes. All that the "Fram" had won by months and years of northward creeping, our balloon had covered and outstripped by a few short hours of eagle flight,—and still we swept on northward towards the great goal.

As the full realisation of our good fortune dawned upon us, we whirled our woollen caps overhead and yelled like madmen. Not until Black popped up from the car and set a savoury meal under our noses—and even then not until our hunger overpowered us,— did we cease shouting. After months of famine and raw meat, however, even the Pole itself could not long have kept our thoughts from Black's steaming dishes. We fell to upon them like savages, and no one stood on the common decencies of etiquette.

Each devoured what first came to hand, and the meal ended only when the dishes had been scraped.

As the last morsel disappeared in Thord's cavernous mouth, Balderston turned with a sigh of contentment, and took up the binoculars. Leisurely he leaned upon the bearing-ring and raised the glasses to sweep the horizon. From northeast to north they turned. Suddenly they stopped, and I saw Balderston's lithe figure stiffen as though he had received an electric shock. Then he whirled about, his blue eyes and fair face beaming like a bride groom's.

"Land ho!" he yelled.

9

In an instant we were beside him, striving to see with the naked eye what was barely discernible through the binoculars. Realising this, I reached for the glasses.

"What's it like?" I demanded.

"Black and cloudy."

"It _is_ a cloud! I can see it change shape. If that is your land—"

"Look at the lower edge."

"The lower edge?—A-h; mountains! I see them well now, with the dark background. Not large—but they can't be ice. They stand too high above the horizon."

Thord took the glasses and gazed long and steadily. When at last he handed them on to Black, he spoke with conviction "Never before have I looked at land so far; yet doubtless those are fells or jokuls. The black cloud is smoke from a burning jokul beyond."

"A volcano!"

"Why not?" said Balderston gleefully. "Think of warming our toes at a crater on the Pole! Now, old boy, we'll soon see what's what."

"Ay; and see about Jarl Biorn," muttered Thord.

"Jarl Biorn—what of Jarl Biorn?" I asked.

"Have you never heard the saga of Jarl Biorn and the storming of Jotunheim?"

"Did Snorre Sturleson write of him?"

"No, but my father had a very old writing in Runic which told of him. He was a jarl outlawed from Norway about the year 925. He came to Iceland, and organised a large expedition to colonise the fair land which, Biorn said, they should find by sailing due north. They thought that by storming the icy walls of the frost giants they would come to a rich and beautiful country."

"Did they turn back?" asked Balderston.

"Not one of all the ships that sailed. All vanished into the north, never to return."

"The first Arctic explorers. Poor fellow they head a long list of victims.

"Perhaps; and yet, Doctor Godfrey, is it not possible they may have escaped? All the early writers agree that the Icelandic climate was far milder in the tenth century than now. The East Greenland pack did not then exist, as it does to-day. I believe it possible that such bold and hardy sailors could have crossed the Polar pack even this far north, and if that land is habitable, we may find their descendants living about the Pole."

10

Balderston and I roared with laughter at this absurd fancy, and the lieutenant replied flippantly: "We may find white Biorn, Thord, warming his toes; but I have my doubts of any Biornsons."

"That is to be seen," the giant coolly rejoined. "I'm glad you two are well versed the Eddas. Biorn must have sailed before Christianity reached Iceland, so no doubt we will find the colony's descendants still worshippers of the Asir."

"I differ with you there," said I. "If we find them at all, I bet we find them—well packed in ice."

"As some one may find us a few centuries hence," suggested Balderston.

"_Ugh—_ don't mention it!" I exclaimed. "The mere prospect of stalking about over the Pole is chilly enough for me."

"On the contrary," said Balderston, "that prospect is warming to me. To think that a few short hours will bring us to the Pole!"

"Ay, or past it," replied Thord. "Another observation wouldn't hurt."

"True. Frank will see to it, while Black and I take stock of the balloon's stores."

With no little caution, the sergeant and I drew ourselves up among the suspension ropes and began overhauling the great storage sacks. Our work in such a position was of course hurried and cursory, and we had dropped down again upon the platform, when Balderston announced the result of his work.

"Eighty-seven degrees!" I repeated—"eighty-seven degrees!"

Then Thord's deep voice rolled out in triumph: "_Skoal, skoal_ to our Skidbladnir! She's truly an Eagle! Five hours more will bring us to the Pole."

"Hurrah! We's gettin' dah. Jes' see dem mountings grow!" shouted Black.

We turned to look. Already the mountains were visible to the naked eye, being distant about a hundred miles. The glasses showed that they formed a jagged chain of peaks, somewhat higher at the east end, and trending off to the left until lost in the iceblink. Over their crests, and backed by the black volcanic cloud, appeared a broad white plain, but whether a snow-covered plateau or a cloud-bank we could not at first determine. Minute after minute, however, the view became clearer, until Thord at last declared that the white plain was a sea of fleecy clouds, floating at an elevation somewhat higher than that of the mountains.

"Looks like a warmer temperature beyond the peaks, judging from the appearance of the clouds," observed Balderston, when the glasses passed around to him.

11

Thord's big face lighted with sudden humour.

"No doubt it's Paradise we're coming to," he said. "Some of you scientific fellows say that man first came from the north."

"Well, it may be the Garden of Eden," replied Balderston smilingly; "yet I look more for the other place,—fire and brimstone—a big crater, you know."

"We may find both," remarked Thord in a serious tone. "It may be the Niflheim of our heathen ancestors."

"Don't talk crazy!" said I. "All we'll find would pass for Iceland in winter dress."

"Maybe!" retorted Thord. "At any rate, we'll find nothing if we keep at this altitude. Beyond the fells, that cloud-sea blankets the whole earth. We must dip beneath if we wish to see anything."

"True," said Balderston; "and yet that would likely bring us into a cross-wind, or even a counter-current."

"We might try it," I replied. "If the wind is wrong, a sack or two of ballast will bring us up again. Being so near the Pole, we can well spare the gas and stores to survey this _terra incognita_. What do you say?"

"You're boss, doctor," said Thord laconically.

"Well, Frank?"

"All right. It will give us a chance to christen our discovery. I suppose there is no champagne aboard; but no doubt I can rummage out a bottle of brandy."

"Will we lan', sah?" asked the sergeant, who was already making arrangements for his next culinary triumph.

"Land?—Well, it is possible," I replied.

"Any Apaches up dis way, sah?"

"Hardly."

"Ay; but my Biornsons may have run wild," put in Thord, with his broad grin.

"Den I'll look to de guns, sah," said Black, taking the matter seriously. Without a moment's delay, he started in to inspect and load the guns with the utmost care. Thord and I grinned at each other, but we did not interfere. Neither of us expected to come across even the amiable Esquimo here in the heart of the Polar world; but we did look for white bears and Polar wolves.

Every minute of the balloon's swift flight was now bringing out to our view the details of the Polar range. Already the white slopes and wind-swept peaks stood out clear to the unaided eye. Beyond the first ridge, however, the veiling cloud-banks and the great black pall of volcanic vapours still concealed all that lay beneath. Only the ragged peaks and crags of the range, rearing up a

12

thousand feet above sea-level, stood out intensely black against the snow, and Balderston presently declared that they were basaltic.

"But what will the Pole be, lieutenant?" asked Thord in an anxious tone.

"The Pole?—Oh, the Pole is a shaft of pure gold, seventeen feet three inches high, with a nice place on this side for us to cut our names with our penknives."

"Am dat really true, sah?" cried Black, his eyes bulging.

"True as the world is flat," said I. "Unfortunately, gold is so heavy, we will be unable to carry any away with us."

"Besides, sergeant, the earth might get to wobbling, if we took off the end of its axis," added Thord.

"Some folks's tongues is wobblin' now," muttered Black, as he saw the Icelander's blue eyes twinkle. "We'll see no gole pillows dis side Johdan."

"'In the sweet fields of Eden—that's what we're coming to now," rejoined Thord.

"We're coming down, at any rate, and pretty soon, too," said I. "Get some ballast handy, in case of accidents. Frank, you can look to the valve, seeing you have run balloons before."

"All ready, whenever you say go," replied Balderston, and he took the cord of one of the escape-valves high up on the balloon's side.

"Ten minutes from now should bring us down just short of that long ridge," observed Thord.

"In ten minutes then," said I, and with quickened pulse, we waited the moment for our return towards Mother Earth. Eagerly we stared down upon the serrated peak crests while the last few miles of icefield glided beneath us. Six miles—five—four—three—two—

"Let her go!" I shouted.

I saw Balderston tug at the valve cord. Almost instantly a little gust of air fanned my face, like the waft of unseen wings. I hastened to gaze down over the bearing-ring. We were sinking—falling—with startling rapidity. It seemed as though some buried Titan was heaving mountains and floes alike swiftly upwards into mid-air.

Even Thord, fearless as was his nature, could not stifle a cry of alarm. But I found assurance in Balderston's cool bearing. Cord in hand, he gazed over at the upheaving mountains, with no other expression on his handsome face than quiet curiosity. Yet he was none the less fully alert to his duty, as I could see by his quick glances at the barometer before him.

13

Down, down we plunged, until Thord shouted that we should be dashed on the hummocks.

"Steady—steady!" commanded Balderston, as the Icelander heaved up a sack of ballast, and with that he closed the valve.

"You've dropped us too far!" I exclaimed, turning from the hummocks, in appearance so perilously near the car's bottom, to the mountain crests, which seemed to tower far above our level. But our eyesight was deceived by the sudden descent from the great altitude. Balderston only laughed at our dismay, and, after a little pause, held his barometer out to me.

"See," he said, "twelve hundred feet."

"Twelve hundred inches!" muttered Thord, and we stared down again at the hummocks. But already our eyes had begun to adjust themselves to the altered perspective, and we realised that Balderston was right. The balloon's descent had terminated at an altitude between eleven and twelve hundred feet.

The next question was the direction of the wind at our new elevation. Thord was first to answer it.

"Good," he said, closely eying the ice pack beneath us. "Our luck still holds—about a ten-knot breeze, bearing us towards the left end of that long ridge."

"We will just scrape over the crest," remarked Balderston; "then, clear sailing. I see no other range in below the cloud-bank."

"Those under mists obscure the view," I replied. "But if they hide any loftier peaks, we will have ballast ready, and can rise. If I'm right on the compass variation, we are heading only a little west of north, and the breeze is moderate enough to allow us a good view of the country in passing."

"Reglah 'commodashun train to de Pole," observed the sergeant, no less elated than the rest of us.

"Right you are, Black," replied his lieutenant. "But Station No. I is only a siding. I will heave out my brandy bottle, and we will not stop unless there are passengers."

"Better get your bottle ready," said I. "If it is the ridge you are calling your station, it is not over three minutes off—and you have a new land to christen."

"Don't worry; I have both liquor and name ready. But the honour should be yours, John."

"Too late," I replied, waving aside the brandy flask. "I couldn't think up a name in a week. Another minute, and we'll be alongside that top ledge—thirty feet clearance—just nice and handy for your throw."

"Ay; but hold on, lieutenant," cried Thord. "Give me a pull at the good stuff before you waste it."

A smile flickered across Balderston's face, only to give way to deep gravity. He raised the flask in his right hand, and at the moment we were about to cross the ridge, his voice rang out clear and solemn: "In the name of the United States of America, I take possession of this land; and I name it—_Polaria_!"

With the word, out whirled the flask of liquor, and all eyes turned to watch its flight. Out over the crest ledge it whirled, and we listened expectantly for the crash of shattered glass,—a crash which never came. Instead, our ears rang with a bestial howl, and up from the hollow where the bottle had fallen leaped the figure of a savage,—naked, squat, hairy, with the face of a gorilla.

For a moment the creature gaped at us in stupid wonder; then, with a yell of rage, he snatched a stone from the ledge beside him and hurled it at the balloon. The sack might as well have been tissue paper so far as offering any resistance to the missile. Through the lower bend the flint tore its way like a rocket, whirling out on the farther side with undiminished velocity.

But the injury did not pass unavenged. As I craned my neck to stare upwards, aghast at the havoc wrought, Black clapped a rifle to his shoulder and fired. The savage, who had stooped for a second flint, leaped high in the air and pitched forwards over the cliff. His death-shriek mingled with the echo of the shot, which came up from the mountain slopes like a thunder-clap.

"_Huh_—Apaches!" grunted the sergeant, and he slipped a fresh cartridge into his rifle.

"Apaches? Bah, worse!" cried Balderston, staring back at the brown, misshapen body on the snowy slope. "Makes one feel queer; eh? Lucky you took him so quick, Black. That stone fairly sizzled—a second, better aimed, might have done for one of us."

"Better aimed!—You say that, with those great rips in the balloon!"

"Don't worry, John. The holes are not so large as you fancy, and after the gas we've let out, they are too far down for much more to escape."

"Ay; we're sinking,—but as if we were in jelly," said Thord. "We can make an easy landing across this big hollow, on yonder slope. The friction of the guide-rope is already slackening our speed."

"Yet it will mean a big bump, unless we rig an anchor," said Balderston.

15

"Didn' fin' no ankahs. Yoh mus' hab cut dem loose, sah. But dah's plenty ob rope."

"Yes, here is a thirty-fathom line," I added. "With a sack of ammunition to catch in the rocks, it will be just the thing. There is another question, though—how about more savages? What a brute—"

"That's the word!" cried Balderston. "Why, the creature could have posed for a pre-glacial caveman. See any more, sergeant?"

"No, sah. Single track up de snow to de ledge. But dah might be a whole tribe ambushed ober in dose rocks, sah."

"If so, we'll have to clean them out, that's all. The balloon must be landed in one of the drifts between those rock heaps. We shouldn't waste any more ballast or gas than we can help."

"Drag is ready, such as it is," remarked Thord.

"Stand by, then, you and Black," I ordered. "Frank can manage the landing. Look to him for directions. I will keep watch for savages."

Placing both my express and Balderston's army rifle beside me, I took up the glasses, and as the balloon slanted down across the hollow, I scrutinised every rock and depression within a radius of half a mile. To all appearances, the slope was devoid of life, but I maintained my outlook with the closest attention. For all I knew, every heap of the frost-split basalt blocks might conceal a score of bloodthirsty beast-men. Having encountered one hyperborean on these Polar .Alps, it was not unlikely we should see more. I stood with down-pointing rifle as the balloon glided a few feet above the first outcropping ledges.

"No enemy!" I cried; but my sigh of relief choked short—we were drifting straight upon a second rock heap. Though checked by the friction of the guide-rope, our movement was yet swift enough to dash the car in flinders on the sharp edged basalt cubes. But already Thord and Black were lowering the drag. At the right moment Balderston gave the word to let go, and the balloon, relieved of the weight, bounded upwards.

"Steady now, steady," exclaimed Balderston, gripping the anchor line with Thord and Black. "Pay out—pay out, I say, else the jerk will snap the line, or pull us overboard. Good! it's caught fast. She's coming to. Now, hold her!"

Only Thord's giant strength saved all three from going overboard during the final tug; but somehow or other, our aerial craft was snubbed without too severe a jerk, and the last fathom of the anchor line was at once knotted to the bearing-ring. "Well done!" I exclaimed.

The balloon, lying over before the pressure of the breeze, swayed gently from side to side above promising snowdrift. At once Balderston drew himself up above the bearing-ring, and, securing the necessary materials, climbed into the netting to mend the holes torn by the stones. We watched him until he was at work on a patch for the hole to windward. Then we divided our time between eying the nearest ledges and gauging our descent upon the snowdrift.

Steadily but gently we sank as the leaking balloon sagged under its load. The loss of gas was now very slow, and it was some time before the car's bevelled bottom broke through the crust on the drift and settled in a bed of the loose dry snow beneath.

Chapter III
The Valkyrie

"At last," said I—"we have arrived!"

"Yes; thank heaven!" answered Thord. "This plaguey car is cut too small for me. I'd as soon be a sardine for the trip back. I've just been longing for a good stretch, and here goes," and he laid hold of the bearing-ring to vault out.

"Stop!" I yelled, none too soon. The giant paused, surprised. Then the truth flashed upon him, and he glanced quickly about at the barren slope and then skyward.

"Thank you, doctor," he said huskily, his face a shade less ruddy than usual. "This is not a pleasant station to stop at alone—with a horde of my Biornsons, like as not, sunning themselves on the peaks around."

"Yes; I'm afraid we must keep you snug aboard. Better a cramp than a freeze."

"That's all right for you who can stretch out on the platform. I'll have to dangle my legs through the ropes. I'd give anything to stretch them on the ground."

"Huh—pull de rope inboa'd den."

The solution to his difficulty was so simple that Thord paused to kick himself before laying hold of the guide-rope. Black and I took the line behind him, and, hauling together, we soon had the platform full of the coils.

"Hold," I said. "We certainly have enough aboard."

"Not yet, doctor. Black will want out, to use his stove. He can't light it here so near the balloon's neck; but we might as well have a meal while we wait here."

"Shuly, sah," assented the sergeant.

"How are you making out, Frank?" I called. "Will you be much longer?"

"Just finished one,"-came the cheery reply, and Balderston swung down to pass under the balloon's neck and ascend to the opposite hole.

"You're in for a tough job now," remarked Thord.

"Sure!" replied Balderston, and clinging to the netting cords with hands and feet, he climbed up and out under the overhang of the great sack. It was a feat to make a sailor dizzy; but the lieutenant reached the hole in safety. Hooked fast in the netting, he hung suspended head down, like a fly on a swaying ceiling, and started in on his half-hour's job with serene assurance. The danger and difficulty of his position only served to stimulate his venturesome spirit.

"What a man, doctor! You couldn't find many to whistle while head down."

"You would growl, either end up, eh?"

"So would you, with this cursed rope. It catches back there."

"'Nuff boa'd now foh you."

"Ay—but yourself, Black?"

"We don't want any more coils inboard. There's hardly room to stir now. You get out, Thord, and fetch some of those basalt blocks. Four or five would let us all out."

"All right," said the Icelander, and swinging over, he let himself down knee-deep in the drift. But he held cautiously to the rim of the car, lest we should have miscalculated the weight of the guide-rope coils. Greatly to his relief, the car merely stirred in its bed, and he at once left it to wade through the snow to the nearest rock heap. Swinging up with ease one of the square black cubes that could not have weighed less than two hundred pounds, he waded back and laid it on the platform. A second, no less weighty, was soon placed beside the first. The task was mere child's play for the Icelander's giant thews. Without a moment's pause, he turned to fetch a third stone.

"Out with your stove, sergeant," I ordered, and Black was overboard and had his stove blazing on the nearest ledge before Thord brought my release.

18

"Ho, doctor!" exclaimed the giant. "This is jolly work to stretch the muscles. I'll fetch one more stone, in case the lieutenant wants to get out; then I'll go and free the guide-rope. It's caught in between the rocks."

"Yes, we must keep it. Though to ascend again, we will have to cast out a lot more of the stores."

"Not a funny thing to do this side the Arctic Circle, doctor,"— and Thord looked about at the desolate waste of snow and rock with a grim smile. "We might make a virtue of necessity, and say that the stuff we leave is wergild to the Biornsons for the death of their solitary chief."

"Very likely the white Biornsons will be the first to find the goods. But, seriously, I hope neither bears nor savages come this way. If we leave food here, it may prove invaluable to us on our return south, should anything happen to the balloon."

"Perhaps we will not return south."

"Well, that's true. Yet, between balloon and wind, Fortune has favoured us marvellously so far; and while I admit that many an Arctic explorer has perished—"

"I didn't speak of perishing. We may stay here alive," rejoined Thord, and with a jerk of his thumb northwards, he strode off down the slope. I smiled upon his great back, much amused by the absurdity of his remark. It was true that this Polar land was habitable—that was proven by the presence of the bestial savage. But who would choose an Esquimo existence?—Still smiling, I waded through the snow to the sergeant, drawn by the savoury odour of his cooking. Black had been more than half a _chef_ when some scrape caused him to enlist in Balderston's regiment. The meal he was now concocting promised to do full justice to his reputation.

I was teasing him for a taste of his half-cooked stew, at the same time listening to the lively tune by which Balderston announced the wind-up of his task, when the gay whistling abruptly stopped in the middle of a note.

For a moment all was silence—the dead, cold silence of the Polar waste. Then, ringing down the slope against the breeze, came a high-pitched musical cry, such as only a woman's throat could utter:

"_Haoi—a-o—haoi!_"

At first I could not see anything. It was otherwise with Balderston, who shouted something in an astonished tone, and swung down the netting with reckless haste. Puzzled and alarmed, I followed Black, who, with a soldier's instinct, dashed instantly for

19

the guns. As we floundered through the snow, I heard Thord's deep voice roar out a word that sounded like "Biorn," and a side glance showed him coming up the slope at a tremendous pace. Over the rocks and drifts he bounded like a deer, but he was not making for the balloon.

"Biorn! the Valkyr!—Bring the guns!" he roared, and cutting across our tracks, he rushed on up the slope. Breathless with excitement, I leaped to the side of the car, where Balderston and Black stood staring up the mountain-side. I stared also, expecting to see a second brute-man. Yet the halloo and Thord's shout might have forewarned me.

Instead of the savage my fancy had pictured, I saw bounding toward us down the slope a creature beautiful as a Norse goddess. It was a girl, tall and fair, in the costume of a huntress, and she was running as though for life. Dumfounded, we stood gaping beside the car, while the maiden sped swiftly over a stretch of bare rocks. Suddenly she flourished overhead a long lance, and repeated her strange cry, "_Haoi—a-o—haoi_!"

"An attack!" I gasped.

"Hardly—I—"

"De guns!" shouted Black, and then all saw what Thord had meant. Up from a hollow behind the girl loomed a shaggy grizzled beast. It was a bear, larger than any polar or grizzly I had ever hunted.

"Curse that twist!" cried Balderston, and snatching his rifle, he limped forward to kneel behind a ledge. He had his rifle sights up as Black and I spurted past him. And it was none too soon. I could see the huntress struggling across a broad drift, through which the bear ploughed a path without the slightest hindrance. Thord was yet many yards distant.

At first girl and bear were so directly in line that Balderston could not fire; but when the girl leaped from the drift out upon a bit of rocky ground, she swerved a little to one side and faced about, too hard pressed to run farther. Down went the lance butt against a stone, and the girl bent forward, one knee upon the shaft, to meet the onrushing brute.

Already the monster was at the edge of the drift, when I saw him spin around in his tracks and roll sideways. The crack of Balderston's army rifle told me the cause. But the beast was up again, like a cat, and charged upon the spear, with a roar of fury. Again Balderston's rifle rang out—once, and then three times more, in quick succession. The bear kept on—and the rifle was empty!

The ground reeled before me as I ran, and I uttered a frenzied cry. I flung myself down to shoot, but was far too shaky to aim straight. Black was staggering in my wake, more breathless and spent than I. Thord still lacked fifty yards of the bear, and he had no weapon. For all we could do, the girl's fate lay in her own hands. Gazing over my wobbly rifle barrel, I saw her poised like a statue, her lance pointed straight at the beast's shaggy breast. It was a wonderful sight—that bright, graceful figure, so still and resolute, awaiting the shock of the furious monster.

Great as were the odds, my hopes rose at sight of the girl's courage. Should she gain but ten seconds of respite, I knew I could kill the beast. The range was not great, and already my hands were steadying. Yet it was not to be.

Straight upon the levelled spear charged the bear, and at the instant the point pricked his breast, he struck nimbly at the shaft. Away flew the splintered wood, and I looked to see the girl fall forward into the monster's jaws. I could fancy the sickening crunch of bones as the great fangs mangled her white flesh.

But I had failed to estimate the girl's skill. Quick as was the blow that broke the lance, she sprang back like a flash, and plucked from her side a short-handled axe. Up went the weapon in a sweeping circle, and I saw the beast stagger as it whirled down upon his skull. Well he might—the blade shore through hair and skin and bone to the very brain cavity. Fearful as was the wound, the beast reared up and struck a blow in turn that swept the girl from her feet. She fell in a drift, five yards away, and lay maimed, helpless to save herself.

The beast turned to rush upon his victim. I gasped—then shouted wildly. A sixth shot from Balderston had pierced the beast's foreleg, and it gave a moment's delay. I drew a deep breath and raised my rifle. With one shot I would end the matter.

But my chance was gone. Thord, running on like a madman, leaped between me and the bear. Straight upon the beast he rushed in reckless fury, empty-handed but utterly devoid of fear. What followed was the grandest feat I had ever seen. The bear reared up, with a terrible snarling roar, to confront this new foe; but the giant Icelander leaped on without a falter.

Suddenly he stooped, not six paces from the grey beast. I saw him clutch downwards—then up he straightened and swung high overhead a massive block of basalt. Forward hurled the great stone between the threatening paws, driven by all Thord's giant strength and the momentum of his rush. The beast, monster though he was, went down before that missile like a cardboard puppet. There was no need of a second blow.

When I came up, on a run, the iron claws were still feebly beating the air; but it was the beast's death throe. One glance I took at the massive limbs, waving spasmodically above the shapeless mangled bulk—and I knew I beheld the cave-bear of the Stone Age— Ursus Spelaeus, the terror of early man.

But my thoughts flashed from the dying beast to his victim. I sprang past him to where Thord was lifting the girl from the snow. The moment I looked at her, I saw that Thord's Biornsons were not a myth. The girl was as purely Norse in type as Balderston himself. But the impression of her appearance that I had received from a distance fell far short of the reality. Her lissome figure, nearly six feet in height and beautifully proportioned, was well set off by the huntress costume,—buskins and leggins of otter skin, an ermine blouse, and knee-skirt of blue fox. Her golden-yellow hair was plaited in two heavy strands and crowned by a round ermine cap with scarlet wings.

But it was the girl's face that held my gaze. I had seen beautiful women of many nations, yet never one whose beauty so much as compared with the clear-cut features and exquisite colouring of this Polar Valkyrie. I must confess that for a moment I stood and stared at the girl like a country gawk.

Then she looked wondering at me with eyes of the deepest, tenderest blue, now misty with pain. I could see them widen with a sort of awe; but they showed no sign of fear,—only a wordless appeal for aid. At that I found my wits, and hastened to look to her injuries.

The bear's chisel claws had ripped through the left sleeve and down her breast, and already the white fur was streaked with red. Worse still, the injured arm dangled loosely about as Thord raised the girl to her feet. Though she did not cry out, I saw her face contract with agony.

"Bone smashed, Doctor Godfrey," explained Thord, his rough voice strangely softened. The girl started at his words, and bent forward beseechingly.

"Ah, good Frey, help me!" she cried.

So like the Icelandic was her language, I understood every word. I had expected as much. But I was surprised at the name the girl gave me. Clearly, she thought that Thord had addressed me as the Vana-god, a supposition strengthened by the presence of the balloon, which no doubt she had already taken to be Frey's cloud-

22

ship Skidbladnir. Under the circumstances my godhood was very apt, for Frey was the healer.

"Take comfort, maiden," I replied in Icelandic. "Your pain will soon be eased."

As I spoke I drew open the tattered blouse to examine the wounds. At my touch, however, the colour, which was fast leaving the girl's cheeks, came back in full flood, and she shrank from me.

"Go on, doctor," growled Thord. "It's no time for squeamishness. Her bodice is already full of blood."

I shook my head. The look in the girl's deep eyes compelled me to respect her modesty. I pointed to the balloon.

"You must carry her down," I said, and I waved to Black, who had regained his wind, and was trotting up to see the bear.

"Run down, Black," I shouted. "Hot water and chloroform—lieutenant knows."

The sergeant turned on his heel, saluting in the act, and started double quick down the slope.

"Ready," said Thord warningly, and his voice softened again as he dropped into Old Norse—"Now, maiden, I bear you to Skidbladnir to be healed. There is naught to fear."

Reassured by his tone, the girl made no attempt to shrink from him, and he lifted her in his giant arms like a child. I took my place beside him, to hold the broken arm, and we walked as rapidly as possible down to the car. There she was lifted gently in upon the couch of furs that Black had spread on the platform, and she lay gazing about in awed amazement, while I made my hasty preparations for the operation.

The sergeant already had his kettles full of melting snow, and, best of all, Balderston, up among the stores, rummaged out a surgical case. A moment later I had it down beside me, and was opening a half-pound can of chloroform. With it I turned to the girl, whose white face betrayed the acuteness of her suffering.

"This is a sleep-charm, maiden," I said, again in Icelandic. "Do you fear?"

For answer, the girl looked at me with the utter trustfulness of a child, nor did she shrink when I held the drug-saturated cloth to her face. Steadfastly the deep blue eyes gazed up at me, full of mingled awe and faith, until the life within waned and the long lashes drooped with the coming sleep. A minute later she was fully under the influence of the drug.

"Now," I said, "I want Thord. The rest can go to see the bear."

Thord promptly ran to fetch the hot water, while Black and

23

Balderston set off up the slope. By the time Thord returned, I had everything ready.

"Come aboard," I directed. After you chuck out those rope coils, I want your help with the lint and sponges."

"I know, doctor," replied the Icelander, and his ready aid showed former experience. Before starting to throw out the guide-rope, he thrust a pair of scissors into my hand. With a few snips, I laid open the girl's tattered blouse and bodice and the eider-skin chemise beneath. Another cut bared the round white arm. Greatly to my relief, the fracture proved to be simple, and was easily set. There were splints in the surgical case.

The bandaging I completed with the utmost haste, for the long gashes torn across the girl's snowy breast and shoulders were still bleeding freely. This was the only danger, however, as none of the wounds penetrated the chest cavity. While Thord bathed them with hot water, I plied my needle, and between us we soon had all the cruel gashes stanched and closed. The whole had not taken fifteen minutes.

As I applied the dressings and stitched together the tattered garments, Thord signalled the others to return.

"She's coming to already," he said. "When she can talk, we all want to hear, and consider what lies before us...Think of it, doctor Only a few short hours ago on that cursed floe—and now, at the very threshold of the Pole—and—and this! What next?"

I did not wonder at Thord's outburst. But with me a softer emotion had overcome this excess of elation and amazement. Heedless of all else, I sat watching the bloom creep back into the rounded cheeks of my patient, fascinated by the beauty of her features and the colouring of milk and roses.

Presently the blue eyes opened and looked about dazed wonderment. Then they met my gaze, and at once grew radiant with gratitude.

Chapter IV
Thorlings

For some time the Polar maid and I gazed at each other in mute wonder. But Thord at last thought to fetch a cup of coffee. The stuff had been boiling so long that it was thick and muddy; yet when

I raised the girl's head and held the cup to her lips, she drained it like an obedient child. No doubt she thought the hot, bitter draught some kind of powerful medicine, and indeed it had the effect of counteracting the lingering stupor of the chloroform. Before I could prevent her, she sat up, the movement twisting her arm and shoulder so severely that she was unable to restrain a cry of pain.

"You must keep still, maiden," I exclaimed, and I hastened to adjust the sling for her arm. As I drew back, a sudden sense of awe seemed to overcome her, and she bent her head reverently.

"Lord Frey is very gracious," she murmured. "He acts the Holy Rune."

Before I could reply, Balderston came up, limping from the twist that had aroused the old sprain, but full of cordial greetings for our guest. Forgetful alike of her pain and her awe, the girl smiled back at him. Then she chanced to glance around at Thord's giant figure, and her eyes widened.

"Biorn's bani!—hail to the Son of Jord!" she cried, and bowing to each of us in turn, she murmured in a voice scarcely audible—"I give greeting to the skyfarers. The Asir are welcome to Updal."

"You over-honour us," replied Balderston, smiling. "We are men, not gods."

The girl looked about at us and up at the balloon in bewilderment. Then she thought she understood.

"It is Skidbladnir," she said, nodding to herself—"Skidbladnir; and the Lord Frey has bound my hurt. Yet the sagas tell of like comings, and if they wish to pass as men—"

"She bowed again to us.

"The wanderers are very welcome," she said.

"And who is it greets us?" asked Balderston.

"I am Thyra Ragnersdotter."

Thord took off his sealskin cap and stood with the sun gleaming on his fiery hair and beard.

"Maid Thyra," he began in his deepest voice, "I am Thord, son of Vegtam, son of Bor. This fair one is called Frank Balderston, and beside you stands Jan Godfrey."

Not a word of this introduction was untrue, but if Thord had calculated to confirm the girl's belief in our godship, he could not have done it more effectually by an outright lie. To her ears, my name no doubt sounded like _Vana-god Frey_, while the other names seemed but thin disguises for Thor and Balder. I perceived the awe deepening in the girl's eyes, and cried indignantly: "Shame on you, Thord, to trifle with her!"

25

Thord grinned, highly amused—"Why, doctor, you don't believe she really—"

"Where are your eye? Between the balloon and our looks, and the way you gave our names—"

I dropped English, and turned abruptly to the wondering girl: "It is a jest, Thyra. We are only men—men of like blood to you, descended from your early ancestors in the south land."

The girl opened her lips to reply; but a sudden look of horror distorted her face. Clutching my shoulder, she drew herself behind me and shrieked in terror: "Surt!—fiery Surt! Oh, save me, Frey!"

I stared about in amazement. Sergeant Black, who had loitered by the bear, stood a few paces off, puffing at a cigar and evincing his enjoyment by one of his grotesque grins. We all laughed as the situation dawned upon us, and I took the girl's hand, with a reassuring look.

"Only consider, maiden," I reasoned; "would Surt fare in peace with the Asir? We are all merely men—he also. He is a true carl, despite his colour. His forefathers came from a land where the sun burns men black."

"The dwerger are more ugly," said the girl, panting and still half alarmed; "yet they are brown. He is so black, I thought it must be Surt; and—and he breathes fire—the smoke-!"

"A small wonder—only smoke," said I. "We will show you the mystery soon. But now, tell us,—is it often you hunt grey biorn alone?"

"The others follow the trail of bera and the cubs. I crossed the blood snow to cut them off; but biorn rushed upon me. Few can fight grey biorn singly. I fled to seek my brother. From the crest I saw Skidbladnir and ran towards it for aid. I was hard pressed. But for the thunderstones you cast so far, and the huge rock hurled by this great one, I should have been fey."

"No wonder!" commented Balderston. "What did he measure, sergeant?"

"Muns'ous big, sah—muns'ous big! Ten feet, shuly!"

"Not ten of your own feet!" protested Thord.

"No, sah; no, sah; I doan say dat, sah. Only seben ob _dem_."

"Yes; I didn't think he was quite a whale," said Thord. "But hustle out your knives. We want that skin."

"No we don't," said I. "The thing will weigh two or three hundred, and with our fair passenger, we'll have enough aboard. Leave the bear alone, and help consider what's to be done next."

"No time for that either," interrupted Balderston. "Look there!"

26

All followed his gesture up the slope to the right. Five hundred yards or so away, a man had leaped up suddenly above the sky-line. For a moment he paused on the bare crest of the ridge, to gaze back down the opposite slope; then, with a defiant shake of his lance, he turned and bounded towards us.

"It is my brother, Rolf Kaki!" cried Thyra, and she sent a clear "Haoi!" ringing up the mountain side. The man flung up his hand in response, and came on faster than ever.

"Hello! That looks like flight," exclaimed Balderston.

"I'll get another stone ready," said Thord grimly.

"Yet the man is big enough to do it himself. He can't be a span shorter than I. Bah! with a woman it's different; but a fellow who would run from a bear—"

"Bear!" I cried. "See him zigzag. He wouldn't do that for a bear."

"Must be savages, then," said Thord.

"No; see! There's another like him, on the crest—two!—and they're shooting with bows. He's had a scrap with his comrades."

Balderston was right, at least in part. I even fancied I could see the arrows flash around the fugitive as he leaped sideways in his flight. Suddenly three more men came leaping up on the ridge crest. One of them paused to shoot, but the other two rushed on in chase. Then, all in a body, came a dozen more pursuers, headed by a gigantic woman in huntress dress. At a shout from her, the whole party charged on down the slope.

"Thorlings!" cried Thyra. She stood with flashing eyes, and her nostrils quivered with excitement as she snatched eagerly at her empty belt. Lance and axe lay by the dead bear. As she remembered, she threw up her hand in despair—"Unarmed! unarmed!—and the odds so great!"

"Courage! Here he comes, safe!" I shouted.

"Ay; and the arrows with him," added Thord. "Good Lord! how they shoot! We'll soon be in range."

"Boots and saddles!" shouted Balderston. Black made a dash to bring in his cook outfit; the rest of us seized our rifles.

"We must stop that rush," said Thord coolly.

Balderston's answer was a shot that dropped the foremost pursuer. Thord and I knocked over our men a moment later, and a second ball from the army rifle winged a fourth. That was enough for the Thorlings. Down they went behind a pile of rocks, just out of arrow range, while the hunted man staggered up to the car, all but spent, a great arrow fast in his shoulder and the blood spurting from a sword-cut on his broad chest.

27

He was of huge build, half a head shorter than Thord, but still almost a giant. As he halted a dozen paces off, and leaned gasping on his lance shaft, he appeared, for all his sorry plight, a magnificent type of manhood. Hard pressed as he was, badly wounded, and as yet ignorant of our intentions, he stood like a lion at bay, not a trace of fear in his bold, questioning gaze.

Thyra was the first to speak.

"Friends!" she cried warningly, as her brother caught sight of the sergeant's scarred black face, and gripped his lance.

"Friends?" he repeated hoarsely.

"Ay!" replied Thord, striding forward with outstretched hand. "Come aboard Skidbladnir."

"Come yourself, Thord," cried Balderston. "The gang up there are stretching their bows. See the arrow beside you."

"Yes; hustle aboard, and out with ballast. We don't want the balloon full of holes again. Keep the enemy close, Frank."

"Just what I had in mind," replied Balderston, and he drove a bullet through the forehead of an incautious Thorling. But the other bowmen lay back out of sight and sent volleys of arrows curving high through the air.

"Dey's comin' close, sah!" warned Black, as a long shaft, thick as his finger, glanced down the out-leaning side of the balloon, and buried its head viciously in the car rim.

"Out with the stones!" I yelled, tugging at a huge block. "Look sharp, Thord."

"Coming, doctor."

The two big men released their handgrip, and Thord almost carried the stranger to the platform. In the excitement of the moment we did not think to put the girl down within the car, where she would have been out of the way as well as more comfortable. As it was, between our numbers and the ballast stones, the little space on the platform was all but jammed. But Thord and I quickly tumbled three stones overboard, and a moment later Black, up above the bearing-ring, cut loose half a thousand pounds of stores.

"Look out! They're going to rush us. The big woman is up and calling them to follow," warned Balderston.

"Rush ahead," growled Thord, as he heaved up the fourth stone. The car was already shifting in its bed. I slashed through the taut anchor rope at the instant that the last block went overboard. Up we soared, a grand and marvellous sight to the astonished Thorlings, and an equal wonder to our rescued guests.

The weight of the guide-rope checked our ascent at no great height, but the raise was sufficient to expose the refuge of the

Thorlings. Seeing this, they stood up boldly beside their Amazon leader, and held their bows in readiness as we drifted towards the ridge crest. The breeze bore us somewhat to the left of them, yet not out of arrow-shot of the level on which they stood. Balderston and Thord at once prepared to open fire; but Black, at a sign from me, saved our powder by cutting loose more ballast.

As the sergeant swung down into our midst, we caught sight of a new spectator on the ridge,—a huge Thorling, tall as Rolf Kaki and fully as broad as Thord himself. Through the glasses, I could plainly see the man's evil face, contorted with the ferocity of a wild beast. One of his eyes seemed half-closed by a scar. The other, which was very prominent, rolled uneasily about with a terrible leer. His undershot jaw and brutal expression reminded me of the savage on the peak, but his clothing was of silky furs and a broad band of gold bound his shaggy red hair.

We had no need to ask the name of this ogre. The moment Rolf caught sight of him, he uttered a furious cry—"King Hoding!—Hoding Grimeye! I left him for dead!—Curse the sword which failed me!"

"I'll end the fellow," said Thord, his hard eyes keen for murder. But I struck up his rifle.

"Stop!" I cried. "It will be time to shed more blood when we know the quarrel. There is no need now. We're safe."

"No, by heaven! The others are running for the guide-rope."

"They can't catch it."

"Ef dey do—" muttered Black, patting his rifle.

"If they do, they'll find it hot," added his lieutenant. "Och, me Thorling frins, jes' thread on th' tail o' me coat, now."

We laughed at the invitation, all except Thord. He took deliberate aim at the Thorling who was running with the big woman several yards in advance of the others. With a splendid burst of speed, the unlucky man reached the end of the line and sprang to grasp it as it drew up a ledge. Out roared Thord's express. The Thorling spun around and fell flat.

"Ake-Thor!" shouted Rolf Kaki in wild joy. "That was Eyvind Deerfoot. He it was slew Haldor."

"But the others?" cried Thyra anxiously.

"Arrow-pierced, all three. We were hot on the trail, when the forestmen surprised us. There were five at first, Hoding in the lead; and when the three fell to their arrows, they attacked. Haldor pierced two of them with his javelins, and then fought the second pair, while I met Hoding. It was a hard fight. Hoding cut me, as you see, but I felled him, and Haldor slew the others. Then half a score

29

more came running, led by the woman, who is Bera herself,—Bera of the Orm, the king's half sister. So we fled. But Haldor fell to Eyvind's spear, and Hoding, it seems, was only stunned."

Thyra's eyes overflowed at the recital, but there was no vengefulness with her sorrow. She laid her hand on her brother's arm and said: "Remember, Rolf, the Holy Rune—hold no blood thoughts. The Thorlings have paid doubly, and more. Rather let us thank those who have saved us. But for them, grey biorn would have devoured me,"—and the girl gave a vivid account of her rescue.

Rolf looked at Thord as at a demi-god, and then he turned to me. But I cut short his thanks.

"It is my craft to heal. I will now bind your wounds also," said I, and I opened the surgical case. At once the Polar Northman turned about, and stood without a flinch or groan while I drew the arrow from his shoulder. The tip of the six-inch head had pierced through until it showed in front, but there was no barb, and neither the lung nor any artery had been injured.

I had the arrow wound dressed in short order, but the ugly sword gash was a different proposition. To close it required thirty or forty stitches, yet the man bore the painful operation with wonderful fortitude, almost with indifference. While I still sewed away at the quivering flesh, Balderston picked up the heavy Thorling arrow and wiped the blood from its head.

"Hello!" he exclaimed. "This isn't steel. It's platinum, or I'm a fool!—and the lance head, too."

Thord and Black, who were still watching the Thorlings, now gathered on the crest near their king, at once wheeled about to examine the weapons; but I was so absorbed in my work that at the time the discovery made no impression on my mind.

Chapter V
Niflheim

After I had finished with the needle, it did not take me long to apply my dressings. Not until then did I become conscious of a pair of deep blue eyes that followed my every movement with flattering constancy. Their look put me in a glow, as I realised the advantage I had gained over Balderston by winning the girl's gratitude. To tell the truth, I was already head over heels in love with our fair Polar Valkyrie, and it seemed impossible to me that Balderston should be indifferent. Therefore I was filled with jealousy of the best of friends, and thought enviously of his handsome features. I forgot my dark eyes and black Van Dyke, which, among a blond people, gave a novel attraction to my homely phiz.

"All right, friend Rolf," said I, as I pinned the last bandage. Then, anxious to take all possible advantage of my opportunity, I turned at once to his sister. But before I could speak, our attention was drawn by a shout from Black—"Golly!—red snow!"

I stared down over the bearing-ring, side by side with Thyra. Black's surprise was easily explained. The balloon had crossed a hollow beyond the crest where the Thorlings yet stood gazing after the cloud ship, and now, skimming close above a second ridge, she floated out over a vast glacier field, the nearer side of which was belted with a broad streak of crimson.

"The blood snow," explained Thyra.

"Yes; _Protococcus nivalis!_"

I replied absently, my gaze following the line of the glacier. It descended into a narrowing valley that seemed to extend downwards to an astonishing depth. For the first time an inkling of the truth entered my mind. I raised my eyes quickly. Thyra stood puzzling over my scientific remark, but the big Northman caught the question in my gaze.

"The Ice-Street," he said, nodding downwards. "It leads up from the Thorling Mark."

"Thorling Mark—a forest?"

"Ay; that of the Ormvol—on the mid-land."

"Betwixt Updal and Niflheim," added Thyra; and I found myself more perplexed than before.

"Niflheim?" I exclaimed, in a voice that attracted the attention of Thord and Balderston.

"Niflheim—Dwergerheim," repeated the girl, puzzled in turn by my surprise. "Surely you know of Hel's under-world—of Hela Pool, where Nidhug lies."

"Oh, she's talking mythology," explained Balderston, laughing.

"Not so," protested Thord. "I really believe—"

"A heavy lurch of the platform flung us in a heap against the bearing-ring—almost overboard. All uttered a cry of alarm, for close in the balloon's wake a great cliff of black rock seemed to shoot up into the air. So swiftly were we falling, I thought the balloon had burst. Yet that did not explain the violent lurch. Then, in a flash, I understood. The trailing portion of the guide-rope had dropped into some deep chasm, and its weight was dragging us clown. A glance at the basalt cliff showed that the speed of our descent was already lessening. But my sigh of relief was answered by a groan from Black. He was glaring down over the side, his face blanched to ashen grey and his eyes almost starting from their sockets.

"Good God, man! what is it?" cried Balderston.

"Lawd—O Lawd!" gasped the negro, his teeth chattering. "_De bottomless pit!—O Lawd_!"

Seized by a contagion of terror, we peered fearfully down over the side of the car. No wonder the negro was terror-stricken. The balloon hung suspended over the gloomy depths of a vast gulf—a chasm yawning in the earth's crust like the empty bed of an ocean. Overcome with vertigo, we clutched the suspension-ropes, and stared with dizzy eyes at the black wall of the pit, running down, down, down in grand sheer precipices, thousands upon thousands of feet, until lost to view in the gloom of the great deep.

Our blood ran cold in our veins, and every nerve in our bodies tingled with fear of the awful abyss. It was as if the solid earth had collapsed beneath us. For a time we could neither move nor speak, so great was the shock of the discovery.

At last, however, Thord and Balderston and I realised that the balloon was no longer sinking, and the knowledge somewhat restored our presence of mind. Our rigid muscles relaxed, and we gazed about, half fearfully, to measure the extent of the gulf. Eastward the black precipices of the mighty escarpment jutted out in a Titan buttress that hid from our view all the land beyond; while to the north the whole abyss was veiled by wisps of vapour, floating up out of the black depths to the cloud sea. In that direction we could see neither earth nor sky. To the west, however, across a great southward bend of the gulf, we caught vague glimpses of a faraway land, sloping up from the gloom of the lower pit to a dim white sierra of icy mountains.

Balderston was the first among us to speak, and his voice sounded harsh and strained.

"Symmes' Hole!" he muttered.

I shook my head, and, with much effort, managed to reply: "No; I see bottom—miles down—where the sun strikes through the vapours."

"Niflheim!" cried Thord meaningly.

"Ay!" gasped Rolf Kaki, panting as when chased by the

Thorlings—"ay, Niflheim—yonder in the lower depths. We float above the Ormvol."

"Lower depths—lower depths!" I repeated, and my jaw fell.

"Where lies Updal?" demanded Thord.

The Northman pointed to the dim outlines of the icy sierra.

"Yonder, beneath the Utgard Jokuls," he answered. "If we float on as now, we shall soar across."

"Good!" cried Balderston, and we breathed easier. The dread of the abyss that had so dazed and appalled us, fast gave place to other emotions. An oath from Thord broke the last bond of the spell. Angry at his own panic, the giant turned upon Black, who still crouched in his place, ashen-faced and rigid, exactly as at first.

"Here, you blasted nigger! Stand up, or I'll kick you over!"

To the rest of us the brutal words acted as a powerful tonic, stimulating all our self-control. But the sergeant only licked his blue lips and moaned hoarsely: "_De bottomless pit!—de bottomless pit_!"

The man was half crazed with terror. But for his lieutenant, another hour would have seen him raving. With ready wit, Balderston adopted what was perhaps the only way to reach the man's tottering reason.

"Attention!" he commanded, in curt martial tones. "'Bout face!—salute!"

Like an automaton, the sergeant straightened up, wheeled about, and jerked up his hand. Up went Balderston's hand with the same mechanical motion.

"Special order No. 10," he snapped out, "Sergeant Black detailed to cook dinner for the mess."

Again the sergeant gave his jerky salute, and again the lieutenant responded in kind. Suddenly Black drew a deep gasping breath. His scarred face lost its ashen hue, and the hideous glare of his eyes softened to a more human look. His reason was saved. But still he stood at attention, dazed and hesitating.

"Damn you! Step out, sir! What you standing there for?"

"Yas, sah! Goin', sah!" stuttered Black. Then abruptly he flung up his arms and burst into tears.

"There, there, sergeant; don't make a fool of yourself," admonished Balderston, in a tone of womanly tenderness, "Come now, you're not scared of a hole in the ground—so long as it has a bottom. There is one. Look and see it."

"Yas, sah; yas, sah," replied Black, and he sought to hide the shame of his panic and tears by close attention to his duties.

The whole scene was laughably grotesque, but the narrow

33

escape of the man's reason was quite enough to sober us, even had we not been smarting under the mortification of our own panic. Even Thord unbent, and, with rough sympathy, helped Black lower his stove and dishes into the car.

"A strange thrall," commented the big Northman, as Black laid aside his fur cap and slipped through the trap after his cook outfit.

"Thrall," repeated Thord.

"Is he not? His hair is cropped," said Thyra, peering around my shoulder. One of the scarlet wings on her cap brushed my sleeve, and I was so interested in observing her lovely profile, just visible from the tail of my eye, that I only half heard Thord's reply. He said something explanatory of negro wool and of Black's relations to Balderston. Then he added, _sotto voce_, in English: "It's well, fellows, that we've had no haircut for so long. Otherwise, I venture to say, these latter-day Norse would look on us as we regard clipped convicts."

Instinctively I put up my hand and twisted the point of my beard. After the months of neglect, my hair hung about my shoulders, rough and unkempt. But my Van Dyke I had managed to keep in very fair shape, considering that the trimming had been done with a pocket-knife. Greatly pleased over this and the recollection of our baths during the last weeks on the floe, I set about the agreeable task of entertaining Mistress Thyra.

"So we float about the Ormvol," I observed, as I readjusted the sling for the girl's arm, which had been wrenched about when the lurch of the car into the abyss so nearly threw us out. With a grateful glance that repaid me a hundredfold for my attentions, the girl soberly answered my remark: "The Ormvol?—Yes, Lord Frey."

I smiled at her serious face. It was evident she still entertained a suspicion that we were gods _incog_.

"My name is not Frey, but Godfrey," I protested; "and I am neither drott nor hersir,—just plain John Godfrey. Call me John."

"Jan," repeated the girl, and she smiled in turn, showing a dazzling line of teeth. This was an excellent beginning; but Balderston interrupted.

"Would the daughter of Ragner like to draw up the pit's bottom?" he inquired.

"Thanks, Frank. I'll show her," said I, and I appropriated the glasses.

"Oh, John, you don't play fair!" he remonstrated; but good-natured as usual, he turned at once to join Thord in the entertainment of Rolf Kaki. The girl's naive smile told me that she

34

understood the meaning of this little by-play. Very demurely she gazed from Balderston's blond poll to my plain and swarthy features. As the blue eyes met mine, they fell in sudden shy confusion, and a delicious thrill stirred my pulse at sight of the quick reddening of the girl's cheeks.

Fortunately I managed to keep my head, and pretended not to notice her confusion. My heart was thumping like a trip-hammer, and my hands trembled with joyful excitement as I adjusted the binoculars for her use. Yet somehow I constrained myself to speak in a matter-of-fact tone. My self control was to be still more severely tested.

As the girl could not, with only one hand, both support herself and hold the glasses, I placed my arm before her as a bar between the suspension-ropes. The bearing-ring was too low to safely lean out over, unless one had hold of the ropes. But my arm formed a higher support, and Thyra trustfully accepted my invitation to make use of it. Any one who has been a lover can realise the feeling that all but overcame me as I felt the weight of the girl's person upon my arm. The touch filled me with a sort of blissful intoxication, and I was seized by an impulse, almost irresistible, to fling my arms about the beautiful girl and draw her to me.

A cry from her diverted my thoughts none too soon. Her first look through the binoculars had very nearly startled her into dropping them. She started back and exclaimed in astonishment:

"It is _seid_—the crystals are bewitched! When I gaze through them, the whole Ormvol rises!"

"Not in truth, Thyra. It is but seeming," said I, and to hide my feelings I took the glasses. One glance was sufficient to give reality to my simulated interest. Far down in the gloom of the abyss I could discern a wide extent of hilly land, which seemed to be clad with thick forests of a strangely pallid hue. Eager to learn more of this weird subterranean world, I was straining my eyes to make out its features, when a flash of reflected sunlight half-blinded me.

"There is a lake on the Ormvol!" I exclaimed, as I handed back the glasses.

"Yes; Vergelmer. I see we soar above its lower end. It is the lake where the bergs gather from the Ice Street ere they roll down Giol to plunge into Hela Pool."

As she uttered the last name the girl shuddered, and lifted the glasses eagerly towards Updal.

"Ah, Jan," she cried in delight, "they are wondrous crystals! I see the very walls of Biornstad. Look in line between the twin-peaked jokul, in the belt of green."

35

Already I could see with the naked eye what I knew to be Updal; a huge natural terrace on the side of the pit, sloping down from the snow line at the base of the Updal Jokuls, to the brink of a long, broken escarpment. The latter, which varied in height from hundreds to thousands of feet, bounded the upper edge of the Thorling Mark.

Since the most of Updal lay only two miles below sea-level, it was not so obscured from view as the greater depths. The glasses quickly confirmed my impression that it was a land fair to look upon. The higher parts were dark with pine and spruce; but lower down grew woods of deciduous tree between which I could see meadows and, I thought, tilled fields. Of this last I was not certain, as the base of the nearest jokuls was yet forty miles distant, and wisps of vapour interfered with the view. I did, however, catch a clear glimpse of the walled town pointed out by Thyra. It stood midway down the terrace, about thirty miles distant from us.

"So that is Biornstad, Thyra—the red walls with the smoke above?" I said.

"It is Biornstad, the home of the Runefolk."

"Then they are few in number?"

Thyra shook her fair head so that one heavy braid came over her shoulder and fell across my arm like a strand of gold.

"Nay, Jan," she exclaimed; "the benches in the Runehof seat seven score udallers, each the leader of a fylki."

"And a fylki numbers-?"

"Half a hundred warriors."

I whistled with surprise. Seven thousand able-bodied men!—that meant a population of thirty thousand or more. The figure could not include the Thorlings, who were evidently a hostile clan of these Polar Northmen.

"Are not your people the descendants of a certain Jarl Biorn and his following, who, in ancient times, came like us from the Southland?" I asked.

Thyra's lovely face beamed with joy.

"You know of the Hero!" she cried. "You have heard how he stormed Jotunheim—how he steered his ships through the ice-world, till the bergs ground them in splinters—how he then led all in safety over the floes to the Utgard Jokuls and across their crest, down into Updal."

"I have heard of the Hero's venture—of his sailing to storm Jotunheim. So all your race sprang from those dauntless vikings?"

"The Runefolk are of pure blood," replied the girl proudly. "As to the base Thorlings, many have mingled with the dwerger brood."

"But who are these Thorlings?"

"In the early years when first the Allthing voted the Rune-law, the fiercer warriors would not bend to it. So they were driven beneath the Gard Fells, into the forests of the Ormvol, where they have never ceased to welcome the thieves and berserks and other nithings outlawed from Updal. They own no other laws than guest-troth and the Orm-peace, save only the will of their king, and even that little beyond the sweep of his sword."

"How of your king in Updal, Thyra?"

"We have none. The eldormen sit in turn on the high-seat, judging by the Rune-law and the will of the Allthing."

A hundred eager questions crowded my thoughts, but while I hesitated which first to ask, Sergeant Black popped his head and shoulders through the trap-door and spread a meal on the platform with deft swiftness.

"Dinnuh's sahved!" he observed. "Doan step back, Mistah Thod. De beans is behin' you."

Everybody promptly faced inward and settled down on the rim of platform between Black's dishes and the guard-ropes. The little space was somewhat cramped; but the sergeant, standing in the midst, half out of the man-hole, served his dishes with great dexterity. I, for one, had no objection to the arrangement, since it fenced me in on one side with the fair Norse maiden. She and her brother proved to be fully acquainted with the use of their forks, but the disability of the girl's arm gave me an excuse for numerous little attentions.

The great variety of food in the stores of the balloon had given Black ample opportunity to prove his culinary skill, and our guests fell to on the novel dishes with keen relish. Our own appetites were nearly as sharp, but Balderston found time between bites to describe in graphic terms our swift flight over the Polar Ocean. Then, in response to eager inquiries, we told of the marvellous Southland, where the sea rolled free without floe or berg, and the sun, the year around, rushed straight across the sky and under the world, bringing night and day all in the period of a _ring_.

"Wondrous!" exclaimed Thyra. "The skalds sing of these strange things; yet few men believed the tale."

"It seems beyond reason," added her brother, and he stared upwards at the sun, circling around the sky in the noon of its six months' day.

"Yet your piy-world is no less wonderful to us," replied Thord; and while the balloon sailed steadily on across the mighty gulf towards Updal, we listened with deepening interest to weird stories of the lower pit—of its fierce beasts and the great stone Orm; of the Orm Vala and the peace-holy Orm-ring, where Hoding Grimeye, the terrible Thorling king, held rude court with Bera, his sister; of the fiery Nida Mountains, the home of elves and sprites, far out across the impassable abyss; of the beast-like dwerger horde, swarming up the sides of Niflheim to adore the Snake; and of the living Orm, the great dragon Nidhug, down in the uttermost depths, where the blue death-glow flickers on the stagnant waters of Hela Pool.

Chapter VI
Biornstad

Dinner was over, and Black cleared away the empty dishes; but still we listened, half doubting, to Rolf's tales of the dragon and his stone image. As to the living monster, we were somewhat sceptical, since all evidence of his existence rested on the assertions of the dwerger. But we could not do else than believe in the mammoth stone reptile on the Ormvol; for Rolf had himself seen it, while on a mission to King Hoding.

His account of the gigantic saurian, chiselled from a glassy cliff, filled our minds with strange fancies. What vanished race could have conceived that monstrous image and graven it in flintlike obsidian?

Our speculations were cut short by a cry from Thyra—"The Gard Fells! We soar above Updal."

Gazing downward, we saw the pit slope falling away behind us, and even Thord heaved a sigh of relief. The balloon had drifted above the brink of the escarpment, and was floating over Updal towards the Utgard Jokuls.

"We drift to the right of Biornstad," remarked Rolf, and he pointed out the red walls of the town, now only ten miles distant.

"I suppose, Frank, we must land at the nearest point, and finish the trip afoot," I observed. "It will be four or five miles."

"But the town would then miss the sensation of our descent out of mid-sky. Think of that! Why not try for a more favourable current?"

"All right; I leave it to you."

"Very well. But have you ever been in a compressed-air chamber,—a caisson?"

"No. Why?"

"We are about at sea-level now. Down there in the pit the atmospheric pressure must be very great, even on Updal. Our guests, of course, are used to it; but it may affect us. Remember, all of you, to keep swallowing, if you feel uncomfortable."

Assured that every one understood his warning, Balderston opened one of the valves long enough to send us down a thousand feet. The drop brought the balloon into a different current, but it was even less favourable than the one above. Again the lieutenant dropped us,—with no better result. However, the third descent, which brought us down within four thousand feet of the terrace land, accomplished the desired purpose. The balloon entered a cross-current flowing directly towards Biornstad.

Gazing down over the bearing-ring, we saw Updal spread out beneath us like a huge topographical chart; a parklike land, belted with spruce and pine along the upper side, and crossed by numerous glacial streams from the gorges of the snowy sierra. Towards Biornstad the sun's rays struck on fields of yellow grain.

"A fair land!" observed Thord. But our interest was mainly centred on the red walls of the town.

Nearer and nearer we drifted, until we could discern the general features of the place. It lay on a wedge of land between the forks of a large stream, and the walls of red stone, forty feet high, stretched along the banks and across the base of the wedge in the shape of a huge triangle. The apex of this enclosure, at the junction of the streams, was filled by a large edifice, of which the converging town walls formed the sides. This, Thyra said, was the Rune-hof, which we took to be a sort of temple and town-hall combined.

What most surprised us, however, was the appearance of the town proper. Instead of the high-gabled wooden houses which we had expected to see scattered about the enclosure, we perceived that fully half of the remaining space was laid out in a great park or common, intervening between the Runehof and the unbroken facade of the town. The latter seemed to consist of one enormous building, for all the space between the facade and the walls was covered by a continuous area of shining roof, rising here and there terraces, and pitted by garden courts, but nowhere betraying the outlines of separate structures. Towards the rear, this roofing sank beneath the level of the walls, and the lofty chimney-stacks towering up through it indicated the location of forges or factories.

With what wondering curiosity Ave studied that broad stretch of roof and the great facade with its colonnades and stately stairways! To call it a town seemed most incongruous. It was rather an enormous spreading palace,—a people's palace, as Balderston observed.

But presently the question of our descent demanded our attention. We had entered on our last mile's drift. A few minutes would determine whether we could effect a landing in the town park. Straight towards it we soared, and presently Balderston, with a satisfied nod, seized the valve cord.

"Remember what I said about swallowing," he cautioned. "The halt at this level has eased the change for us. But this last will be a big drop. Make ready. I'll pull in half a minute."

"All right," said I, and we braced our nerves for the plunge. Balderston, however, paused with up-raised hand, to watch the vulturine flight of two great birds, circling swiftly up from the pit. Another grand sweep around their spiral course promised to raise the soarers to the level of the balloon, and a premonition of the truth filled us with curiosity to see what manner of feathered creatures these might be. Now they were on a level with the car. Around they swung, attracted by the balloon, and glided swiftly past within ten yards of us, filling the air with their harsh croaks. We stared at their long tails, undulating strangely to the breeze, at their broad wings and naked reptilian heads. It was only a hasty view we had, as they shot past with arrowy speed, but it left the four of us gaping and astounded.

"Foh de Lawd's sakes!—day's got teef!" gasped Black, rubbing his eyes.

"Jaws!" shouted Thord, and he struck his great chest. "No beak at all, but jaws full of fish teeth! What do you call them—toothed birds—opterix—?"

"Odontornithes—reptilian birds...But they've been extinct since the Cretaceous!"

"Evidently not here in this pit world," rejoined Balderston. "Did you notice their tails, John? They're vertebrated!"

"We pass the Runehof!" cried Rolf. To him and his sister the odontornithes had of course been of little interest.

At the warning, Balderston started from his daze, and tugged quickly at the valve cord. The rush of air in our faces as the balloon shot downwards drew our gaze once more to what lay below.

The balloon, already shrunken from loss of gas to the shape of a withered pear, drew out longer and flabbier as it sank down through the dense atmosphere, and presently we found ourselves swallowing air with great energy. In this our guests soon joined us, for the increase of atmospheric pressure was too sudden even for them. These efforts to meet the effect of our descent did not, however, prevent our watching the town with keen interest.

While we were yet quite high, some sharp-eyed person must have perceived the strange object falling from the sky. A group of men on the green common, tiny midgets from our altitude, suddenly spread out and ran towards the archways of the facade. Hardly had they disappeared, when from every arch and portico the townfolk, men, women and children, began to stream out into view.

Fully six or seven hundred people had gathered on the common before the tip of the guide-rope touched the ground. The town roof also was fast becoming dotted with spectators, who stood gazing from the higher parts, or ran to the great stairways that led down from the crest of the facade. Throngs of others came jostling through the archways below, and among the bright-hued costumes we noticed the glint of weapons and armour. At this Balderston promptly eased up on the valve cord, so that we descended more slowly.

"Those arrows are nasty customers," he explained. "We'll give ourselves time to parley."

"Dah's a fellah drawin' now!" exclaimed Black, and he reached for his rifle.

"Not that—not that!" I commanded, and I grasped Rolf by the arm. "Show yourself! Hail your people!"

But Thyra, her cheeks flushed and eyes sparkling with joyous excitement, was already waving a white cloth—one of the sergeant's dish-towels. At the signal, the hostile bows were lowered, and the swelling crowd of townfolk sent up a deep responsive murmur.

Slowly the shrunken balloon let us down into the circle of upturned ruddy faces. One could scarce imagine a more attractive assembly. The pick of all Scandinavia and North Germany could not have been more stalwart and fair. Men, women and children all alike seemed perfect in health and physique, and bright with intelligence. I did not perceive a single stupid or evil face among them. The effect of their blond hair and ruddy cheeks was in nowise lessened by their costumes, which, though much the same in design, varied greatly in colour and material. The brightest dyes had been used on the manufactured goods, and many women wore mantles of brilliant feather-work. Add to this various beautiful furs and the glint of polished steel helmets and ring-mail, and the effect can be imagined.

But we soon had other thoughts than the dress of the Runefolk to occupy our minds. At a hundred feet, Rolf began

41

shouting to various individuals whom he spied out in the crowd. Almost at once the people recognised both him and Thyra, and raised a great cry that half deafened us. After that shout of surprise, the crowd stood in silent wonder, while the car settled slowly down into their midst. We stared back at them with equal interest, our thoughts in a whirl. What manner of people were these?—in what ways had they altered from their bold viking ancestors?—what meant the great town house and the Holy Rune?

Thord was first to waken to action. When we were about twenty feet from the ground, he leaned over the bearing-ring and addressed a big Runeman whose mail shirt only half covered a leathern blacksmith's apron.

"Ho, friend," he said, "fetch stones to anchor Skidbladnir."

The warrior turned with a gesture, and at once seven or eight brawny young men ran through the opening crowd towards the nearest town wall. They returned, each staggering under a heavy piece of metal, just as the car touched the ground. Obeying a sign from Balderston, all placed their burdens on the edge of the platform. The lieutenant gravely thanked them, and they drew back to the ring of spectators, evidently pleased to have been of service to the strangers.

"Now out we go," said Thord, as he caught up Thyra in his giant arms. In a moment he had lowered her gently down upon the turf. Then he turned to me with a twinkle in his hard eyes.

"You're next, doctor."

"That's true," I replied, and without waiting for his intended aid, I vaulted over beside the girl. The others, after helping Rolf over, sprang after in quick succession. As Black leaped down behind his lieutenant, I saw the nearest Runefolk start and push back before his ebony face and its droll grimace. But at the moment the crowd parted towards the Runehof, and Thyra turned to speak to me—"See, Jan; the eldormen come."

I looked, however, at the big man in armour, who was staring at me with keen interest. His eyes were bold and hard, like Thord's, and I fancied their gaze expressed disapproval of the maiden's friendly tone and bearing towards me. In his eagerness to speak with my beautiful companion, he ignored the respectful courtesy which kept his fellow townfolk at a little distance. Almost immediately he stepped forward and, with evident concern, asked the girl about her injuries. By the man's bearing and the slight flush which reddened Thyra's cheeks at his approach, I felt certain he must be one of her suitors. That she had many, I took for granted, and with good reason. There were numbers of very handsome and pretty maidens in the crowd around, but not one of them, to my mind, could so much as compare with our sweet huntress. Therefore I waited anxiously for Thyra's reply, to see how she would address the warrior. Both he and I were to be disappointed. The arrival of the eldormen interrupted her answer.

The judges, nine dignified greybeards, were costumed the same as the other Runefolk, but distinguished by the headless spear shafts which formed their staffs of office. They marched gravely down the lane through the crowd, and halted just before us. Then all raised their spear shafts in salute, and their leader made a gesture which, Thord whispered, was the sign of Thor's hammer.

"The skyfarers are welcome," he said, "whether they come from Dwergerheim, or Jotunheim, from the Southland, or the Nida Mountains."

"'To a good friend the paths lie direct, though he be far away,'" responded Thord, quoting from the High Sang of Odin. The eldorman bowed, evidently pleased, and quoted from the same Edda: "'Food and raiment a man require; who o'er the fell has travelled.'"

We bowed, in turn, and the eldorman continued: "The skyfarers are guests of Updal; but if they be not weary, let Rolf Kaki tell how he and his sister come home wounded, in the cloud-ship."

Thord at once drew forward the big Northman, who saluted formally and replied:

"Eldormen and folk of the Rune, a great honour has come to our hearth. We have guests from the mystic South—from the land of the Hero—friends who have sailed in Skidbladnir over the ice of Jotunheim...On the fells beyond the blood snow this great one, whom they call Thord, crushed grey biorn with a stone, saving my sister from his maw. Godfrey, he of the swart beard, bound the wounds the beast had given her; so likewise my own, when, fleeing from the Thorling band that slew my foster brothers, I was rescued by the strangers, and, with Thyra, borne hence in their sky-ship."

At the terse recital, the crowd turned to Thord in added wonder, and the faces of all fairly beamed with friendship and hospitality. The spokesman expressed the general feeling with eager warmth—"Thrice welcome are the skyfarers! All Runefolk owe them gratitude for the saving of Rolf and Thyra. They are guests of Updal,—friends whom all will honour."

We bowed in acknowledgment, and Thord made answer for us: "We give thanks for the greeting. The Runefolk shall not sorrow for their welcome. From the home of Jarl Biorn we come, and

43

though our hands are light, our heads are not empty. We will strive to repay our hearth-cheer."

One of the eldormen who had turned from us to the balloon, and back again to Thord, in a puzzled manner, now stepped forward and addressed the big Icelander in a tone almost of veneration "That the guests may not lack the full honours which are their due, I pray them to disclose their rank. Rolf has called this sky-ship Skidbladnir. If, in truth, it be Frey's cloud-ship,—if our guests come from Asgard in human guise—may they grant us knowledge of the fact, that we may do them reverence."

Thord hesitated a moment, but caught my eye, and at once answered with decisive emphasis: "We are men from the Southland, and neither Asir, Elves, nor Vans. As common men we stand before you, begging hearth-peace and guest-cheer."

"For such," answered the eldorman, "not even the dwerger need beg in Updal. What says Holy Rune?

"'Be your deeds unto men Such you wish back again.'"

"Hello, Frank," I exclaimed; "that sounds familiar—the sentiment of it. Where have I heard it before?"

Balderston turned to me, his eyes shining with the look which so irresistibly drew people to him. Long as I had known him, his answer for the first time revealed to me the broad altruism of his nature, to which his charm owed all its force.

"Surely you remember, John. 'Do unto others'—"

"That's it! How did you come to have it on your tongue's end? By George, Frank, I believe that is your creed!"

Balderston blushed guiltily, and his hand went to the pocket which held his Testament.

"Well, John, I've never sought to hide—"

"You've never been able to hide that you're the best fellow out."

"Listen! They are inviting us to the Runehof."

"For a feast to-morrow,—or should I say, next _ring_?"

"Meanwhile we stick here as a town-show, I suppose," muttered Thord, impatient at the prolonged greeting of the eldormen. I turned to Thyra, who had been relating to the big warrior the details of her own and Rolf's escape.

"Will the daughter of Ragner tell us where we are to go?" I asked.

"To my father's house, Jan—where else?" she exclaimed, evidently surprised at the question. "See; the eldormen lead the way to escort us. Farewell, Smider."

The big warrior stepped back, with another hard look at me,

44

and I promptly took his place at the girl's side. As the crowd opened, and our party moved forward, I said: "You are pale and faint from your hurt, Thyra. Rest your arm on mine."

"I am weary, Jan," she answered simply, and did as I bade her. So we walked through the bright-clad throngs of Biornstaders, meeting everywhere, from men, women and children alike, a warmth of hospitable friendliness that both charmed and puzzled us. Taking it with the quotation from their Holy Rune, it set Balderston and myself to thinking.

Chapter VII
Hammer-Drott

We approached the great red stone facade of the house-town with our interest keyed to the highest pitch. Nor were we disappointed. From the park the front of the immense building looked all the more like some vast spreading palace of mediaeval type, the town walls answering for a court of like proportions. The architecture was massive in effect, yet relieved by the stairways and numerous porticoes, balconies and archways that broke the continuity of the surface. There was no suggestion of the rounded arch to be seen, all openings being either lintelled or arrow-arched.

As we passed beneath the lofty archway of the facade's main entrance, I wakened fully to the fact that the Runefolk were far other than the half-barbaric viking sons we had pictured them before our landing. Before us stretched a long straight passage, smoothly paved with grey stone and shut in by walls like the facade. The greenish tinge of the light at once struck us. We looked up and saw that the whole passage, or street, was spanned by a glassy roof.

"Stained glass!" muttered Thord. "These folk are thundering stylish."

"It's volcanic glass—obsidian," replied Balderston. "See the panes, set in a bronze framework. There is a section open. The whole roof of the town is like this. Remember how it shone. The place is just a great human anthill, with a glass top."

"You've hit it," said I. "This is not a street, but a main corridor of the big house. Look at the galleries bridging across the next story."

"Pow'ful strange!" commented Sergeant Black, and the further we went, the more fully we agreed with his statement.

After leading us past a great bazaar, in which we saw displayed nearly all the products and wares of the town, the eldormen turned up a flight of steps and along a hallway that brought us to a large court. The air was sweet with the perfume of flowers, and looking over the bronze balustrade of the gallery in which we stood, we saw the space below, like a bit of Paradise, full of brilliant flowers and blooming shrubs. In the centre rose a glossy-leaved tree, somewhat like a magnolia, with great bell-shaped scarlet flowers, large as a child's head. The tree reached up almost to the metal framework of the court's roof, from which the obsidian panes had been removed.

Beneath us, in the porticoes facing the four sides of the court, were numbers of men and women, spinning and weaving woollens. The implements of their industry were only the old-fashioned spinning-wheel and handloom; but the workers chatted and sang over their tasks as though at play. Well might they be light-hearted in such "an ideal workshop, with their babes and little tots rolling on the grass plot before their eyes.

"That don't look much like your friend Baxton's mills, John," remarked Balderston.

"Oh, go 'long! You're an anarchist. I suspect you believe all that socialist rot."

"I believe in what Jesus Christ said, and I'd like to see some of it put into everyday law. We need it badly at home. Look down there, and then think of our Christian sweat-shops!"

I had a flippant reply on my tongue, but at the moment we entered a portico before which stood a full-sized figure of a white bear, splendidly modelled in ivory. Beside this work of art the eldormen formed in two opposite lines, and crossed their headless spear shafts overhead. Rolf at once took Thord's hand and passed in under the arch. When we had followed, the eldormen bowed gravely and withdrew.

"Welcome to our home," said Rolf, and the simplicity of the words emphasised their sincerity. "Sit here with Thyra, and rest."

We turned gratefully to the stone bench in the cool shade of the portico, for the heavy air of the pit still oppressed us, and its warmth made our fur clothing burdensome. This last was also the case with Thyra, who suffered as well from her wounds and broken arm. So white and exhausted did she appear, that I insisted that she should at once leave us and try to gain some sleep. She was too weary to insist upon entertaining us, and so, with a grateful clasp of my hand and a little bow to the others, she followed her brother. We were left alone only a short time, for Rolf soon came striding back beside a stately matron, whom I knew at a glance as Thyra's mother. After the two, a maimed old giant stumped forward on his wooden leg.

"These are Astrid, my mother, and Ragner, my father," said Rolf, and he named us in turn.

"Our guests are very welcome," said Dame Astrid, mustering a smile even for Sergeant Black. Her grim old husband nodded hospitably, and gripped hands with us all. But I noticed that throughout Rolf's explanations he kept his eye fixed on Thord, and as we rose to follow our hostess into the house, I heard the old giant mutter: "By the beard of Odin, that were a deed for the skalds! Man or god, would I had seen him cast that rock! He will have play in the Thorling Mark."

Entering a doorway ornamented with Runic designs, Dame Astrid led us to seats at a table of polished redwood, on which she set a cold roast and wooden bowls filled with a drink like honey-mead. She then excused herself to go to Thyra. The lunch was ample, coming as it did so soon after our meal aboard the balloon.

When we were satisfied, Rolf and his father led us through a hallway glazed above with obsidian. We heard the gurgle of running water, and passing two or three doorways, came into a room whose centre was occupied by a bronze basin, twelve feet square.

"Your rooms are ready," said Rolf, pointing through an archway on the left. "If you would bathe before sleep, the bowl is here to your it use.

"We thank you—" I began. But old Ragner interrupted.

"Are we not Runemen?" he said. "Moreover, we owe you two lives. Ragner of the Mark will not soon forget the service—may bright visions fill your sleep!"

With that Rolf and the old giant gripped our hands, and withdrew. The sergeant followed them to the doorway and promptly shut the bronze panel, fastening it with the bar.

"What is that for, Black?" demanded Balderston.

"Best be on de safe side, sah."

"Throw it out," I ordered.

"That's right. But now, I'm going to turn in," said Thord, and he fetched a yawn that threatened to engulf the whole room. The act was infectious, and we all started for our beds, too sleepy to stop for a plunge, or even to talk over the amazing sequence of events that had so swiftly followed our sighting of the derelict balloon. The very magnitude of the wonders crowded into such a short space of time had blunted our sense of their strangeness, while the excitement due to them had added not a little to our bodily weariness. We were therefore quite ready for sleep, and the single cots, sheeted with cool linen and set each in its little apartment, by no means discouraged our retiring. The rooms were provided with movable screens to shut out the sunlight which poured in through the obsidian roof. Everything, in fact, tended to make our sleep a long one.

I awoke to find Balderston standing beside me in a handsome costume of woollens, just suited to the warmth of the season in Updal. In material and design it was the usual town dress of the Runemen,—an open-necked blue shirt, bordered with Runic designs in white, and fastened loosely with ivory clasps; knickerbockers of a heavy, brownish material like hemp cloth; a belt of metal links that looked like dull gold; light buskins, and striped woollen stockings.

"Pretty good golf outfit," suggested Balderston, with a smile. "But there is more. See here."

He held up a jaunty purple-winged cap, and a short cloak of beautiful yellow fur that displayed an iridescent lustre like the fur of the golden mole.

"You're in luck," I remarked.

"No more than the rest of you. There are your own new duds at your side."

"Good for Biornstad!—How long have you been out?"

"Long enough to take a plunge. The others are still snoring."

"No wonder! After the floes, this is bliss. Wait a minute while I run for a dip."

The bathroom proved to be furnished with almost all the conveniences of civilisation. I missed a brush, but with scissors and comb, managed to get my hair and beard into very fair shape. My new clothes, like Balderston's, fitted as though made to measure. Such, in fact, was the case. While we slept, Rolf had carried off our clothes to the tailors' garden, to furnish the necessary measurements, and the guild had turned out complete suits for the guests of the town within a few hours' time. Even Black was outfitted in the same manner, the only difference being that his cloak was of some red skin, instead of the iridescent yellow fur. His belt, like ours, was of solid gold links, engraved with Runic figures.

While I was still prinking, with the somewhat unsatisfactory aid of an obsidian mirror, Rolf came in to waken us for breakfast. He aroused Thord and Black, and after explaining the change of clothes, led Balderston and myself, by another door, into the portico, where we waited while the others bathed and dressed.

"How are your wounds?" I asked, when the big man cut short our thanks for the suit. He smiled at the question.

"Fast healing. In Updal a hurt heals quicker than down the Mark, but your balm is magic. Already I feel the flesh joining."

"Antiseptic dressing, under aseptic conditions," I commented to myself. How does your sister fare?"

"Very well, Jan," answered a soft voice, and the girl herself came forward beside the great ivory bear. At sight of her, my heart began to thump with almost painful force. If Thyra the Valkyrie had been stately and beautiful, Thyra the maiden simply ravishing. In place of her huntress dress, she now wore a natty blue skirt, and a scarlet bodice that exposed her white throat. Across her injured shoulder she had flung a cape of brilliant feather-work, and there was a scarlet ribbon entwined in each heavy plait of her golden hair.

"That make-up is for you, old man," whispered Balderston, and he gave me a sly poke in the ribs. I shook my head, though the possibility that he might be right was enough to fill me with an intoxicating joy.

Thyra meantime eyed our costumes with a critical air, that ended in a nod of approval. "Now you are Runemen," she said.

"Whatever the word may hold, I am glad to be so called," I replied with fervour. The girl blushed and dropped her eyes.

"Meat awaits us," she said, turning away. Her brother looked at me curiously, but spoke in a friendly tone: "I trust, Jan, that with the Vana-god's name you bear his heavy fist."

"Why so?" I asked.

"You remember Smider, who spoke to Thyra beside your cloud-ship? He will ask you to fist-play, or I am dog-wise,—and he stands second to me in the Metal Guild."

"He can call on either of us for fist-play," answered Balderston, with a readiness that brought a glow of satisfaction to Rolf's somewhat anxious face.

"It is well," he said. "Yet Smider strikes like grey biorn."

"A blow must hit to hurt," said I, as we entered the eating-room.

Thord and the sergeant were just seating themselves on one side of the table, at whose ends sat our host and hostess. Thyra had taken the place on the opposite side next her father, and I hastened to slip into the seat beside her. Balderston looked at me reproachfully, but soon began making himself agreeable to Dame Astrid. While I filled Thyra's ivory plate and my own with the roast

49

meats and succulent vegetables that covered the board, the lieutenant ventured to compliment the handsome old dame on her cooking. She looked at him in surprise.

"Do you not know?" she said. All food is from the Cook Guild Hall above. I was a member in my girlhood; but now I oversee the flax spinners."

"What do you do, Thrya" I asked.

"I weave with feathers, such as this cloak. They chose me at the Thing because of my gift for designs."

"Do all Runefolk work?"

"Assuredly, every one within the work age who can. Is it not so in your land?—"

"'Each for all, and all for each, Happiness and welfare reach.'"

"But what does your father do?" I inquired, my interest deepening.

"He has reached the rest age, and need do nothing, unless the Thing requires the service of his wisdom as eldorman. He has worked in the Metal and the Hunter Guilds, and, like all other men, has taken part each year at tillage and harvest."

A question asked Thord by old Ragner started the Icelander on quite an extended account of early Norse history, during which I was quite content to sit in silence, feasting on the savoury dinner— and the beauty of my sweet neighbour. Thord was still immersed in that rather misty period of Scandinavian history which preceded the advent of Christianity, when a large metal basket came sliding down a rod from an aperture in the side of the room. Dame Astrid at once went to the basket and took from it two large dishes, one heaped with sweet-cakes and the other with fruit. The latter looked like the bursting buds of thick-petalled white flowers, and such proved to be the fact. They were large as oranges and very sweet and juicy, with an aromatic flavour unlike anything we had ever tasted.

When we had finished this novel dessert, old Ragner gathered a few fragments of the meal on his plate, and rose with it uplifted in both hands.

"We thank the Father," he said simply, and response each of the family made the crosslike sign of Thor's hammer. This ceremony marked the end of the meal, and Dame Astrid promptly cleared the contents of the table into the metal baskets. Both were then hoisted up a shaft through the roof, whence, as Thyra explained, they slid back to the Cook Guild Hall on a return rod.

Ragner now excused himself to go to the Runehof, where he had been asked to give the eldormen his advice on some question that came within his special knowledge. As he left, Thyra suggested that she and her brother should introduce the guests of the town to Rolf's guild. All thought the idea a happy one, and it was acted upon without delay.

Balderston and Thord, and even Black, were as eager as myself to see more of the Runefolk and of their wonderful town. Nor were we disappointed. For the next hour Rolf and Thyra led us through passages and colonnades innumerable, up on the pavilioned roof, and down into court gardens, explaining the customs and arts of the town, and introducing us to the people, who, with friendly curiosity, thronged to meet us.

Everywhere was to be seen the same cheerful industry as in the Weavers' Court, and almost every moment some interesting new point came up. Balderston was wreathed in smiles, for a few inquiries had confirmed his surmise that Updal was a fully organised social democracy.

"Think of it, John!" he exclaimed. "This is indeed a true people's palace. We'll find no slums here. And their government— it's nothing but pure out and out democracy and Christianity."

"But how could they have gotten the idea? The old Norse had their kings and classes."

"Yes; but with them the law was supreme, and they had direct legislation through the Allthing. We think of them as heathen pirates, yet many of their laws and customs would put our own to shame. We send to the penitentiary the man who steals food when without work and famished; they pardoned him. We have fire companies, but they had community fire-insurance. When a homestead burned, the owner had his property restored by his district, except luxuries—mark that!"

"Well," said I, "that was no more socialistic than our public schools, or post-office. It does not explain this development of a full-fledged social democracy."

"Perhaps they took the hint from the ants, if there are any in this pit-world," suggested Thord. "Ask Rolf."

Rolf explained that the present social conditions of Biornstad had existed for two hundred years or more, and, so far as he knew, had been due to a gradual application of the principles of the Holy Rune to practical affairs.

"I should like to sec that Rune," remarked Balderston.

"You will see it presently, when we go to the feast," replied Thyra. "Now we come to the Metal Guild, as you may know by the din."

"And by the stacks," added her brother, pointing up through an open skylight to a group of lofty chimneys.

Once more we descended to the ground floor, where the brother and sister led us through court after court of metal workers. The first were finishing shops; but soon we entered an immense forge hall, where hundreds of hammers were clanging upon their anvils.

At the largest anvil we came upon my friend Smider, welding together two white-hot bars with a huge platinum sledge. Upon our approach, he paused to nod at Thyra and addressed her brother.

"Ho, Rolf," he said. "Would that I had your arm here. It is a stubborn piece."

"It must needs be, if Smider's arm flags. But my hurt would burst open at the first swing."

"Give me a hammer," said Thord shortly. One of the men holding the bars ran to fetch Rolf's sledge, which was even larger than Smider's.

"The metal cools," said Rolf.

"There is yet time to work it, if your hammer is good. Stand clear."

Tossing aside his cloak and hat, Thord stepped before the anvil and twirled up the massive sledge like a plaything. For a moment he held it poised overhead; then brought it down with tremendous force.

"Good. A well-balanced tool, observed the giant coolly. He shifted his grip a little, balanced the sledge, and suddenly began to strike so fast and powerfully that from all over the hall men came running to see the new smith. Down rained the terrific blows, like the concussion of a steam hammer, and the great metal bars could not but yield obedience.

"So; it is done," said the giant, abruptly pausing. The dozen assistants lifted the forging aside, and Thord caught up Smider's sledge in his left hand.

"I have wielded hammers before," he said, not vauntingly, but as one states a simple fact. As he spoke, he shortened his grip on the sledge handles, and swinging them up, one in each hand like forehammers, began to play with them on the anvil.

By this time all work in the all had ceased, and hundreds of members of the guild gathered around the giant smith from Biorn's Land. They had good cause to throng about that towering form. It was a wonderful sight to see Thord play the two great hammers on the ringing anvil. But there was a far greater treat before the guild. Suddenly the Icelander burst out in the forge-song from "Siegfried," his mighty voice rolling through the hall like thunder. On all sides I saw the broad faces of the brawny smiths flush with fierce pleasure.

All the old viking blood in their veins surged hot and strong at the Nibelung lay. So too did Thord's. He dropped the smaller sledge and whirled Rolf's about his head.

"Look out!" warned Balderston, and I pushed Thyra behind me as I caught the glint in the giant's eye. He had reached the point where Siegfried cleaves the anvil with his sword. The sledge, gripped in both his hands, swept around a broad circle and hurled down, driven by all the Icelander's vast strength. It fell like a thunderbolt. There was a rending crash, and the great anvil, shattered by the terrific impact, fell from its block in a dozen fragments.

For a time we were deafened by the shouts of the guildmen. Soon the cries began to take form—"Hammer-drott! Hammer-drott! Call husthing, Rolf. Husthing bode!—Lot! lot!"

"What does it mean?" I asked of Thyra, as Rolf sprang upon the anvil block and raised a sledge.

"A great honour to our friend. The smiths have not named a hammer-drott in fifty seasons. Even Rolf failed to split Thor's Stone."

"Such was the anvil's name?"

"Yes. It is a guild custom, Jan. When the Stone is split, the breaker is named as hammer-drott, and he makes another Stone. Whoever can split the new Stone becomes hammer-drott in turn."

Smider turned about in the crowd just before us, and said: "The skyfarer has my vote. It will be long ere another breaks the Stone he forges. He strikes like Ake-Thor, his namesake. Do his fellow farers wield the hammer?"

"No. But Rolf tells me you are fond of fist-play. We have some knowledge of that."

I felt Thyra's hand suddenly clasp my arm.

"Do not talk so," she whispered hurriedly. "In the idrottir he holds only to the letter of the Rune-law. Do not anger him."

Though he could not have heard her, Smider saw the troubled look the girl's face, and he smiled rather grimly.

"Frey's namesake should bear a heavy fist," he said with taunting irony.

"Choose your time. I will not be the one to shun a bout," I rejoined. The uproar of the smiths, voting for Thord, prevented any further talk.

As Balderston, Black and I accompanied Thyra from the hall, leaving Thord to his triumph, the lieutenant inquired what the title of hammer-drott implied.

"That is for the guild to say," the girl answered.

If he be wise as well as strong, he may fashion their work as he thinks best."

"Does it bring no other power or rights?" I asked.

"All powers and rights rest in the voice of the Thing. The guilds have honours, such as this, but no more," replied the girl; and while we wandered through the halls and roofed streets of the wonderful house-town, she unfolded the whole grand but simple scheme of the social organism. So far as I could see, the sole liberty lost by the citizens was the right of preying on fellow townfolk by crime or sharp dealing. True, no one could be a millionaire, an aristocrat, or a tyrant, but neither could one be a slave or a beggar. They had put in practice the abhorrent theory that flesh and blood weighs more than gold,—that man should be considered before the dollar.

Chapter VIII
The Orm-Crown

Our trip through the town ended in a visit to one of the school courts, where children were taught poetry, music and drawing, writing in Runic character, and all branches of manual training. Thyra said that the Holy Rune and a synopsis of the Rune-law constituted an important part of every child's education; but we saw nothing of either rune or law at the time.

After this we returned to Ragner's portico, where we sat talking and admiring the great ivory bear, until Thyra returned with her mother, to accompany us to the Runehof. Thoughtfully considerate of my feelings, Balderston stepped out beside the dame. I nodded the sergeant to follow, and myself fell in behind with Thyra. No doubt I too plainly showed my eagerness to walk alone with the girl, for a sudden shyness and confusion fell upon her. She dropped her eyes and held her face half averted, so that I could only see a bit of rounded cheek glowing softly through the maze of golden hair. However, by the time we reached the green her reserve had vanished, and she was chatting and laughing in the gayest spirits.

We found the balloon exactly where it had descended, the car now buried beneath the folds of the empty sack. Even Black, who still harboured suspicions of our hosts, was satisfied at sight of the spiked fence that had been built about it to keep off children. We were passing by, when a short, thickset man came forward with a roll of parchment.

"Greeting," he said. "Will Skidbladnir's owner stay a little?"

"What can I do for you?" I asked.

The man unrolled his parchment, and exhibited plans for a building much like a kiosk.

"The Builders' Guild has been asked by the eldormen to shelter the cloud-craft. We will store it, if you wish; yet all would be pleased should you consent that it be hung within the building here planned. Every one then might view it as it came."

"I owe both the guild and the eldormen thanks for their trouble, and am glad to furnish the folk with an object of interest," I replied heartily. It was indeed a pleasure to make some little return for the hospitality we were receiving, and, moreover, I thought it just as well, in case of a possible emergency, to have the balloon so conveniently placed for inflation. The architect bowed, rolled up his parchment, and walked briskly away towards the main archway.

Thyra and I strolled on across the common, which seemed one huge playground. In every direction we could see men, maidens and children engaged in all kinds of outdoor sports. There were running, jumping and wrestling, slinging and hammer-throwing, a ball game much like lacrosse, fencing with edged weapons, spear-throwing and archery. The little we saw of the last in passing was enough to explain why Rolf had so wildly dodged the Thorling shafts. One of the archers, a mere boy, shivered war arrow against the town wall at two hundred paces.

"Golly! Dat beats de 'Patches," called Black, and I saw his hand go instinctively to his hip. But, if anything, there was more cause for alarm on the other side. The townfolk could not accustom themselves to the ebony skin and grotesque features of the outland carl. Even the men avoided the uncanny stranger, and a group of young girls in his path scurried away like frightened rabbits. A few of the most daring boys on the green proceeded to put each other's boldness to proof by dashing across in front of the sergeant. The bravest spirit among them, however, incontinently fled, when Black fished out the stub of his last cigar and set it in operation.

"There goes Surt again," said I, smiling at the children's panic.

"It is wondrous that a man should drink fire," replied Thyra, who was still ignorant of the process. I called the sergeant back, and had him illustrate my explanation. She watched him gravely, sniffed the smoke, and then expressed her candid opinion on the subject. It was, indeed, very candid, and I concluded not to mention the fact that I, too, was an adept at "smoke-swallowing." To retain the respect of the most charming maiden in the world, I was quite willing to give up tobacco,—besides, we had none left.

A quarter mile more brought us across the common to the Runehof. Like the facade of the town-house, the Biornstad temple was ornamented by numerous archways and colonnades, porticoes and buttressed stairways. There were towers as well, which, with the convergence of the town walls, made the height of the edifice more in proportion to its width than was the case with the great facade across the common.

The centre archway led us directly into an immense arsenal, extending, like a broad, transverse corridor, almost entirely across the Runehof. The apartment was stacked to the roof with shields, mail, helmets, swords, sheaves of arrows and javelins,—all the various arms and armour of the Runefolk.

Fascinated by this remarkable display of weapons, the sergeant stopped to examine them; but Thyra and I crossed over and entered a doorway arched with spears,—the sign of Odin. It was the private hall of the eldormen, a long and rather narrow room. The furniture consisted of carved chairs and tables, fur mats and a tapestry of enormous shaggy skins. On the dark background of these monstrous hides, other smaller skins were arranged in unique colour designs. I was astonished at the great variety of the furs, both in size and hue. The skins of all the well-known Arctic animals, as well as of the grey bear, I at once recognised; but the majority were entirely new to me.

One skin in particular attracted my eye even more than the huge hides of the background. It was a silky fur, blotched with dark leopard rosettes, but large as a tiger skin and of a vivid scarlet between the spots. I pointed this out to Thyra.

"A fire-cat," she said, and we advanced to examine it closer. As we moved forward, I noticed for the first time that Balderston and Dame Astrid had entered the room before us. They stood on our left, and were talking with a small, gipsy-looking girl, at sight of whom Thyra uttered a cry of astonishment and delight. In an instant she had darted forward and was greeting the other maiden as one risen from the dead. Laughing and sobbing, the two fell into each other's arms, in such an ecstasy of happiness that it was some time before they could think of anything else. Meantime we stood back a little, and Dame Astrid explained:

"It is Jofrid the Orm Vala—poor lass! She was Thyra's heart-friend, the merriest maid Updal. But five seasons ago her father slew a man who had thrown him in wrestling. He fled to Hoding Grimeye, bearing with him the maid. She tells me that the Thorlings chose her for Vala last Yule, and she bent to the Orm to avoid a worse evil—the wooing of their king."

"If the valaship is hard," I asked, "why should not the maid stay in Updal? Though a thousand Thorlings came to stand guard over her, surely Biornstad could protect its own."

"She gave her vow to return, so the Thorlings had no need to put her under guard," replied Dame Astrid simply. "Her escort stopped at the Updal Gate, and the only Thorlings who accompanied her on to Biornstad were two of Hoding's heralds. They come direct from their king where you met him on the fells, and overtook Jofrid just at the foot of the pass. She thinks that their mission is in regard to you and your fellow skyfarers."

"I say, John, it looks as if we'd stirred up the pit," remarked Balderston. I hope our grim-eyed friend has not sent to demand our heads."

"If he has, there will be war, sure. These Runefolk are not the men to give us up."

"You're right there. But doff your hat. The young ladies are about to remember our existence."

The girls had just parted, and they now turned to us, the Vala once more calm, almost lethargic, but Thyra radiant with joy. Never had she looked more lovely than when, flushed and bright-eyed, she drew Jofrid forward to introduce us,—and yet I found myself turning from her to fix my gaze on the Orm priestess.

Beside Thyra's stately figure, so tall and lissome, the Vala looked very small and frail—almost fragile. Not only was she the smallest Rune maiden I had yet seen,—she was also the first whom I could have termed a brunette. Her hair was dark brown, and fell about her shoulders in wild elfin locks, which seemed writhing to escape the clasp of the gold dragon crown that bound her forehead. This horrid emblem of the valaship was a masterpiece of the most _outre art_.

At first I thought it was intended for a serpent. A closer view, however, showed it to be more of a saurian form, snaky in its proportions, but with spiny crest and whale-like flippers. The upreared head, with gaping red jaws and opal eyes, gave the strange image a weird semblance of life that made me shudder.

Yet notwithstanding its uncanny verisimilitude, the gold dragon was far less striking than the face it surmounted. It was a face one could never forget,—the features of a child, stamped with the seal of the knowledge of evil. The deepset grey eyes, full of mystic wildness, seemed darkened by the shadow of an unutterable sorrow. Their look recalled to me that fearful painting of the Druid priestess forced to officiate at a human sacrifice.

As the strange girl paused before me, her eyes seemed to light up with an inward flame, and their burning gaze searched into my very soul. To all appearances, she was quite unconscious of Thyra's half-shy, half-proud introduction. "It is Jan, sweetheart,—Jan Godfrey. He it was bound my hurt when biorn struck me:"

The Vala made no response. Silent and motionless, she gazed at me with dilating eyes, while I stared back, my nerves tingling as though I held an electric battery. At last, greatly to my relief, the priestess lowered her eyes and released me from their sombre spell. She even smiled faintly with her lips as she moved aside.

"I give you joy, Thyra," she said. "You have both chosen well."

I saw Thyra look at me in a startled manner, and then she ran to hide her blushing cheeks on her mother's shoulder. Jofrid, however, gave no heed to her friend. She seemed to have lapsed into unconsciousness of her surroundings. She was only aroused by a direct question from Balderston, who, with thoughtful tact, sought thus to divert attention and cover Thyra's confusion.

"Will the Orm Vala foretell my fortune?" he asked.

The priestess raised her eyes and fixed on Balderston the strange gaze that had so fascinated me.

Before it his smile vanished, giving place to a look of deep sadness. Presently his eyes began to glare, as though looking upon some terrible spectacle, and his face whitened until it was no less pallid than that of the girl before him.

At last the Vala spoke, very slowly: "I see Hoding's court...Hoding and his Thorlings, Bera and Godfrey and the great one whom you call Thord...There are others—but you are not with them...The time for sacrifice draws near...Nidhug hungers in Hela Pool...I see the Orm—"

The seeress paused, and a violent tremor shook her slight frame. But some unseen power seemed to compel her to speak on—"The mists rise—it is dark; yet I see them gather the foul dwerger...The Orm jaws gape...I see—-I see."

Suddenly the Vala thrust out her hands before her eyes, and pitched heavily forward into Balderston's arms. She was in a swoon when Dame Astrid lifted her up and bore her off like a child. Thyra, with eyes carefully averted, hastened out after her mother, and left me in a quandary whether I should follow. I ended by turning back to Balderston. He was gazing moodily at the Vala's crown, which had fallen off when she swooned and now lay at his feet. The image seemed to irritate him strangely, and in a minute or so he gave it a savage kick.

I did not ask the reason for his temper. My thoughts were in a whirl over the Vala's words to Thyra. The girl's blushes had confirmed all that the remark implied. Whether through clairvoyance, or merely by acute observation, Jofrid had perceived that her friend loved the swart outlander. With all my joy at this disclosure, however, I had my misgivings whether it would further my wooing. It was evident that the open announcement of her heart's secret had alarmed the girl's modesty, and already I was beginning to experience the effects. As I thought over the situation, I half wished the Vala had not spoken.

Presently, while I stood musing, Balderston went and fetched the Orm-crown.

"What the devil is it?" he asked.

I examined the gold reptile closely, and the thing appeared to follow my every movement with its fiery eyes.

"Ugh! It's horrible enough for Satan himself," I replied. "It doesn't look like the conventional dragon, though,—but more like one of Marsh's Mosasaurs. Perhaps the stone Orm they talk about is a fossil—a real _Tylosaurus dyspelor_, petrified in soft strata and exposed by erosion."

"It's a monster, at least, if this is its miniature. Think of that girl wearing such a thing!"

"She certainly does not enjoy the privilege."

"Privilege!—You should have seen her eyes before she swooned."

With a curse, Balderston snatched the evil emblem from my hand and sent it spinning down the room. At the moment, old Ragner appeared at the farther end of the apartment with two strangers. The latter, both very tall men, were decked out in all the barbaric splendour of furs, Runic bractreates and enamelled armour. So unlike the Runemen were they, both in dress and bearing, I at once took them to be Thorlings, and my surmise was borne out by their actions. At sight of the dragon crown, whirling towards them along the floor like a living snake, each uttered a cry of fear and anger, and sprang forward. One stooped for the rolling image and lifted it reverently to a table, while the second man came striding up to Balderston, his face ablaze with wrath.

"Who is he casts _nid_ on the Orm?" he demanded. "A guest of Updal," answered Balderston in his mild voice.

"And a coward!" shouted the Thorling. Balderston measured the man contemptuously. "You lie," he said.

At the deliberate insult, the Thorling uttered a yell of rage and tore his dagger from its peace-thongs; but before he could raise it, Balderston struck out, right and left. The second blow, on the Thorling's jaw, brought him down like a felled ox. Balderston stooped for the dagger at his feet; then rose to face the second Thorling, who came running, sword in hand. I was unarmed, and though old Ragner stumped forward to intervene, he could not overtake the Thorling. For a moment matters looked serious for us. But then I heard a muffled oath, and Sergeant Black sprang to the lieutenant's side with upraised revolver. The Thorling stopped short, sword in air, and stood glaring at this unexpected apparition.

"Faul!" he gasped—"black Faul!"

"Stand where you are!" commanded Balderston. "Another step, and my carl slays you."

"Sheath your sword, Varin!" cried the first Thorling, as he staggered to his feet. He stared wonderingly at Black; then turned to Balderston.

"By Frey!" he exclaimed; "that was a good cheek-horse. Yours is a fist for a warrior to clasp."

Balderston gripped the man's extended hand without hesitation. The other Thorling, however, leaned morosely on his sword, and muttered "Yet there is _nid_ on the Orm. Had he a sword, he should fight me."

Balderston raised the dagger and answered the man: "Hearken, Thorling—but for the coming of my swart carl, this should have been your bane. Watch!"

The hand with the dagger went up to Balderston's shoulder and forward sharply. There was a flash in the air, and the dagger struck through the centre of a tapestry panel across the room, shattering on the stone behind. The Thorling thrust his sword back in its sheath and came forward with outstretched hand.

"Hervard is right," he said. "It is doubly pleasing to find the skyfarers such kempermen. We are heralds of Hoding Grimeye, and saw you on the fells when you slew our fellows with thunderstones, and bore off Rolf Kaki and the maiden in your cloud-ship. Hoding was wild for vengeance, but Bera, his sister, wished to look upon you, and so persuaded him to send you greeting to his court and kingdom. Asir or men, whichever you may be, we bring you welcome to the Ormvol. May you grant Bera's wish, and come with us. There is wild play for warriors in the Mark."

"That I doubt not," replied Balderston, glancing at the great skins on the walls. "When would you have us go?"

"That is for our guests to say; though we would ask a _rings_ delay to rest. We have travelled far and fast. The Vala left the Orm three _rings_ since and came by way of the Strand Bridge, yet we overtook her at the Updal Gate. Now I would ask, how comes the Orm-crown in this hall?"

"The Vala swooned, and the crown fell," said Balderston tersely. "It is a heavy burden for the maid."

"True," replied Hervard, and I thought I saw a glimmer of pity in his grim, scarred face. "The Orm-crown will crush her yet it is lighter than Hoding's love."

I could well believe this assertion as I recalled to mind the Thorling king, snarling on the ridge like a baffled hyena. The remembrance of his ferocious face awoke in me a sudden doubt.

"What pledge have we of King Hoding's guest-troth?" I demanded.

Hervard held out a ring rudely shaped to resemble the Orm.

"This is the king's guest-pledge," he said. "Whoever bears it is peace-holy to every Thorling,—he and all his following. It is none the less binding though the king bears you no love. Having sent his token, he dare not seek your harm, for even he fears Bera, and the Orm yet more. Furthermore, should you stay a little and come from Updal with the Vala, the very dwerger would bow before you."

Both Thorlings looked significantly at the dragon crown.

I was about to reply, but Balderston cut in very decisively: "We fear neither dwerger nor beasts; yet we are the guests of Updal. It would be unmannerly to leave the Runefolk so soon. We will wait for the Vala."

"Well said," remarked old Ragner.

As he spoke, eldorman entered to announce that the feast awaited us,

Chapter IX
Holy Rune

After our excursion through the house-town, I was fully prepared to find the Rune hall grand, perhaps magnificent, in its size and decorations; but my anticipations fell far short of the facts.

The hall was an immense triangular apartment, occupying the greater part of the edifice. Across its width extended three rows of gigantic redwood columns, which towered up forty and fifty feet to the support of the obsidian roof. The walls were completely covered to a height of thirty feet with trophies of the chase,—the strange skins, gigantic horns and ferocious heads of beasts unknown without this Polar world.

Yet all these wonders failed to hold my eye for a moment. Over the heads of the guests we looked into the apex of the hall, and saw the Runestal gleaming in its marvellous white beauty, like a bit of fairy land. Such a piece of ivory carving I believe was never seen elsewhere in all the world. It was a masterpiece that must have taken years to complete. From floor to ceiling, all the angle of the converging walls was filled with a maze of graven ivory,—a jungle of ivory palms and reeds and strange exotic plants, peopled with ivory beasts, ivory birds, ivory reptiles. We even saw ivory insects on the perfectly carved vegetation, when, bursting with wonder and admiration, we pushed through the crowd to the front of the hall.

We had little time, however, to study the fairy scene. The eldorman, who had followed us with old Ragner, called us all to our places at the guest table. The interruption, unwelcome as it was, brought with it an answer to the puzzle whence the Runefolk could have obtained such a vast quantity of ivory. In our impetuous rush up the hall, we had scarcely noticed the numerous long tables and benches between the pillars. These, for the most part, while of good material and finish, were plain and unpretentious. But only the closeness of the Runestal itself could have kept our eyes from the two remarkable seats which flanked it. They stood behind long narrow tables of ivory, bound with bronze, and were themselves constructed of the same artistic materials. What surprised us, however, was the row of enormous upcurving tusks which supported the blue canopies of the benches.

"Mammoths!" cried Balderston. At the word, I thought of the huge skins of the eldormen's tapestry, and understood. Truly, we had strange adventures impending. The beast-man, Polar Northmen, the cave-bear, the reptilian birds, and now, mammoths!—what next might we expect in this weird underworld? I gazed about at the spoils of the chase that told of so many strange and ferocious beasts. In the medley of trophies, one, a splendid skin of inky blackness, caught my eye. Though it was some distance away, I could distinguish a monstrous tigerish head, armed with frightful serrated tushes.

"The sabre-toothed tiger!" I cried, and before me stalked the grim vision of that Quaternary terror, _Machairodus latidens_, the greatest of all carnivora. My exclamation drew Balderston's attention, and together we advanced to obtain a nearer view of the black tiger. At the first aisle, however, we found our way blocked by a long line of men and women laden with table service. Before these representatives of the Cook Guild had passed, we caught sight of Thord's giant figure looming up in the hall's main entrance.

"Hello! the show is opening," said Balderston. "Guess we had better take our seats. We can look around afterwards."

"True; there go the harpers, or skalds—or whatever they are called now," I replied, and we returned to Black and the two Thorlings at the ivory bench on the left of the Runestal. By the time we were in our places, the half-dozen skalds at the hall entrance had joined in a deep-toned chant of welcome, and started up the hall before Thord and the eldormen. The crowd was so dense that at first I could see only the Icelander's fiery head, towering above his neighbours; but as the little procession drew near, I perceived the skalds with their harps, the dignified eldormen, Dame Astrid and Rolf, and—what put my heart in a glow—the lissome figure of Thyra.

"The Vala! She, too, is a guest. She will sit with us," whispered Balderston, in suppressed delight.

"The Vala?" I replied. "Where is she?—oh, Thyra. I did not see her. But will Thyra sit with her friend, I wonder?"

"Ask her father."

Old Ragner, who stood waiting at the end of the guest bench, nodded pleasantly in answer to my question.

"Ay," he said; "the family of him who acts as town-host sit with the guest, if they so wish, and there be room. The Thorling heralds have chosen the hearth of Ingemund, the eldorman, but we will have Jofrid, as well as you."

"That's good," murmured Balderston.

"What?" I asked; but just then the skalds came up beside us, and twanged their loudest, while the rest of the procession filed by. The eldormen turned to the ivory seat on the right of the Runestal. Thord and the others came in with us. Thyra shyly avoided my gaze, and though I sought to gain her side, she slipped in between Balderston and the Vala. I was not to be frustrated, however, and promptly nudged Balderston, who was staring at the Orm-crown. He caught my meaning and rose with a readiness that surprised me. The reason was apparent when, bowing his apologies, he deliberately wedged himself in between the Vala and Dame Astrid. There was no escape for Thyra. As Balderston seated himself, the

63

attendants shoved our ivory table closer, and penned us in our places.

For some time I refrained from pressing my advantage. Thord sat on my right, and we talked over our prospects of lively hunting in the Thorling Mark, when we should go to visit King Hoding. The array of gigantic horns and ferocious wild beast heads promised all the sport the most ardent hunter could desire. Drawing upon my Indian and African experiences, I was telling Thord the chief characteristics of the great cats, and speculating how best to hunt mammoths, when old Ragner opened the feast with a toast to the guests.

The deep-toned "Skoal!" that rolled across the hall made the very pillars tremble. Before the great cry had died away, two of the skalds came across from the eldormen's seat, bearing between them a gigantic drinking horn, mounted with gold. This huge loving-cup was placed upon our table and slid along from end to end, each of us in turn taking a sip of the honey-mead it contained. We out-landers all stared with deepest curiosity at the polished black horn, which was exactly like a bison horn many times magnified.

However, I did not stop to speculate on the beast whose head had furnished the giant flagon. After drinking from it I was required to push it along to Thyra, which gave me an excuse for edging nearer. Nor was that all. As the girl was unable to manage the vessel with one hand, I of course had to hold it for her and then help her move it on to the Vala. Balderston promptly offered Jofrid a like service, and as the horn passed on, I ventured to address my fair neighbour.

"What have I done, Thyra, that you should be angry with me?" I asked.

"Angry? I am not angry, Lord Frey," she protested.

"Why then do you turn away, and call me by a name I dislike?"

"I am not angry, Jan," she repeated. In her eagerness to deny the charge, she forgot her shyness.

"That is better," said I, as the blue eyes met mine. "Now I trust that you will remember that guest-cheer is due me. You may leave the Vala to my friend. He talks like a skald."

"Is it true what he told Jofrid—that you are to go with her to the Ormvol?"

"We expect to go. The Thorling heralds, at the end of our bench, bring us their king's pledge and a guest-welcome from his sister Bera, that giantess."

"Ah! if only my arm were well!" exclaimed Thyra, her eyes

sparkling. "I have never seen the Orm, and the chances are rare. Hoding is so savage and morose that he seldom sends his pledge of hearth-troth to Updal. I also long to be a few _rings_ more with Jofrid!"

"Why should you not go? Must you and Rolf so soon return to your guild work?"

"Oh, no, we have yet many free _rings_ in our favour. But my arm—"

"That will shortly heal, and we may not start for some time. Anyway, you would have little need to use it. Your brother already regains his strength. Between his sword and our thunder-tubes, there will be small danger from wild beasts."

"I had no thought of the beasts, Jan. It was that I should fail to bear my share of the journey toil. As to danger, the score of Thorlings who brought Jofrid to the Updal Gate will return to guard her down the Mark."

"But do you not fear their king—Hoding Grimeye? From the glimpse I had of him on the fells, he is more to be feared than grey biorn."

At the Thorling's name Thyra shuddered; yet she shook her golden head—"There is naught to fear. Hoding is bound by the Orm-pledge. With all his dwerger blood, even he dare not break guest-troth."

"So the heralds say. I am glad to know that the forestmen acknowledge one good law," I replied; and then we fell to comparing the Thorling monarchy with the social democracy of the Runefolk.

Meantime the feast went on, enlivened by songs from the skalds and the drinking of healths in the mild honey-mead. The merriment was at its height, when two of the eldormen rose from their places and disappeared in the ivory maze of the Runestal. At once the skalds gathered before the shrine, and as the two eldormen reappeared, the harps thrummed the prelude of a solemn chant. All other sounds in the hall were hushed, and the chanting skalds began a solemn march up and down the aisles, followed by the two eldormen. Each of the latter exhibited to the eager spectators a flat ivory case, glazed on the top with a thin facing of obsidian.

"What is it?" I asked Thyra—"what do the eldormen show?"

"It is the Rune, Jan."

"The Holy Rune!" repeated Jofrid, in a tone of great longing. And what is the Rune?—who wrote it?"

"It is the Word of the Father, of him who shall be after Ragnarok," answered Thyra, and she bent her head reverently. "The skalds have a saga which tells how the Rune came. When Jarl Biorn

65

sailed from the Southland, he brought with him a thrall of another blood, a man blue-eyed but dark, who was a master of many runes. That thrall carried always in his bosom the writing which we call the Holy Rune, and when, after many years in Updal, he was about to die, he copied the Rune in the tongue of our people. Both parchments have come down through the ages. The eldormen bear them in the cases."

Balderston leaned over with an eager inquiry—"You are telling of the Rune and a thrall—who was the man?—of what people was he?"

"The saga tells only that he was of another blood. Jarl Biorn freed him and gave him his daughter in marriage, and thereafter he toiled for the good of others throughout his life. So men remember his love, and read his Rune as he bade them."

"They bring it to us now," murmured the Vala, her mystic eyes fixed on the approaching eldormen. The final turn of the little procession brought it before our table, where it halted while the Rune was shown to the guests. The Thorling heralds sought to mask their curiosity by a look of haughty indifference. What was this old Rune to free men of the Mark? We, however, had no motive for hiding our interest, and craned eagerly across the narrow table to obtain a better view of the faded writings. Both parchments were just legible, and I was trying to spell out the Runic characters of the first, when a cry from Balderston drew upon him the eyes of all the feasters.

"Greek text!" he shouted, as he took the original Rune out of the hand of the astonished bearer. "Look, John; it's Irish script—of the tenth century!"

"But the words—what does it say?"

"Say—say! No wonder they call it the Holy Rune!—It's the Sermon on the Mount!"

"What?" I cried.

"The Sermon on the Mount, as I'm a living man. That thrall must have been an Irish priest."

Highly excited, Balderston laid the Rune before him on the table, and tracing the lines with his finger, he rendered the whole manuscript in sonorous Norse. He had not read a dozen sentences before every person in the hall sat silent and spellbound, drinking in with rapt attention this strange new wording of the Holy Rune. As Balderston's clear voice proclaimed those Divine rules of life and love and right, the pleasures of the feast were forgotten in a higher joy—a happiness which brought its spiritual glow to the sternest faces. As I watched the hushed feasters in their solemn joy and

66

wonder, I could have imagined myself in an assembly of the early Christians.

At last Balderston's finger traced along the lower edge of the parchment:

"Ye shall know them by their fruits," there the Rune ended. With barely a moment's pause, the reader drew out his Testament and continued to the end of the chapter.

Had Balderston saved the land from invasion and conquest, he could not have received a greater ovation. For an instant the people sat motionless; then, as if moved by a single impulse, they came surging to the front of the hall, wild with delight.

"He has ended the Rune!" they cried. "He will tell us of the Father! He has the Rune—the whole Rune!—Tell us of this Jesus who spoke it."

Smiling down upon the excited crowd, Balderston held up his hand, and as the uproar died away, he began the story of the "White Christ."

Chapter X
The Shadow of the Orm

After the feast, our relations with the Runefolk became fully settled. The people did not treat us with greater hospitality than before, because that was impossible; but their friendliness had deepened to fraternal love. No longer were we wanderers or guests,—we were brothers in the great Rune family.

The two weeks of the Vala's visit were very happy ones. Balderston and I spent much of our time in the Metal Guild, giving Thord pointers on metallurgy, and figuring out an electric plant and factory, which, being owned by the community, could not but prove a blessing to all alike. Even Black found a place in the Biornstad life. At a hint from his lieutenant, Dame Astrid introduced him to the Cook Guild, where he spent much of his time, swapping receipts. He quickly began to pick up Norse, and in spite of his uncanny appearance, became a general favourite, even with the children. When not in the Cook Guild Hall, he was usually to be found on the common, engaged in some game with the Thorling heralds and the Biornstad athletes.

Thord was far too busy directing his great force of metal workers to join in any games, and though Balderston and I allowed ourselves more leisure, we found little time for athletics. As may be surmised, I sought the company of my lovely sweetheart upon every possible excuse, and neither Ragner nor his good dame made any opposition to my wooing. The old hunter, I fancied, would have preferred Thord as his daughter's suitor, and Dame Astrid was plainly captivated by Balderston. But the girl herself could not hide a preference for me.

Had Balderston put himself forward as a rival, I should have feared for the outcome. Fortunately, he did not enter the field. I believe that at first his only reason for not doing so was his friendship for me, for no man heart-free could have been indifferent to Thyra's beauty and noble character. After the first meeting with the Vala, however, he had another motive for his course. It very soon became apparent that the pity which had filled him when he learned the little maid's sad fate was fast ripening into a still more tender feeling.

Girt in by the friendship and affection of her own people, with the Orm-crown hidden from sight, and Balderston so often at her side, Jofrid forgot for a time her dreaded valaship. She put aside the terrible memory of the Orm, and drank in eagerly all the joy and happiness that came to her. This interval of peace and enjoyment in her wretched life was all too brief. It was not even to last out her visit.

Shortly before the time set for our departure from Biornstad, Black requested us to be present at an archery contest. Thord, as usual, was too busy to go, as were also both Rolf and Dame Astrid, while old Ragner was called upon for counsel by the eldormen. The four remaining members of our hearth, however,—Jofrid and Balderston, Thyra and myself,—gladly accepted the sergeant's invitation. We went in anticipation of an interesting, perhaps exciting, diversion, and I, for one, found the realisation only too full.

One of the most successful bowmen proved to be Smider, who saw us standing among the spectators, and promptly challenged me to shoot with him. When I replied that I was not a bowman, he smiled scornfully, and cried in pretended surprise: "What! A namesake of Frey, yet cannot draw a bow?"

"No more than you or your fellow-bowmen could shoot with our thunder-tubes," rejoined Balderston. "Ask the daughter of Ragner how we slew the Thorlings while yet beyond bowshot."

"I have heard. But, if I remember, you are versed in some at least of our idrottir."

"Is it the fist-play you would have?" said I. "If so, the time and place could not be better."

"I am of the same mind," answered Smider, and he flung aside his cloak, unable to conceal his eagerness and exultation. Confident in my training, I was not behind in preparing for the contest. But Thyra sought to intervene, her cheeks pale with anxiety.

"Is this hearth-peace, Smider?" she protested. "Is it thus we give cheer to the guests of Updal?"

"True, maiden; I have done wrong. He is a guest, and peace-holy," replied Smider ironically.

"Do not fear, Thyra," I interrupted. "After the great kindness your people have shown me, I could not but give pleasure in turn."

My irony stung no less sharply than Smider's, and the flush still reddened the face of the big smith as we took our places. At the moment the Thorling heralds joined the crowd of spectators, and Hervard called out in mock anxiety: "Ho, my Updal friend; if Godfrey's fist be as weighty as Balderston's, you had best pad your jaw."

At the jesting words, Smider's anger burst all restraint. It was enough to have his wooing crossed by a meddlesome outlander; but to be taunted by a Thorling was beyond endurance. I saw murder in the man's eye, as the mad berserk blood surged through his veins, and for the first time I felt some misgivings of the outcome. I had made due allowance for my rival's great size and his strength, which, among the Runefolk, was second only to Rolf's. But I had not counted upon facing a madman.

However, it was too late to draw back. Smider was already gnawing his moustache in speechless rage. Though my heart was beating somewhat faster than usual, I managed to give Thyra a nod and smile and to face my opponent with seeming calmness. I did not have long to await the attack. The instant I raised my hands, Smider threw up his great fists and came at me roaring. It was a rush that might well have appalled a professional prizefighter. I was quite satisfied to avoid it by side-stepping.

"Good!" shouted Balderston. "Keep away!"

The advice was needless. I well knew that a single one of the Runeman's tremendous swinging blows would end the contest on the spot. But it was not easy to keep him at arm's-length. He followed me up with savage eagerness, his fists whirling about in clumsy but sledge-hammer strokes. Luckily for me, the very excess of his fury blinded him, and his ignorance of boxing laid him open to my blows. This advantage, however, was more seeming than real. Before I could strike a knockout blow, my arms were so numbed with warding his heavy fists that my throat and jaw blows barely staggered him. As yet I had managed to dodge or ward every blow, but now my wind began to fail me, and I realised that I could not avoid those savage rushes much longer. Once in Smider's grip, I should be lost.

At the thought, all my coolness left me, and for an instant I stood unnerved. Only by a hair's-breadth did I escape Smider's exultant attack. But as I dodged aside, I caught a glimpse of Thyra's face, white and terror-stricken. The sight stung me to desperate fury. Around swung Smider, like a charging bear; but this time I did not wait his attack. Heedless of guard myself, I sprang in and swung an upper cut to his chin with my left fist. The big man stopped short and reeled in his place. Then, before he could recover, I drove my right straight to his jaw, with all the weight of my body behind the blow. It was my last effort, but it was enough. Smider went down, all in a heap, and lay senseless.

"Thor's Hammer! That was a shrewd blow!" shouted Hervard, and the onlookers closed in about me with hearty congratulations. I thought only of Thyra, however, and my first glance surprised a look that repaid me amply for all my bruises and the danger I had risked. All the girl's Norse blood was roused by the fierce contest, and she was unable to hide her joy at my victory. With cheeks flushed and bosom heaving, she faltered a moment, and then came towards me, her eyes beaming with love and admiration.

But a groan recalled me to my fallen opponent. He was just regaining consciousness, and I bade the crowd fall back, that he might have air. I awaited his recovery with a bold front, though I was inwardly quaking lest he should demand a renewal of the fight. I had had my fill of slugging with a mad berserk. Greatly to my relief, the Smider who staggered to his feet was a different man from the Smider who fell to my blow. He eyed me for a few moments in a dazed manner; then, as the full situation dawned upon him, he thrust out his great hand and burst into a hearty laugh.

"By Frey!" he cried, "you bear the Vana-god's fist. I could not wish a braver foster-brother!"

"Nor I!"

My bleeding knuckles were buried in Smider's palm, and I feared he would crush the bones, in the excess of his cordiality. But he released his grip, to snatch a knife from his belt.

"Let us mingle blood!" he exclaimed, and he gashed his bared arm with a blade. As the blood trickled down into his palm, he again grasped my bleeding hand—"Hearken, Runefolk, and may Var bear

70

witness!—we two are now of one blood,—foster-kin for weal or woe."

Remembering the words of an old Norse oath, I added— "Come weal or woe, till fire and pyre."

Smider suddenly leaned nearer, his stern face softened by generous emotion.

"The maid is yours to woo," he said in a low tone. "Henceforth she is my sister."

I sought to answer, but the words choked in my throat. I could see in the man's eye what his generosity was costing him, and no words were adequate to express gratitude for such a sacrifice. But Smider understood my look. We were, in truth, linked together by the strongest bonds of friendship. Hiding his emotion with a deep laugh, he gripped my shoulder and swung me around beside Thyra.

"A warrior fostering," commented the Thorling Varin, as the crowd dispersed. The two heralds turned away with the other people; but a little later, while we were inspecting the half-finished balloon kiosk, Hervard again joined us. He lingered about several minutes, and though, as may be imagined, I had little thought to give any one beside Thyra, I noticed that the Thorling was watching Jofrid and Balderston with unmistakable pity in his grim face. However, he said nothing, and I had forgotten the incident when, some time after, he met us near the Runehof.

"What is it, Hervard?" asked Balderston, as the Thorling stepped before him.

"A wolf's hair for you, skyfarer. Though we have not sworn brotherhood, as your friend and Smider, I am loth that ill should befall a kemperman."

"You have my thanks," replied Balderston. "But what is your warning?"

"No Thorling would have need to ask. I wonder that the Vala has not told you. But doubtless, while her brow is free of the Orm-crown's weight, she forgets her valaship."

The words were kindly said, yet their effect on Jofrid was pitiable. Her cheeks, which in the last week had gained a tinge of colour, became deathly pale and seemed to fall in, while her eyes, just now so full of quiet happiness, clouded with an anguish so terrible that the stern Thorling turned aside with bowed head.

"What is it?" demanded Balderston hoarsely.

Hervard stood silent until the question was repeated. He answered slowly, without lifting his head—"This is the law of the Orm: 'Whoso raises his hand against the Orm Vala, or seeks to woo her for wife, he shall go to the Orm.'"

71

With a shriek that pierced the heart like a knife stroke, Jofrid thrust herself away from Balderston and fell swooning on the grass.

"You have killed her, Thorling!" cried Thyra, and she began to weep over the insensible girl.

"She will wake to thank me for the warning," replied Hervard. "If Hoding Grimeye dare not woo the Orm Vala, do you think others can break that law and live? Wherever falls the shadow of the Orm, all else gives way,"

Chapter XI
Down the Mark

Far from altering our plans to accompany Jofrid on her return, Hervard's warning only increased our desire to see the Orm. But we added a few more pounds of cartridges to our packs, and gave Smider a hearty welcome to our party. At the last I tried to dissuade Thyra from going, and had she been thinking only of herself, I might have succeeded. All my arguments, however, failed utterly, for the girl's purpose was to lessen the bitterness of the Vala's return. She laughed at the possibility of danger, and I was estopped from mentioning her arm. It was healing rapidly, and I had myself given assurance that it would not suffer from the journey.

One of the last acts of Balderston and myself before leaving Biornstad was to determine the town's position on the chart, by a series of careful observations. They placed us at longitude 71 deg 11 min west, and latitude 89 deg 3 min 17 sec north,—a distance from the Pole no greater than is covered by a fast express within an hour. But the line northwards ran directly out over the abyss of Niflheim, and, much to our disappointment, we figured that the Ormvol could be little nearer the Pole than was Updal. For the time being, therefore, we had to give up The hope of obtaining the great objective point of our expedition.

At the time set for our departure, the Runefolk poured out upon the common to give us a grand farewell. Choice presents were showered upon Jofrid and the Thorling heralds, while the universal anxiety for the speedy return of the skyfarers proved in a gratifying manner the feelings with which the people regarded us. Shouts of good fortune followed us through the city gates and out across the great bronze drawbridge.

"Now for the Updal gate," said Smider, as he waved his lance back at the crowded walls.

"The Gate; then the Mark," added Varin, whose wild spirit rejoiced at the freedom of wood and meadow. "We will show our guests play."

"You are ever ready at that, guest or no guest," laughed Rolf, drawing a finger down his broad chest over the scar of Hoding's sword gash.

Hervard nodded towards the Orm-crown on Jofrid's bowed head as he answered: "With that in our company, there will be no sword-play. No dwerger dare approach the Snake Vala in anger. But those who have walked the Mark know well it has other games to offer."

"Who should know better than Rolf and Smider?" said Thyra. "It is but two seasons since they slew swartbani on the shore of Vergelmer."

Varin turned with keen interest to the two Rune-men, and exclaimed "You, then, are the hunters whom swartbani saved. There were five of us hot on your trail; but when we came upon the naked body of the beast, we gave over the chase. We thought it nithing's deed to rob from such kempermen the well-earned joy of bringing home their trophy."

Smider and Rolf hastened to grasp the Thorling's hand in acknowledgment of a chivalry not common in the Mark. After that the relations of our party became more cordial than ever, and we lightened the remaining twelve miles to the Updal Gate with such a round of songs and stories that even Jofrid for a time forgot her ill fate. Part of the way we rode in a heavy waggon, drawn by three span of small heavy-headed horses, indigenous to the pit. The driver was going for a load to the Updal Gate. Many others had preceded him, for we met a long line of waggons returning to Biornstad with great blocks of obsidian.

The source of this mineral became apparent when we reached the Updal Gate. The Gard Fell, or escarpment of the Updal terrace, was here only three hundred feet high, but nothing else than pure green obsidian from brink to base. The Gate proved to be a steep, narrow gorge, blocked by stone barricades and commanded by a fort at its head, where resident members of the Hunters' Guild formed a permanent garrison. In case of need, men serving their turn in the adjoining quarries were within call to reinforce the garrison, while a beacon would bring down quick relief from Biornstad.

As the escarpment could not be scaled at any other point, the position of the Runefolk seemed impregnable, and yet, four times in the history of Updal, the Thorlings, by treachery or surprise, had won their way up from the Mark. It was during the last of these forays, when the Thorlings brought with them a horde of dwerger allies, that old Ragner had lost his leg, leading a sortie from Biornstad.

The udaller of the garrison reported that the Vala's escort had been waiting at the foot of the pass for two or three _rings_; so, after a meal and a short rest, we leisurely descended the gorge. At the cliff's base we came out on a rocky stretch of ground, dotted here and there with clumps of magnolia-like trees. A thin column of smoke drew our attention to the nearest of these little woods, and a closer view showed us a round white shield hanging from a limb.

"The camp of the Vala's guard," said Varin, pointing to the shield.

As though in answer, a voice among the trees roared out a deep hail, and twenty or thirty skin-clad Thorlings came running from the wood to salute their Vala. Having bowed low before the wearer of the Orm-crown, the shaggy, wild-eyed forestmen greeted the heralds with scant deference, and promptly gathered round to stare at the skyfarers. Though neither Balderston nor I could complain of lack of attention, the baud's interest centred Thord and Black. The latter aroused even more curiosity than he had among the Runefolk. It was very amusing to hear the comments on his features and complexion. One man actually rubbed his hand to see whether the colour would come off. But when a second drew a knife to carry the experiment further, I thought it high time to interfere.

"Hold, Thorlings," I said. "Do no harm to the swart carl. We are the guests of your king and of Bera, his sister. Behold the pledge."

The Thorlings at once drew back a little, and one who seemed their leader answered me: "Greeting to the skyfarers and their company. They are welcome to the Mark."

"Well said, Ingolf," replied Varin. "Now choose four bearers for the Vala. The rest can follow later, or go home by another path. We would not have our hunting marred by numbers.

"The Vala's safety is chargeable upon our band, protested Ingolf.

"Varin and I answer for her safety," answered Hervard. "Go

without fear. Here is Rolf Kaki who struck down Hoding on the fells, and Smider, another Runeman not unknown in the Mark. Nor are any of the skyfarers children, even if measured by the Thorling ell."

"Farewell, then. Here are six trusty men. The rest go with me by way of Vergelmer."

Saluting the Vala, Ingolf and his band set off southward along the foot of the escarpment, while two of the men he left returned to the trees to fetch the white shield and a light palanquin for Jofrid. Her visit, however, had so greatly benefited the Vala that, for the time, she preferred to walk with Thyra. This cheated me of my intended company and Balderston of his. Rather disconsolate, we fell in behind with Thord, who was loading his express.

"Now for the fun, boys," he said. "I hope, lieutenant, you haven't loaded up with regulation bullets, like the time with the grey bear."

"No. I don't see how those got in the magazine. Now I have the soft-nosed beauties all right. I'll trust them to stop almost anything. Still, with the girls along, we must be careful."

"Yes; we may have our hands full to protect them," said I, and I pointed before us into the gloomy, steaming abyss of the pit. What might we not chance upon in that mysterious underworld? We gazed down the long slope of the Mark,—down, down the vast green mountain side to where its base was lost in the vapoury depths. With that sight before our eyes, and the memory of the toothed birds yet fresh in our minds, we found ourselves recounting the stories of the living Orm with a sudden absence of scepticism. If such ancient types of fauna as the Odontornithes had survived the ages in this Polar zoo, was it not reasonable to admit, that, under the same conditions, some of the huge contemporaneous saurians might also have lingered to the present period?

Yet the possibility of a dragon-hunt did not cause us to forget such small game as mammoths and sabre-toothed tigers. Even Thord was quite willing to wait a while for the dragon. We were, however, eager to test our guns on the other beasts of the pit, and kept a sharp lookout on all sides as the Thorling heralds guided us down the long slope through a jungle of pale green palms.

For five or six miles we saw nothing larger than a flock of pheasant-like birds and two or three lemuroid animals. Wearied at last of our fruitless watch, Thord and Black jogged along in silent disgust, while Balderston and I turned all our attention to the girls. Thyra was as fresh and lively as when we left Biornstad; but Jofrid now began to show signs of fatigue. Balderston's solicitous eye quickly took note of this. He had just suggested that the Thorling

75

bearers should be called into service, when Hervard suddenly halted and made a sign for silence.

"A chase!" exclaimed Thyra, as all stood listening.

We outlanders could hear nothing; yet Rolf confirmed his sister's assertion, and the Thorlings hurriedly led the party off to the right. Presently they again halted, at a point where the jungle came to an abrupt end on the bank of a thirty-foot cliff.

"Be silent, on your lives," muttered Varin, in a tone which spoke of imminent danger.

We crouched on the edge of the cliff and peered down at the open level below. There was nothing in sight, and I turned to question Smider. But an outburst of hideous yells in the thickets to the right told the source of the alarm.

"Werewolves!" whispered Thyra in my ear, and she crouched yet lower. I did not reply—I was staring, open-mouthed, at the gigantic moose which came crashing from the bush.

"The Irish elk!" cried Balderston, and he and Thord thrust out their rifles. On the instant, however, both dropped flat upon their weapons and lay silent. The colossal deer had no more than cleared the thicket, when after him leaped out a pack of wolfish red beasts. At the heels of their huge quarry the pursuers seemed small—almost puny. But a nearer view dispelled the illusion. One of the red beasts would have made two grey wolves, and their heads, which were so big as to look monstrous and unwieldy, gave evidence of jaw power far greater than that of the laughing hyena, the cruncher of ox bones.

As the chase swept in under the cliff, the giant elk made a last desperate effort to outdistance his pursuers. But it was in vain. For a little his tremendous strides carried him clear of the yelling pack; then their leader closed up and leaped in to hamstring the quarry. He fell short, and was spurned aside by the flying hoof. Yet the effort showed the elk that the pack would soon be at his flanks. Snorting with rage and fear, he wheeled sharply about and stood at bay.

In a twinkling the terrible beasts leaped in on their prey, yelling with the blood frenzy. The immense palmated antlers swept down into their midst like giant scythes, flinging the foremost beasts to right and left. In two strokes the ground was strewn with red bodies, pierced and mangled by the keen tynes. Yet, with a ferocity that appalled us the pack closed in around their quarry and fairly buried him beneath a wave of bristling red forms.

We heard the crunch of bones in the iron jaw and the gallant stag was literally torn limb from limb. So swiftly did the beasts rend him, I believe he was half devoured while yet alive. Many of the pack were unable to force a way through the mass that covered the carcass. Ravenous for blood, these fell upon their wounded comrades, with fiendish yells, and tore them piecemeal.

I am not ashamed to acknowledge that I lay prostrate on the cliff edge, fairly overcome with the horror of that hideous spectacle. Nor was I alone. Beside me Balderston and Black and the girls gasped and shuddered, and even Rolf turned pale. Thord alone showed no fear. He was the first to speak, when, at a sign from Varin, we crept away from the cliff and around out of the jungle.

"How is this?" he demanded. "We cower and fly like children. What are these red beasts, that men should so fear them?"

"What are they?" cried Rolf.

"They are werewolves—spawn of Loki—blood-kin of Hel and the Fenris-wolf! Not even swartbani stands before them."

"But men," sneered Thord,—"men should—"

"Hark!" cried one of the Thorlings. "I hear the trail yell!"

"Thor aid us!—they have caught our wind!" shouted Hervard, and the Thorlings huddled together, panic-stricken.

"To the trees!" roared Smider. "To the trees with the maidens!"

"Save the Vala!" shouted Varin.

"Nay; look you to Ragner's daughter," rejoined Thord, and he caught up Jofrid in his giant arms.

After him we rushed along the open slope towards a group of large trees. We ran our swiftest, for we ran from certain death. Yet the trees were still many yards away, when a terrible yelling outburst told us that the red beasts had view of their new quarry. Spurred on by that appalling clamour, we fled over the grass like deer, Thyra leading all except Thord.

Suddenly Balderston stumbled and fell headlong.

His weak ankle, strained again on the fells, had turned with a loose stone and thrown him.

"Go on!—go on!" he shouted, as he staggered up. For answer, Rolf and Smider seized him on either side and dragged him along between them, while Black turned on his heel and opened fire. I could not do other than follow suit, though my very knees shook as I looked back at the oncoming horde of red monsters. How I managed to shoot straight I cannot imagine, for I was frightened out of my wits; and yet my shots counted with as deadly effect as the sergeant's.

So quick and accurate was our fire, we mowed down a dozen of the leaders, and the whole pack came to a sudden halt. It was not, however, the death of their fellows that stayed their advance. Had we slain them with arrows, they would have kept on until the last one fell. But though they feared no living creature,—not even the black tiger,—these beast fiends were for a moment checked by the flash and roar of our rifles.

Shot after shot we poured into the hesitating pack, fast as we could fire. But already the red beasts had begun to creep forward, and we had drawn our revolvers for the last stand, when we heard Thord's deep voice, bellowing to us to run. Down went our rifles, and we fled for the trees. The sound of the pack, yelling in hot pursuit, lent wings to our feet.

As we ran, we saw our companions scrambling into the nearest tree. Rolf and the Thorling were already in the branches, and Thord was lifting the girls up to them. Balderston followed in the same manner, and then Thord leaped up and drew himself on one of the lower branches. This left Smider alone on the ground. I wondered why he should so linger even for an instant. Then, in a flash, I understood. The loyal fellow was waiting for his foster-brother. I made a vehement gesture upwards, and at the same moment Thord shouted to him. He sprang into the air, and was hauled up bodily by the Icelander.

A few seconds more, and we dashed in under the tree, the terrible pack leaping at our very heels. Had we attempted to climb, we should certainly have been caught and torn to pieces. But eager hands were downstretched for us, and Smider had given us the cue. Black was a little in advance. He leaped first, and I saw him swung up in Thord's mighty grip. Then I sprang for the branches where Rolf and Smider lay outstretched. Strong hands grasped my upraised arms, and I was jerked upwards. It was none too soon! I heard Thyra scream. Something sharp grazed the calf of my upswinging leg, and a pair of empty jaws clashed together like a steel trap. The foremost of the red beasts had leaped at me in the air and missed only by a hair's-breadth.

An instant later the whole pack was beneath the tree, leaping and howling in a frenzy of rage at the escape of their prey. Safe as was our position, we could not but shudder at the mad ferocity of the beasts. They danced about with a grotesque eagerness which would have been ludicrous had it not been so terrible. They were frantic with baffled fury, foaming at the mouth and biting the earth. Such as could leap to the lower branches tore out great splinters of wood and bark in their iron jaws.

At first I could only lie across the limb upon which Rolf and Smider had drawn me, my lungs pumping for air, my eyes glued on the red fiends below. The thought of Thyra at last brought my head up. She was just above me, in a fork of the tree with Jofrid. On either side of the two girls stood Hervard and Balderston, to make certain their safety. The Vala showed not the slightest sign of terror, and Thyra, though very pale, met my gaze with a happy smile.

Before I could speak to her, Thord motioned Varin, who was the nearest Thorling, to hand over his sword.

"Take the blade as a gift," shouted the herald above the howling uproar of the pack. "You saved the Vala, hero."

Thord shook his head.

"Only a loan," he roared back. "I have a game to play."

It was indeed a game—a very grim game—that the giant had conceived. Sword in hand, he stretched himself flat on a lower limb, and coolly swung his right foot down within reach of the red beasts. The daring invitation was accepted without delay. Up sprang three great brutes, every yellow fang showing in their open jaws. But quick as they leaped, the massive leg was deftly raised above their reach, and Varin's sword whistled through the air. Even in a position so awkward, Thord wielded the blade with terrible effect. Of the three beasts, one was killed outright and another fatally wounded by the stroke. The two had no more than touched the ground before they were being devoured by their fellows. Yet the frenzied pack took no warning from their fate. The moment Thord again lowered his foot, a dozen of the beasts were ready to leap at the bait.

"Well done!—a kemper game." cried Rolf, as a second pair of brutes fell dying into the jaws of the others. "I will try the reach of my lance on the evil brood.

"And we our bows," added Hervard. "Here are four of us with full quivers."

"But waste no arrows," replied Varin. "Drive every shaft home. We cannot leave this tree with safety till the last werewolf lies dead."

"Dah's de revolvahs, sah, suggested Black to his lieutenant.

"No," replied Balderston. "We'll save our shots until needed. The arrows should settle these brutes. By the way, John, I owe you and Black for—"

"Bosh!—Here, Hervard; I will take your place, as you have a bow."

The Thorling willingly swung down to my branch, while I climbed up beside Thyra. Like Balderston, the girl tried to make a good deal out of my stopping to hold the pack in check.

"It was gallantly done, Jan," she said, and I was very glad.

I could see the love light shining in her beautiful eyes. Yet I knew how little I merited the praise.

"Black was the hero," I protested. I but followed his lead. How I aimed straight, Thyra, I am unable to imagine. My very blood was frozen with terror."

"Hardly that, Jan. But my heart stood still when I saw the beasts so close upon you. My hero!—Had they caught you, I should have flung myself down among them."

"Sweetheart!" I exclaimed, and I clasped the girl's free hand. Every one else was engrossed by the yelling fiends below, and in the uproar I kissed Thyra's averted-cheek without being seen or heard— "Dearest, this pays me doubly for my fright."

Thyra turned to me, her face rosy with blushes, but she drew back shyly as I sought to kiss her on the lips.

"Nay, Jan," she protested; "is this a time for wooing? Wait, I beg you—let us watch the werewolves. The Thorlings shoot well. Already the beasts fall on every side. And see the Hammer-drott— what a giant! He still swings the heavy sword like a wand."

"Ay; he is a giant hero, and he does not know the meaning of fear."

"_He will know_," interrupted the Vala, and she lifted her grey eyes, dilated with the same fearful look they had borne when she foretold Balderston's fortune. Before the agonised horror of that look I shuddered and stood silent. But Thyra, who was watching Thord, answered her friend quickly: "Ah, Jofrid, how can that be? Even swartbani is not more feared than the red beasts, yet see the big man make sport of their ravening."

"You know not the horrors of Niflheim. There is one in the pit before whom these are gnats."

Balderston raised his head alertly. "How, Jofrid," he exclaimed, "of whom do you speak?"

"Of the living Snake—the Orm in Helapool!"—and the strange girl, though she had watched with calm indifference the blood frenzy of the red beasts, now shuddered and turned livid at a vision.

A shout from Varin drew our attention once more to the red beasts. The last one had just fallen, pierced by Rolf's lance, and every man was swinging down to despatch the wounded. Thord led the attack, and it was well he did. Hardly had his feet touched the ground, when, from the heap of red carcasses, one of the wounded beasts leaped straight at his throat. Before Thord could strike, the monster was upon him, snarling horribly. A lesser man would have been overthrown by the shock. But the giant caught the mad brute by the throat, and holding him out arm's-length in his left hand, cut him in twain with one tremendous sword stroke.

At this Balderston could not restrain himself. Out came his revolver and he swung down after the Thorlings. I turned appealingly to Thyra, who smiled and nodded.

"Follow him, Jan," she cried. "I can look to Jofrid. But beware. The beasts are yet dangerous. Guard yourself—for my sake."

Already I was swinging down. At her words I glanced up into the girl's eyes; then dropped on Thord's heap of slain werewolves. Already Rolf and Smider and the Thorlings were thrusting and slashing at the wounded with fierce energy, and the crack of revolvers told that Balderston and Black had their share in the melee.

"You're too late, doctor," called Thord, as he turned to wipe his dripping sword. Hardly had he spoken when a bloody form sprang up almost beneath my feet. The beast had only been stunned by a glancing sword stroke. The bullet I fired down his yawning throat, as he reared to seize me, only doubled his fury. His hot, fetid breath struck in my face; his little, bloodshot eyes glared into mine with murderous hate. Already I could feel the yellow fangs closing on my throat. Only just the nick of time a long missile came whizzing to hurl the beast aside. As I tottered back, Smider sprang to support me. He pointed to the dying beast, transfixed by his great lance, and grimly remarked: "You were close to Valhalla, foster-brother."

"True," I cried. "Now I owe you life, as well as happiness. Never shall I forget the debt."

"Nay; we are foster-kin," he answered, and he gripped my hand until the joints cracked.

A triumphant shout parted us—"All dead! all dead! We have stamped out the pack!"

"Ay; all dead, and a merry game in the doing," said Thord, and he handed Varin his bloody sword. The Thorling looked at the blade, all hacked and twisted by the giant's mighty blows.

"A merry game," he muttered—"true, a hero's game—such Tyr, or Thor himself, might play!"

"May we have more of the like," laughed Thord, and as the Thorlings stared at him open-mouthed, he turned unconcernedly to us—"Here, sergeant, trot out for the rifles you all dropped, while I shin up for the girls."

"Right, sah," answered Black promptly; but he stopped to get the Icelander's express before venturing away from the trees. Balderston or I would have accompanied him had we not been more interested in another quarter. Before Thord could turn, we both sprang up and climbed into the branches. Thyra greeted our return with a sigh of relief. She was worried over Jofrid, who stood in the fork beside her, white and rigid, with open, glassy eyes. I saw at once that the Vala was in a trance, and shouted down for the Thorlings to make ready her palanquin.

"Fear nothing, Thyra," I continued. "She will presently recover."

Balderston gripped my arm with a shaking hand.

"Thank you for that, John," he muttered. Thyra said nothing, but her eyes expressed her gratitude.

With a little aid from me, Balderston easily lowered the Vala's slight figure within reach of Thord. He swung down himself immediately afterwards, either forgetting Thyra, or rightly thinking that she had no need of assistance. Single-handed though she was, the girl was quite capable of descending alone. However, as all the others except Rolf were gathered about the Vala, my sweetheart blushingly permitted me to aid her, and I had the pleasure of lowering her into her brother's arms.

As I sprang down after, Black came jogging back with the three lost rifles. Two of the Thorlings now aised the palanquin pole to their shoulders, and at a word from Varin, we started on down the Mark, leaving the red beasts untouched where they had fallen.

We might well turn from their mutilated carcasses with loathing; and yet the great peril we had suffered from the fearful beasts was not without some recompense. The common danger had brought all our party into the friendliest relations. For the time being at least, Thorlings, Runemen and outlanders mingled without distinction. All were boon comrades. Our mutual cordiality was further strengthened by the deep sympathy and concern for the Vala, in which all alike shared.

Personally I had still more cause for gratitude to the red beasts. The terrible encounter had gone far towards breaking down Thyra's reserve. There in the tree she had shown her love so openly that she could not well seek to hide it from me any longer. Therefore, much as I regretted the condition of Jofrid, I tramped along beside the palanquin with Thyra, in a very happy frame of mind. Indeed, so interested was I in talking with her about the Vala's condition, that, had not Balderston called my attention to the fact, I believe I should not have noticed how curiously the vegetation was paling. At the foot of the Updal Gate it had been a vivid light green. But as we descended we found that the green of the foliage was gradually giving place to a yellow tinge. This phenomenon we attributed to the lessening power of the sunlight in the depths.

Three miles on down the Mark, nearly all the vegetation was of a light lemon shade. Here it was, near a cool pure spring, we came upon the cave where we were to rest and sleep. It was a large triple grotto, whose narrow entrance was blocked with stones to keep out wild beasts. While the others opened the cave and built a fire, Thyra and I succeeded in reviving Jofrid with the cool spring water. The poor girl was greatly exhausted, but after taking a bowl of beef juice prepared by Black, she fell into deep reposeful slumber.

Chapter XII
Over the Giol

The rest and sleep benefited not only Jofrid, but every other member of our party. As to the Vala, the reaction from her trance seemed to bring about a state of almost feverish unrest, and she insisted upon beginning the second stage of our journey afoot. This, in a way, was fortunate, since the last mile of descent to the Ormvol was very rough and in places precipitous.

As we clambered down the rocky base of the great slope, I confess that I gazed out over the mysterious subterranean forest beneath us with no little doubt and apprehension. Our gradual descent and the stop at the cave had accustomed us to the tremendous atmospheric pressure,—to the strange, sickly-coloured vegetation,—even to the weird sensation of plunging down such vast depths below sea-level. The light, however, even on the open hillside, was so dim and shifting as to be very unsatisfactory for shooting. How, then, beneath that ocean of foliage, could we hope to defend ourselves from the ferocious pit beasts?

Seen from above, the forest was by no means gloomy, even in the faint light, for on the level of the Ormvol all vegetation was bleached to a pallid hue, little more than tinged with green and yellow and red. The warmth of the interior fires of the earth, however, had forced this sickly-coloured vegetation to such a rank growth that nowhere could the feeble rays of diffused sunlight penetrate the leafy canopy. I shook my head at the worse than Egyptian darkness which must await us in the heart of the pallid jungle.

My misgivings were interrupted by the roar of a great torrent. We had heard its distant boom soon after our start from the cave, and the sound had grown in volume, until now, as we descended the foot of the slope, it swelled into a continuous, deafening thunder.

"The Giol!" shouted Rolf, and a last turn around a rocky point brought us out on the steep bank of a swift-flowing, turbulent river. Above its foam-flecked surface hung a white fog, condensed from the moisture of the warm air. This and the chill which struck up to us on the edge of the bank showed the extreme coldness of the stream. At once I remembered that Thyra, during our flight over the Ormvol, had spoken of this torrent as the outlet of the glacier lake Vergelmer, in which the Ice Street terminated.

A moment later Thyra's account was verified full. Our ears were stunned by a terrific crashing uproar, and down the centre of the river's channel tumbled a long line of enormous ice-cakes. Many of these bergs were too large to float free, and we could see their dim outlines revolving high in the fog as they rolled down the rocky bed. Here and there the bigger ones caught and held, until the river, piling up behind in sudden flood, gathered sufficient head to drive them onward.

In the mystic gloom of the pit, this swift, fog-veiled torrent, sweeping the bergs down into the very bowels of the earth, seemed more a wild chimera of the myth-makers than a real river. Nor was the illusion lessened by the shifting cloud-world above us, through whose dark vapours the sun now and then shone down like a disc of red-hot iron.

While we stood resting on the river's bank, Black began to pick with his knife at one of the broad veins which seamed the mountain side. Suddenly the negro snatched out something from the loose quartz, and sprang up, greatly excited.

"Gole!—gole!" he cried, holding his hand beneath Balderston's nose. "Look, sah, look—a whoppin' big nugget! Dah's gole heah by de hatful!"

"What of it?" rejoined his lieutenant, unmoved. "This is Hoding Grimeye's kingdom. Even should the Thorlings permit us to work the vein, what use would we have for gold in Updal?"

"But when we goes home, sah—"

Balderston stared gravely into the gloom of the Ormvol, and then looked at the Vala with a strange expression.

"Home!" he muttered—"home If ever leave this Polar under-

84

world, it will not be gold shall take with us! No, sergeant; gold is a drug here. Among the Thorlings, I venture to say, we shall find it of no greater value than iron."

"That is true," said Thyra, when I interpreted. "The Thorlings can pick up gold at pleasure, and platinum the same. Neither are found in Updal, but the forestmen gladly barter both in the crude state for platinum wares. They can forge good steel, but the grey metal is too stubborn for their rude methods. The line yonder, by which we shall cross the Giol, is a platinum rope, made in Updal. It was given the Thorlings, long since, as ransom for a party of Updal hunters whom they had taken thrall."

I looked at the long, thin line stretched between opposite crags, high above the torrent. From where we stood, the grey-white strand seemed little more than a thread of gossamer. Even when we climbed the crag to which the near end was anchored, we could hardly believe that this slender woven line was strong enough to sustain any weight. Upon it, however, a light trolley basket or car hung ready for use, rigged with a continuous line of hemp-like rope.

Varin at once stepped into the car and motioned for Thord and Balderston and myself to follow. Though, from his expression, this was evidently intended as a mark of distinction, I, for one, did not appreciate the honour. However, we climbed aboard, and one of the Thorlings promptly gave the car a vigorous shove.

Before we could so much as draw breath, we found ourselves whirling down the bight of the line, far out over the fog-veiled river. A huge ice-cake thundering in mid-channel beneath us did not tend to lessen the strain on my nerves. Thord sat calm and fearless as usual; but Balderston met my look with a shrug and smile which confessed that he felt no less uneasy than myself. Greatly to our relief, the car swept past the lowest sag of the line in safety. As its speed slackened on the upward curve, Varin began hauling in on the endless line, and we seconded his efforts with hearty good-will.

At last we drew ourselves up to the crag on the farther bank. With a shout, all sprang out on the landing platform, and Thord sent the empty car whirring back across the river for a second load. This time Hervard brought over Black and the two girls. We were able to help them by hauling the rope about the pulley at our end, and neither Balderston nor I spared our muscles. Though we had ourselves tested the strength of the platinum line, both of us heaved sighs of joy and thankfulness when the girls were at last over the perilous crossing.

Rolf and Smider and the remaining Thorlings now followed us

across, three and four at a time, until all our party stood grouped on the crag, ready to plunge into the pallid forests of the Ormvol.

"Now we'll have to look sharp, Frank," I said. "Sergeant, if you see a pair of green eyes in the darkness, put a bullet between them, and ask questions afterwards."

"Yas, sah; yas. I'se met grizzlies and mounting lions in de dahk. I knows."

"Then don't forget. If one of those fire-cats or black tigers drops on you, there won't be a grease spot left."

"Huh! I'se all right, sah. De black tiggahs won' eat no black sojah. Dey all has a pruf'runce foh lightah complexshuns."

"We'll see about that," rejoined Balderston, and as the heralds led the way down the crag, we four outlanders fell in about the girls with rifles ready. To tell the truth, none of us quite fancied the plunge into the blackness of the forest depths, and we wondered not a little at the indifferent bearing of our Updal and Thorling companions, as they wound down the ridge which dyked in the Ormvol side of Giol. We had descended only a little way, however, when the reason for their calmness became apparent.

"Whut's dat light, sah?" asked Black suddenly. "Looks like de moon am in dem bushes."

"Shoot me if it don't," answered Thord. "It's lighter there under the trees than here in the open. What can it be?"

"Phosphorescence!" cried Balderston. "See this fungus under the bush—it glows as though afire! The pit gloom has developed luminous fungi, just as the deep sea abounds in phosphorescent animal forms."

"True," I replied, as we filed down a narrow trail in under the dense, pallid canopy of the Ormvol forest. "This is better than moonlight. Seems as if the whole ground is afire."

"That's not all, doctor," broke in Thord. "Look above!—I've heard of luminous fish and flies, but never of luminous flowers!"

We stared about us, half inclined to believe that we had entered fairy-land. The ground was everywhere covered, as it were, with myriads of pale white flames, the glow of the luminous fungi. This was the main source of the weird forest light; but above, the flowers, though far less abundant, furnished a second illumination of incomparable beauty. Not only were they of various fanciful shapes, from grotesque to exquisite,—each variety possessed a different tinge in its phosphorescence, running through all the colours of the rainbow.

One gorgeous blossom, in form like an immense dragon-fly, was a veritable floral chameleon. In as many minutes it glowed with

86

five distinct colours, all of flaming brightness. Nor did its brilliant changeful hues fade for several hours after Hervard brought it to the Vala. As the entire plant had been torn from the limb with the blossom, Balderston and I were able to give it a thorough examination. Its classification was very difficult, but we at last concluded to place it tentatively among the orchids. The other flowers proved to be closely related to the great dragon-fly, and it was evident from the numbers of insects which hovered about the glowing petals, that their luminosity was a lure for the purpose of aiding fertilisation.

So engrossed were we in our admiration and study of these marvellous flowers, that an hour or two passed before we could think of anything else. But when our narrow path turned into a great game trail, beaten like a roadway beneath the overarching jungle, we bethought ourselves once more of the pit beasts. It was high time to finger our rifles and keep a wary eye on the pallid thickets; for Smider observed that we should now be certain to meet with formidable animals. The great trail, though maintained and dominated by the mammoths, was used by many others of the pit beasts.

Fortunately, the luminous plants continued in the same abundance as at first; so that we were not placed at the disadvantage which we should have suffered from the darkness. Indeed, we could see with remarkable clearness the small birds and lemuroid animals which pursued the insects among the fire-flowers. Only now and then did we pass an unlighted patch of thicket. At such places our escort kept close to the opposite side of the trail, and carried their weapons brandished as though in expectation of attack.

"Swartbani," muttered Smider significantly, as we passed one of the dark spots. Thord uttered a contemptuous grunt at the extreme wariness of the Thorlings. But I had hunted tigers, and could better appreciate the reason for such caution. The dark bits of jungle were ideal lairs for the gigantic cat, which could lie in wait among the shadows, black as itself, and at a single bound strike down its prey anywhere within the breadth of the trail. I was giving the others pointers on tiger-shooting, when Hervard and Varin halted abruptly and made a sign. Instantly the men wheeled about and ran with the Vala to the last dark thicket. "After them!" exclaimed Rolf.

Thord stared scowling down the trail.

"Why run?" he demanded—'red beasts again?"

"No,—jotunkaki? Follow the Thorlings," shouted Smider.

I looked for a stout tree in the tangle of whitish jungle; but the others were running straight for the black thicket. Thyra was already once more at Jofrid's side. Then the heralds urged us to follow, and even Thord thought it as well to join the rout. Heedless of tigers or other lurking beasts, our whole party plunged headlong into the blank darkness of the thicket. Varin, who brought up the rear, paused on the edge of the trail to snatch from his pouch a handful of withered berries, which he crushed in his fingers and flung about him. Then he, too, pushed through the bush to where we crouched in the shadows, four or five yards from the trail. As he slipped in beside me, I noticed that his hands gave out a powerful musky odour.

Scarcely had we settled into quiet, when a dull heavy sound broke the silence. Quickly the sound gained volume; the ground began to jar, and we heard shrill outcries, something like the trumpeting of elephants. We drew back a little farther and stared out into the open trail, where every object was plainly visible to us, though we ourselves were hidden.

We had not long to wait. Louder grew the trumpeting, heavier the tread of ponderous feet. Suddenly across our range of vision rushed a gigantic shaggy figure, with snake trunk and enormous upcurving tusks. Beside that creature, Jumbo would have seemed a dwarf.

When almost opposite us, the mammoth swung out his trunk towards the spot where Varin had thrown the crushed berries, and swerved aside from it, with a shriller note in his trumpeting. The cry was taken up by every other mammoth in the herd, and as the huge creatures thundered past, each sniffed the musky odour from the berries and bolted on with increased swiftness.

As the last of the herd, a magnificent young bull, lumbered by, Thord sprang forward with upraised rifle. But Hervard leaped before him and, grasping the muzzle of the weapon, held it to his own breast.

"Stay!" he cried. "Would you draw upon us the fury of jotunkaki, with two helpless women our company?"

The blood rushed to Thord's face, and as he wrenched his rifle free, he shouted in disappointment: "Coward!—you have marred my sport!"

The Thorling started as though shot, and his hand flew to his sword hilt. But at Jofrid's warning cry, he restrained himself, and answered Thord with calm dignity: "You are a guest and peace-holy, else blood should flow for that word. Know that the great beasts can only be hunted singly. Should one in a herd be slain, the others would trample thickets and uproot trees in their thirst for vengeance. Even so, no Thorling would have stayed your deed, but for the maidens!"

Thord stepped forward with outstretched hand, and exclaimed in his frank manner: "I eat my words, Hervard. Will you grip hands?"

"Gladly," answered the herald, with equal frankness. As the two parted, Varin stepped out into the trail and gave the signal to resume our journey. We had not yet fallen into line, however, when a strange beast, something between a tapir and a pig in size and appearance, trotted out of the jungle a few yards away. At sight of us, the creature wheeled and fled down the trail. A brace of Thorling arrows only caused the beast to run the faster, and it would have escaped had not Thord and Balderston fired. Their bullets brought it to the ground, when it was soon despatched by a Thorling lance.

"Here is the roast. We will rest and eat," remarked Varin, and the Thorling bearer: promptly set about dressing the game. Black joined them, but the rest of us, after examining the curious pachyderm, moved on a little farther and sat down to await the cooking. Thord fell to discussing the habits of the pit beasts with Rolf and Smider and the heralds, but Balderston and I were content to sit quietly by the maidens.

I cannot say just how the two others spent their time. Thyra and I, though, certainly enjoyed ourselves. Side by side, we leaned against the bole of a giant tree, and gazed up at the gorgeous fire-flowers shining in the foliage of the palms and magnolias, the eucalypti and tree ferns that overarched the great trail.

"How beautiful, Jan," she whispered at last.

"I see a sight yet more lovely," I answered.

Thyra lowered her gaze to mine—blushed and looked down shyly; but she did not withdraw her hand from my clasp. We were very happy, and we did not look any more at the fire-flowers.

Chapter XIII
The Black Death

Our quiet happiness was interrupted, not by the dinner-call, but by a word from Jofrid. She replaced the hated Orm-crown, which for a little Balderston had persuaded her to lay aside, and gazing sombre-eyed down the trail, she said gravely: "Guests come. Let all be ready."

"Where? Who are they?" asked Thord, starting to his feet.

"Those to whom you journey. They come beyond the bend in the trail."

Balderston and the heralds sprang up, but they stood staring for several minutes without seeing anything. Then suddenly Varin exclaimed "The king!—it is the king himself!"

"And Bera with him," added Hervard, as two giant figures came into view down the trail.

Close after the royal couple followed half a dozen attendants,—all picked men, like Hervard and Varin, though beside the king and his sister they seemed of small size. We gave little heed to the retainers, however, as the party approached. All our interest was centred on the leaders, as, in turn, Thord and Black eclipsed the rest of us in the eyes of the newcomers.

Near at hand King Hoding appeared even more brutal and ferocious than when I saw him through the glasses, on the fells. Yet, notwithstanding his bulldog jaw and terrible leering eyes, the man's great bulk, set off as it was by a cloak of black tiger skin and the rude crown which bound his shaggy red mane, gave to him a certain air of wild grandeur,—the majesty of a king of beasts.

The giantess Bera was no less imposing than her royal half-brother, and far more attractive. Though not so broad as Hoding, she was half a span taller, while whatever might be said of the king's mixed blood, the woman's was purely Norse. Her bearing was truly grand and noble, and her face, though stern, did not lack in beauty of a severe type. She wore a huntress dress of the fiery leopard skin, and her flaxen hair was bound by a gold circlet, set with rubies.

As the royal party drew near where we stood grouped to receive them, Rolf and Smider and the Thorlings lifted their weapons in salute. Jofrid, however, did not so much as rise to meet the king. When he, instead, scarcely acknowledging the salute of the others, turned to bow before the frail young maiden, we began to comprehend the power of the dreaded Orm. The Thorling suite bowed to the Vala even lower than their king; but Bera, I observed, while deferential in her salute, was in nowise servile or undignified. While the others yet cringed before the Orm-crown, she turned, smiling and curious, to greet the outlanders.

Taking our cue from Balderston, we lifted our caps to the Thorling princess and bowed, as we should have saluted a lady in our own land. But when her brother stepped to her side and glowered upon us with his evil leer, we stiffened our necks and stared back at him with interest. For a moment he was so astonished by Black's colour and Thord's huge size, that he failed to notice our lack of deference. Then he scowled darkly, and spoke in a tone that well matched his face: "Ho, by Loki! These are the outlanders—the skyfarers—who slay men beyond bowshot. It seems to me they are mannerless wanderers, whether they be men or gods."

"They are guests, and peace-holy," rejoined Bera in a deep contralto.

Hoding's pop eye shifted its evil stare from us to Thyra and the two Runemen.

"We sent hearth-pledge for the skyfarers," he said; "not for a crew of skraeling Runefolk, nor for such a one as this black fiend."

I saw Smider redden with anger, but Rolf laughed scornfully, and answered the king with mock approval: "Well said, well said, Hoding Grimeye! The skraeling who felled you on the jotun-rim gives you praise for your hearth-warmth."

At the jeering words Hoding grew purple with rage, and he shook his clinched fists in Rolf's face.

"Ha! Nidhug tear you! It was you then who struck me down— not fairly, but by _seid_—by black magic. By Loki and the Fenris-wolf, I shall flay you alive for that!"

Rolf grasped his sword-hilt, furious at the threat and the false accusation. Thord, however, thrust himself in between the enraged men and said coolly: "Hearken!—King Hoding is dogwise. We and our friends come with his guest-pledge. He shall keep troth."

"And if not, outlander?—Beware for your own skin. I am king of the Mark and the Ormval."

"Bah! Does Hoding think we have sailed the sky of Jotunheim, to quail before man or beast? Even this swart one, though he be but a carl, could blast the stoutest Thorling in this realm, king or no."

"That is true," said Bera. "I saw how you slew my men on the fells. Hoding himself saw Eyvind struck down. There is witchcraft in those hollow clubs you bear."

"Ay," growled Hoding; "they are warlock wanderers. They dare not fight as men."

Thord laughed again.

"Ask Varin who it was nicked his sword on the red beasts, or ask Hervard the weight of my fair comrade's fist."

"Rather, remember what you saw of grey biorn on the fells," added Thyra quickly.

The impulsive words were no sooner uttered than the girl regretted them, for they drew upon her Hoding's special attention.

91

Flushed and indignant, she shrank behind me to avoid the odious leer with which he surveyed her beautiful figure.

"The bear on the fells?" exclaimed Bera, and I was relieved to see her brother shift his evil gaze. "Ha! doubtless, then this big one was he who cast the stone?"

"True," assented Thord.

"That was a hero's deed," said Bera warmly, and she turned to her brother. "Now, Hoding, welcome the guests, or go. One and all, they come to Hela Gard with full guest honour, or Bera of the Orm shall know why else."

"There is one man among them," replied Hoding, as he again measured Thord's giant frame. "He is welcome, and the rest in his following."

Even Balderston flushed at this contemptuous greeting; but before any of us could retort, Jofrid rose and confronted the king with a look which all his brute ferocity was unable to withstand.

"Beware, King Hoding!" she said. "Nithing is he who breaks guest-troth—and the Orm ever hungers."

Even Bera shuddered at the warning. As to Hoding, he bowed low before the Vala, and replied hurriedly: "I give welcome to all the guests, Runefolk and skyfarers alike, let Var bear witness."

"It is well. Now be seated. The meat roasts, as you see."

All complied with the invitation, Thord sitting down with Bera and the king. Jofrid, however, drew a little apart, and I followed her with Thyra and Balderston.

We had not long to wait before Black brought us the choicest roast on the spits. This was flanked by food we had brought with us, while the king's attendants contributed a sort of palm wine. So, as the roast proved to be very similar to young pork, we pieced out quite a hearty and enjoyable meal. Even the Vala had for the moment thrown off the heaviness of her spirits, and our little party finished the meal in a very happy mood. In the midst of our gay chatter, however, we were interrupted by an unwelcome intruder. King Hoding stalked over from the fire, and, bowing sullenly to the Vala, sat down close to Thyra.

"Ho! stay quiet, maiden," he said, with an unpleasant laugh. "There is no need to shrink aside. Hoding Grimeye does not eat Rune maids—when they are fair as Freya."

The Thorling's tone was even more offensive than his words, and I turned upon him, half choked with indignation. But Thyra was quicker. She drew herself up proudly, though her pale cheeks and flashing eyes and the heaving of her bosom told how great was her emotion.

"King Hoding knows little of Rune maids," she exclaimed. "Seven times have I walked the Mark, and never yet quailed before beast or Thorling. If now I prefer the company of my betrothed to that of yourself, it is not because I fear you."

"So Ragnersdotter is betrothed," said Hoding, with an ugly sneer. "Yonder big man, then, is a liar."

I looked at Thyra, now crimson with shame,—almost on the verge of tears,—and my anger blazed to a white heat. But the girl's open confession of her love roused an emotion even more powerful than wrath.

"Let King Hoding be assured," I cried pleasantly. "There is no lie. Thord has yet to learn that I have plighted troth with the daughter of Ragner. True, we are not as yet formally betrothed after the manner of the maiden's people; but that is a matter easily remedied."

I paused to draw a ring from my finger and to raise Thyra's hand.

"Let all bear witness," I continued; "I, John Godfrey, plight my troth to Thyra, the daughter of Ragner and Astrid, and naught shall part us."

As I slipped my ring on Thyra's finger, the girl lifted her blushing face, radiant with trust and love.

"Let all bear witness," she responded, in a voice low but clear, "my troth do I plight to Jan Godfrey, of the Southland, with free and willing heart, and naught shall part us."

Trembling, but happy, the girl gave me her ring in turn, and then upraised her lovely face for the betrothal kiss. It was the happiest moment of my life. Oblivious of Hoding's savage scowl, I slipped my arm about Thyra's shoulders and bent over her. Our lips met—

The tiger's attack came like a thunderbolt from a clear sky. There was no warning. A terrific roar—a shriek—and the awful beast was in our midst, his sabre teeth buried the shoulder of a Thorling. The victim did not move; the brute's mighty paw had crushed his skull like an eggshell. The tiger growled horribly and lapped the dead man's blood.

But the truce lasted only a few seconds. With wild yells, Thorlings and Runemen snatched up their weapons. Hoding rushed forward with brandished axe, and Balderston grasped his rifle to follow. I dragged the girls behind a tree. I heard Thord's express, followed by the crack of Black's rifle; then all sounds were smothered in a thunderous roar. The hunters flew apart like wind-struck leaves, and from their midst the monster charged towards me

93

with enormous bounds, the dead Thorling held his jaws as a cat holds a mouse. I saw Balderston fling himself aside and fire. Black's rifle echoed the shot, and flights of arrows came whirring after the terrible fugitive. But, like a sable incarnation of Death, the beast hurled past where I had crouched, and in two more bounds reached an unlighted patch of jungle.

As I rose, Thyra's arm slipped about my neck, and her voice murmured in my car: "Ah, sweetheart, thanks be to the Father!—you have escaped—swartbani spared you!"

I drew her to me until I could feel the quick throbbing of her heart.

"My darling!" I said; "you love me much, else you would not tremble so. But the game is not ended, dearest. The beast has slain a man, and we must take vengeance."

"Vengeance!" sneered Hoding's brutal voice. "What boaster talks of vengeance on the swart one in his lair?"

I turned to the angry, disappointed group behind the king. Thord stood in the midst, rubbing his arm ruefully, while Bera held up to view the shattered wreck of his express. When the tiger leaped past him, he had thrust out the rifle to ward himself, and it had been dashed in pieces from his grasp by an almost imperceptible stroke of the beast's paw. However, the sight did not daunt me. I had hunted Bengal tigers afoot, and this sable monster was only the same creature greatly enlarged. So, picking up my express, I addressed the party with unassumed coolness:

"Hearken, men I shall go alone into swartbani's lair. Be ready should he charge out upon you."

The Thorlings looked at me as though I had gone mad, and Thord half shouted "Ho, doctor, don't be a fool. You will go to certain death."

I shook my head, and turned reassuringly to Thyra, who was clinging on my shoulder.

"Fear nothing, sweetheart," I whispered. "Soon I shall return to you. I have spoken. To turn back now would bring shame upon me."

"Go then, Jan,—and Thor aid you!" cried the girl. Bravely smiling, she drew back beside Jofrid, while I faced about. Instantly Smider stepped to my side.

"Now, brother," he said, "lead on. You may be mad, but I go to death with you."

"And I also, John," added Balderston calmly.

"Declined with thanks, Frank," I replied, grasping his hand.

94

"You stay here and keep an eye on the other royal brute. Smider, I suppose, must come, though I do not need him."

"All right, then. You know what you're about."

"Sure. Some danger, of course; but I've been there before. Don't fret."

With that, I started off, followed closely by Smider, who carried his sword in one hand and a heavy stabbing spear in the other. As I looked at him, I felt a thrill of proud joy that such a man should be my foster-brother. Though he was going, as he supposed, to certain death, he bore himself with perfect nonchalance, and a grim smile curled his stern lips.

Without a word, we walked straight to the place where the tiger had entered the jungle. Before us rose a mass of shrub mosses, whose graceful foliage curtained the surrounding glow from their unlighted recesses. Within the thicket no fire-flowers blazed among the branches—not a solitary fungus sent up its pale light from the ground. However, I had expected as much. I crouched down at once, and pausing only to fasten a bit of luminous fungus on my rifle sight, I crept straight into the thicket. Smider followed me silently, and in a moment we were swallowed up by the black night.

For three or four yards we pushed in under the dense foliage, straining every nerve to catch the slightest sound which might betray the tiger's presence. At last our efforts were rewarded. Smider tapped me on the ankle as a warning, and I stopped. For a moment all was perfect silence; then, through the thicket to the left, came low mumbling growls and the horrible sound of rending flesh. It was the tiger devouring his prey.

Turning aside, I advanced again until the bones we felt under foot told us we had reached the monster's den,—evidence confirmed by the stench of decay and the powerful catty odour. Here it was I had expected to come upon an open space, and I peered into the blackness before me in search of the beast's eyes. I was not mistaken—the den was clear of leaves to the height of a man. But as I stared across the bone-strewn space, a sudden terror seized my heart in its icy grip. There in the darkness blazed—not one pair of emerald eyes—but two! The tiger had a mate.

For a little I crouched motionless, so frightened that I could not think. But the fit passed, and I steeled myself for the attack. It was too late to retreat. The monsters had ceased eating, and it was evident they scented us. Our only hope of escape was to attack at once. From the position of their eyes, I guessed that one of the tigers stood facing us, while the other held his head half averted. Instantly I raised my rifle until the luminous sight was in line with the nearer

95

eye of the latter beast. I pulled the trigger; then swung the gun a little and emptied the second barrel at the invisible figure beneath the first pair of eyes.

The flash of the two shots, one upon the other, lit up the blackness like a double stroke of lightning. It showed the ghastly bone-paved den, the half-devoured corpse of the last victim, the vast, gaunt forms of the monster brutes, inky black against the pallid vegetation,—and in the flash we too stood revealed.

"Fall flat!" I yelled, and I flung myself down sideways. Then an awful roar stunned my ears, and a great shadowy form crashed down on the spot where I had stood, rending the foliage and branches in a paroxysm of fury. I rolled farther away, just in time to escape a stroke of the great talons which tore up the ground at my side. The tip of the lashing tail struck me on the arm with the force of a heavy rope. I had drawn my revolver, but could not see the tiger's eyes in the whirl of mould and leaves. Every moment I expected to feel the bite of the terrible sabre teeth,—every moment I thought to hear Smider's shriek above the tiger's roar.

But not without reason was Smider called the second hunter of Updal. Suddenly a howl of anguish mingled with the mighty roars, and I caught glimpses of fiery green eyes, as the tiger whirled round and round, biting at the spear in his flank. Smider had drawn aside in the thicket, and as the tiger passed, drove his heavy stabbing spear half through the beast. Then, like myself, he had thrown himself sideways beneath the foliage, leaving the tiger to vent his fury on the spear shaft.

In his frenzy the monster leaped and crashed about through the thicket as though crazed, and most devoutly I prayed that he might sheer off and give us a chance to crawl back into the blessed light. I had my fill of _Machairodus latidens_.

Suddenly the furious turmoil lulled, and my heart leaped with wild hope. The monster had not bounded off—of that I was certain. Could it be he was dead or dying? Even as the welcome thought flashed into my mind, something soft and gigantic bore the branches down across my body and pressed upon my chest with crushing power. Above me loomed a shadow blacker than night. I was under the paw of the tiger!

Paralysed, half dead, I lay inert while the monster's triumphant roar shook the earth. The mighty paw on my breast moved,—the steely talons drew out from their velvet sheaths, to sink their tips into my flesh. I was now past fear or pain. In my apathy I scarce felt the piercing claws. Yet their touch roused in me a sort of dull fury. Very deliberately, as it seemed to me, I raised my revolver until my hand touched one of the great sabre teeth. Guided by the touch, I pressed the muzzle of the weapon up under the beast's jaw, and pulled the trigger.

The next I knew I was lying out in the open game trail, surrounded by all our party. Every face wore a look of deep concern. Smider, I saw, was pale with anxiety, and I guessed that the trembling hand on my head was Thyra's.

"Is he crushed, lieutenant?" I heard Thord ask, and Balderston, tearing open my shirt, answered with a sigh of relief: "No; thank Heaven! Only some slight flesh wounds."

Then Black passed me a flask of palm wine, which sent the life tingling through my body.

"I'm all right," I declared, a little unsteadily. "Did we get both? Only bargained for one. I'm thinking Number Two nearly did for us. He tried his best to push my chest in. It smothered me. I must have fainted."

"Sure! But you got him first, old man. Brace up and look at them. You plunked the first straight through the eye. I doubt she moved a yard."

I sprang up and caught Thyra in my arms. As she drew herself away, happy and blushing, I still further shocked Norse propriety by hugging Smider. Then I wheeled him about to inspect the two huge black bodies which lay outstretched behind us. The female had been instantly killed by my first shot. The bullet, entering her left eye, had pierced the brain and burst out through a gaping hole in the skull. My second bullet had shattered a foreleg of her mate, which accounted for the great pressure of his uninjured leg on my chest and his failure to rend me at once.

The forepart of Smider's broken spear, still buried deep in the beast's flank, was a sting which in time would undoubtedly have proved fatal. Indeed, Rolf and the Thorlings had laid the animal's death to this injury, until Balderston found and showed to them the hole made by my revolver shot. The bullet had pierced up through the lower jaw, the tongue and the roof of the mouth, and buried itself in the brain.

King Hoding was examining the dead monsters with the zest of one to whom sport is half of life. At sight of me, he rose quickly and stretched out a hairy fist.

"Grip hands!" he cried heartily. "Warlock or god, you are at least a kemperman."

"Therein does Hoding speak true," assented Bera, no less heartily.

97

Chapter XIV
Bos Latifrons

With remarkable dexterity, the Thorlings stripped the silky black skin from the bodies, including the paws and the monstrous heads with their terrible serrated tusks. Meantime, others of the party, with fire-flowers for lamps, re-entered the thicket to bury the remains of their unfortunate comrade.

Black went with these men to look for my rifle. He found it uninjured,—a very agreeable surprise to me. Thord's express was a hopeless wreck. He flung it aside, and borrowed a spare axe which one of the men carried for the king. As he swung the weapon on his shoulder, Bera nodded approvingly and stepped to his side.

"You may be my journey-mate," she said, with a slight air of condescension.

Thord laughed, and looked straight into the proud eyes of the giantess.

"Bera will be my journey-mate," he retorted.

The giantess started and reddened with anger. Never had even Hoding himself spoken to her in such a tone. To every Thorling in the pit she was the warrior-woman, before whose might all trembled—and now this outland wanderer dared to question her supremacy! But Thord met her angry stare with a look which compelled her to admit that she had met her master. To the woman he was willing to bow,—the Amazon must bow to him. It was a novel experience for Bera of the Orm; but as she realised its meaning, her anger gave way to a sort of elephantine shyness, and she started off with Thord, blushing like a young maiden.

"Golly! Mistah Thod am kotin' de big gal," ejaculated Black.

"If he is, it will certainly be a big affair," I observed.

"Big? Yes, and in more ways than one," said Balderston. "But we had best keep our mouths shut. Ah, here is Jofrid's litter."

As Balderston helped the Vala into her palanquin, our Updal party fell in about it, and the march down the game trail was resumed. Some of the Thorlings dropped behind as a rear-guard; others, with their king, joined Thord and Bera in the van.

And so we journeyed along the glowing forest archway, straight into the heart of the Ormvol. Within a mile we came to a fork in the trail, where a family of Thorling hunters had made a dwelling in the hollow of a giant tree. A comely woman and half a dozen children rushed out to meet us; but King Hoding, after a few words with the maimed old hunter in the doorway, led us on into the trail to the left.

"The Niflheim Street," muttered Smider. "Both lead to the Orm; but this winds around close to the brink of Niflheim. Rolf and I returned this way last Yule, when we went as heralds to the Thorling court."

"Game?" questioned Black.

"Both trails swarm with beasts, but on this one we may also see monsters from Niflheim."

"I trust we may not," murmured Thyra.

"What are they like?" asked Balderston.

"While Smider slept, I saw one soar over," replied Rolf. "But the light was very dim. I cannot tell the thing's shape. Ask Jofrid."

The Vala shook her head dubiously. "Seldom do the Loki-fowl soar above Hela Gard. They wheel up, only to glide back into the depths of Niflheim. But once, in the midnight, I saw one swoop close around the Orm's head. Its vast wings seemed featherless, and its head was a gaping maw, full of hooked fangs."

I looked at Balderston, and he looked at me.

"Giant bat," he muttered.

"Or pterodactyl!" I rejoined. "At this rate, we'll soon have to swallow Nidhug."

Balderston shrugged his shoulders and stared out into the gloomy forest caverns which yawned on our right. The trail here wound around the edge of a great peat bog, from whose quaking surface giant swamp trees towered up in gnarled columns to support the leafy roof. There was very little undergrowth, and so, though the luminous fungi were absent, the fairy glow of the fire-flowers was sufficient to shed a sort of twilight through the obscurity.

In the air flitted vague bird forms; the black pools rippled with the movements of shadowy figures; amphibious creatures glided to and fro over the treacherous bog. The swamp abounded in life. More remarkable still, it was a vast generator of oxygen. Instead of the miasmas we had expected, we were astonished to find ourselves breathing fresher and purer air. We tested the gas rising slowly in bubbles to the surface of the black pools. It was oxygen, liberated in the depths of the bog,—probably by the chemical action of mineral waters on the peat.

Invigorated by the tonic atmosphere, our party swung along the game trail at a swifter pace, giving little heed to the small creatures which darted into the jungle before us, or peered down from the overarching branches. Once a hippopotamus, with long yellow hair, waddled across our path, and a sounder of hideous swine grunted at us from the edge of the jungle. But Hoding and Bera kept on without a pause, until the bog fell away behind us and the trail wound across hilly land, whose open glades gave us glimpses of the blood-red sun.

When, in one of these glades, we passed, within easy bowshot, a herd of giant elk, an explanation at last occurred to Varin.

"The king's chase!" he exclaimed. "Hoding has heard of visund. He will stop for nothing else."

"Ay, it is visund," said Rolf, and he pointed to the trail. I could see nothing, but Smider and the Thorlings grunted assent. _Visund_,

I remembered, had been the old Norse name for the aurochs, and I therefore concluded that we were trailing some species of wild ox.

Black had just asked Rolf to describe the intended quarry, when our three giant leaders halted on an open ridge before us, and hid themselves behind a clump of ferns. As we hurried up, the king turned with a gesture which sent all the Thorlings but Hervard into the thicket on our right. Silent as shadows, the men vanished among the trees, and we climbed up on the ridge.

"What's up, Thord?" asked Balderston.

The Icelander looked around with sparkling eyes.

"Bison!" he answered—"white bison, and big!"

I drew Thyra up beside Bera, and together we peered through the feathery fronds. Below us was a narrow open ravine, which ran up to the right to a small glade. The sunlight was filtering into the vapoury depth of the pit with unusual clearness, so that every object in the open was plainly visible. Following the gaze of Bera and Hoding, we saw at once the herd of immense creamy-white bison grazing down the glade. I had in mind the German aurochs as described by Tacitus, but these creatures were far larger, and the event proved that they were no less fierce.

King Hoding now turned to us, axe in hand.

"Let the maids and bairns stay here," he said jeeringly. "Those who like kemper play, follow me. I will show how men in the Ormvol meet the visund."

"Lead on. We follow," replied Thord, and twirling his borrowed axe, he stalked nonchalantly after the king, over the ridge and down into the ravine's bottom. Bera followed the two, and stationed herself with them in the centre of the ravine. Smider, Rolf and Hervard, not being armed with axes, took their places partly up

100

the opposite slope, whence they could use their lances to advantage in a flank attack. Balderston and Black stopped with me half up the near slope. Though the girls were in a sheltered position, we wished to stay where we could protect them from possible danger.

Our arrangements were made none too soon. Loud shouts told us that Varin and his companions had reached the head of the glade. At first the huge bison seemed disposed to attack these audacious disturbers of their pasture. They gathered promptly in solid phalanx, and stood at bay, bellowing and tearing up the soil with their ponderous hoofs. The Thorlings, having failed in their first attempt to stampede the herd, sprang back at once into the thickets. We were surprised that they should so soon abandon the attack. But they knew their business. Hardly had they disappeared, when the bison lifted their heads and sniffed the air, bellowing uneasily.

"The Orm-scent!" exclaimed Jofrid.

As she spoke, the herd leader, a gigantic old bull, wheeled about and led the retreat down the ravine. After him followed the herd, their slow trot jarring the ground to where we stood. Soon the herd entered the ravine, and came thundering down upon us in a wide, dense column. Not until then did we fully realise the colossal size of the animals. To set ourselves in the path of such a living avalanche seemed the height of folly.

"Here's sport—with a vengeance!" muttered Balderston.

"I should say so, Frank. Might as well be elephant herd."

"I say, sah, dah's a big tree on de right flank, sah," suggested Black, a trifle nervously.

"Good, sergeant. We'll keep an eye that way," replied Balderston. "I'd like to see how the world looks from it now, but presume King Hoding desires our company."

"We can stand it, if he can. But here it comes. Look to your rifles!" I cried sharply.

It was indeed high time. The herd was ploughing through a bank of shrub moss not a hundred yards away.

"Here goes," said Balderston, and he let drive straight between the eyes of the huge bull. He might as well have fired at a stone wall. The soft-nosed bullet struck a little high in the massive thickness of horn and bone, and flattened without penetrating. The colossus paused for an instant, more in surprise at the report than from the shock of the bullet. Then, catching sight of our party, he charged, bellowing with fury, and after him galloped the whole herd.

101

"Steel point would have been better than shot," muttered Balderston.

"Bad shot for any bullet," I replied, and I took chance aim for the bull's spine. It was a lucky shot. The giant beast crashed down in his tracks, without so much as a moan.

The fall of their leader brought the mass of the herd to an abrupt halt, and we breathed easier despite the five gigantic bulls which came thundering on. It was now the sergeant's turn, and he did well, repeating my shot. Before Balderston or I could fire again, we heard Thord and the king shouting for us to desist. But one of the four bulls turned directly our way, and we fired, all three together. The beast was almost upon us, and each sent his bullet over the huge head, through the thick of his shaggy neck. Two shots pierced the beast's lungs, and the third struck him to the heart, yet only the quickest of dodging saved us, as he lunged forward into our midst, ploughing up the soil of the ravine with his monstrous horns.

We were far too closely engaged for the moment to have eyes for the other visund. But above their hoarse bellows we heard a great shout and the crash of weapons. Then we leaped about from our dying prize, and saw Hoding and Thord before two dead bulls. Each had split the skull of his colossal opponent by a single axe-stroke. The helve of Thord's weapon was shattered by the tremendous shock.

Bera, less fortunate, had struck an instant too late, and the gigantic horns of the third bull had caught her in their sweep as she leaped aside. Dashed violently to the ground, she lay senseless, almost beneath the forefeet of the wounded bull. Shaking off the blood which gushed down his horny forehead, the colossus drew back that he might see to gore the prostrate huntress. It was a question of seconds.

Thord uttered a wild shout, and leaped to the side of the raging bull. In under the mighty body he reached, to seize the hoof of the uplifting foreleg. Then, gripping fast the shaggy limb, he heaved with all his strength against the massive white shoulder. Human giant though he was, the Icelander was little more than a child beside the bison; yet so deft and well-timed was his daring act, the bull went over sideways like a falling house.

"Strike, men!" roared Thord, and he leaped aside with Bera. The bull never rose. Already Rolf and Smider and Hervard were upon him, and their lance tips met in his great heart.

"The play ends," said Hoding, and he pointed to the herd, stampeding through a break in the ridge. But he was mistaken. As I hurried forward to examine the wounds in Bera's side, I heard a shout, and looked up just in time to see the herd leader charging into our midst. My shot had only stunned the beast.

Black, who was first to notice the danger, sprang before us and fired two shots. Both struck uselessly into the horny mass of the forehead, and the bull came on, his broad muzzle grazing the earth. In two immense strides he was upon the sergeant, just as the reloaded express came to shoulder. Black was an instant too late. Caught on the gigantic horns, he was flung up and sideways, clear out of the ravine.

Without a moment's check in his mad rush, the bull thundered amongst us like a charging elephant. Thord sprang aside with Bera, and Hoding leaped to confront the huge assailant. But the king's foot slipped on a loose stone, and he barely saved himself from the keen-tipped horns by falling flat. Right across the prostrate man rushed the bull. His vicious lunge grazed harmlessly over the king's shoulder. But swerving in his charge, with an agility I should have thought impossible for such a ponderous beast, he caught Rolf and tossed him as he had tossed Black. Too late Smider hurled his lance deep into the bull's side, and Balderston and I landed three or four bullets that turned the charge into a headlong flight.

"After him—he's hard hit!" shouted Balderston, and with Hervard he sprang away in hot pursuit of the huge fugitive. Smider and I started to follow, but a scream from Thyra turned us back. The girl had darted down with Jofrid to where her brother lay inert, half up the ridge slope.

A glance showed me Black, limping back into the ravine, and Hoding on his feet again, with no other injury than a hoof bruise on his thigh. Bera, too, stood firmly while Thord bound the long wound gashed across her side and back by the up-lunging horn. Only Rolf's injuries seemed serious.

When Smider and I ran up, we found Rolf still senseless, and bleeding from the mouth and ears, so great had been the shock of his fall. Worse still, his leg was doubled under him in a way I did not like. Aside from possible internal injuries, however, I saw that he had suffered nothing more serious than a broken thigh-bone, a simple fracture, easily set. Smider ran to a near-by spring, while Black and I shaped clumsy but effective splints from pieces of drift wood. The two girls supplied linen bandages from their garments. We had the bone in place and everything shipshape before Smider could return. Rolf still continued unconscious.

"Hurry," I called to Smider.

"Here," he answered, and he sprang down the ridge with his leather cap full of water. Jofrid, who was nearest, instantly dashed a few drops into Rolf's face. The injured man moved his head a little, and opened his eyes, clear and bright.

"Good!—his head is all right," I cried. I had feared concussion of the brain. "How do you feel, Rolf?"

"Sore enough, Jan. By Var! the visund tossed me as I would toss a pebble. But the swart carl went first. How did he fare?"

"He stands before you, scathless," answered Jofrid. "The Norns brought him down upon a feather-bush. You struck the bare slope. Lie still, for your leg bone is snapped."

"I might know as much," muttered Rolf, and he gritted his teeth. "Give me drink, Smider."

"Here is better," said Thyra, and she fetched a flask of palm wine. Rolf drained it, and then made an effort to sit up.

"Stay quiet," I ordered. "You must go to the Orm on your back; though I trust the leg is all. I can find no other hurt."

Rolf breathed deeply and moved his uninjured limbs.

"You are right, Jan," he replied. "Now look to the others."

"Yes; Bera was gored. See to her hurt, Jan," added Thyra.

I bent to imprint a kiss on the upturned lips, and then hurried to obey. But my services were not needed. Heedless of his bruised thigh, Hoding had turned to meet Varin and his fellow beaters. Bera failed to hear my inquiry. Thord's rude surgery had stanched her wound, and she stood with him beside the bull that had gored her, listening, with a strange look, while laconically he described the beast's overthrow. I started and almost laughed, so incongruous did it seem to see the Amazon tamed—the grim giantess hanging on Thord's words like a simple maid of sixteen.

But it was not for one himself a lover to pry into the wooing of others. I turned away to take my first unhurried look at the visund. What giants they were! Even during the fight I had failed to realise their huge bulk. The gigantic black horns spread fully three yards from tip to tip and measured over two feet around at the base. I remembered the guest-cup at the Runehof. It was a visund horn mounted—and these visunds were, in all probability, the descendants of _Bos latifrons_, the huge fossil bison of the American _Pliocene_.

Chapter XV
Dwerger

My wondering examination of the mighty game was soon interrupted. At a word from their king, the Thorlings had started with knife and axe to dress the massive carcasses,—a task far from easy even for these born hunters of the pit. They were working their hardest, when Jofrid came down the ravine side and touched Bera with a trembling hand.

"Princess!" she said pleadingly, "let men at once follow after Hervard and Balderston. They have need of aid."

The giantess did not turn her eyes from Thord.

"All in good time, Vala," she answered respectfully. "We will help them brittle the herd king when the men are done here."

"Brittle!" cried Jofrid wildly—"brittle!—ay; it is brittling—and not of visund! Yet one may live. Follow me, Thorlings!"

The girl's cry rose to a scream, and she darted away down the ravine with wonderful swiftness. With a great shout, the Thorling warriors snatched up their weapons and rushed after, Hoding himself at their head. The Vala had commanded!

Thord, armed with Rolf's lance, was already at the king's side; Black was close behind. I threw out my hand to Smider—"Guard Thyra!" I shouted. One glance at my betrothed, kneeling beside her brother—then I ran after the others.

Half a mile brought us out of the ravine into a grassy plain, bounded on the farther side by a wall of dense red jungle. Dim and shifting as was the weird pit twilight, the trail of the fugitive visund stretched away before us broad and distinct, out across the pallid meadow. Along it fled the Vala with astonishing speed and endurance. Hoding and Thord alone were able to hold their own with her. The rest of us began to lose ground, though Black and I, spurred on by the dread we had caught from Jofrid, forged ahead of the Thorlings. We put the very utmost of our strength into the race, when, midway across the plain, our ears were startled by pistol shots and a horror of fiendish howling. My first thought was of the red beasts; but this frenzied outcry quavered with a semi-human note more fearful even than the werewolf yell.

I looked to see the Vala falter, appalled by the dreadful sound—instead, she fled on as though her little feet were winged. On, on she flew, straight for the thicket whence faint puffs of smoke rose against the red jungle wall and the crack of Balderston's revolver rang out above the howling.

"Las' shot!" gasped Black. My heart was bursting. Yet I followed the negro's crazed rush—past Hoding—past Thord—almost past the Vala. Thord's voice roared above the howls "Dwerger! Fire!"

Up went my rifle, and its heavy report shook the air. If Balderston yet lived, he would know that help was near. But the cunning beast-men already knew. Even as I fired, we saw their misshapen brown figures swarming with apish agility up the face of the jungle. One group, I fancied, bore in their midst a dead or injured fellow. In my excitement I did not perceive that the object they held differed from them in colour.

But at sight of that inert body in the grasp of the clambering beast-men, Jofrid, whose eyes were sharpened by love, or by her vala-power, halted abruptly in her wild flight and stood quivering, her child face drawn and ghastly beneath the evil Orm-crown. I stopped short beside her; but Black rushed on, and after him Thord and Hoding and all the Thorlings except Varin. At my shout, the herald paused to grasp the Vala's arm, and between us we hurried her on, almost bearing the frail little body. She made no resistance, but stared at us with a dazed look, and shook her head.

"Too late!" she moaned. "The dwerger have borne him away."

"We will follow!" I shouted.

"No, skyfarer," answered Varin. "We cannot swing through that forest top, and below is bog that no man may pass."

"Is there then no hope?" I cried in despair.

Jofrid drew a deep breath, and pointed ahead to where the others had halted. "Wait!" she said.

At that and the sight of our silent, stooping companions, we hurried on through the fern brush into the little glade at the jungle edge. One glance confirmed our worst fears. In the centre of the glade lay the colossal body of the bull, and the sallow blood-spattered grass around him was strewn with a score or more of naked hairy beast-men. All were dead or dying, their inhuman faces contorted with hate and agony. Scattered about or clutched in the apish paws were rude weapons,—unchipped flints, pieces of staghorn, shapeless clubs, and, what were truly formidable, great shark-like teeth, large as a man's hand.

I looked at the bright red on the Thorling weapons, and saw why none of the stricken creatures lacked a fatal wound. The cause of the slaughter was apparent in the mutilated figure which lay across the visund carcass.

"Hervard!" I cried, as Thord gently raised the torn and

battered corpse to lay it on the grass. The brave Thorling had gone to seek his seat in Valhalla. Hoding bent over the corpse with the others, even his callous heart softened with pity.

Of all the party, two alone had no thought for the hero. Black stood at the foot of the red jungle, his bloodshot eyes staring up at the crest, his ashen lips pouring forth a torrent of awful blasphemies. But Jofrid was running eagerly about among the scattered beast-men in search of one yet alive. Such as lay on their faces she dragged over with frantic haste. The Thorlings, however, had struck with mad fury. She found only corpses or wretches already in the death-agony. With a cry of despair, she turned upon the Thorlings in fierce anger.

"Fools!—fools!" she screamed. "You have slain them all!"

"Nay; here is one," answered Thord, and he pointed between the horns of the bull.

In an instant the Vala was bending over the huddled brown figure, her finger pointed up at the Orm-crown. A flash of intelligence gleamed from between the creature's half-closed eyelids-. His massive animal jaw dropped open, and he grovelled face down before the Vala, gibbering like a maniac. As he lay extended, I saw for the first time that one of his legs had been shorn clean off by a stroke of Hervard's sword.

Jofrid gave no heed to the wound. In a cold, even voice she uttered a command that brought the beast-man back to his first attitude. Like a trapped wolf, he cowered on his haunches, his slit eyes glaring up at the Orm-crown. The Vala touched the dragonhead significantly, and made a gesture. The beast-man replied with a number of signs so swiftly formed that I could not follow them. Not so the Vala. She raised her head, with a shade of hope in her eyes.

"He lives—he is unharmed!" she cried. "They will not devour him!"

"True, Vala," rejoined Hoding gloomily. "We shall see him again—but at the Orm-blot. You should know the dwerger-right."

"Odin aid him!" cried Jofrid, and she stood white and trembling.

Hoding swung his axe above the dwerger, but checked the stroke and stepped back with a ferocious smile.

"Nay; the wolf-birds shall tear his living flesh," he said.

"Not so," rejoined Thord, and he mercifully slew the wretch with his lance. The weapon was hardly withdrawn, before Hoding's upraised axe threatened the Icelander.

"Ake-Thor!" he bellowed; "who are you to cross my will?—Learn that Hoding's wish is law!"

But if the Thorling looked to see the outlander cringe, he was never so mistaken. Heedless of the great axe, Thord returned the king's ferocious glare with a glance of yet deadlier menace. He stepped back, but only to fling up Rolf's lance. The Lion faced the Boar—death hovered over both. Not an instant too soon did the Vala spring between the furious giants.

"Back!" she commanded, her eyes blazing. "Back, outlander!—and you, Hoding Grimeye, beware the Orm!"

"The Orm!" yelled Hoding, now mad with rage. "Aside—not Hel herself shall stay my hand."

"Ward!" said Jofrid, and the king's chosen bodyguard sprang to face him with upraised sword and levelled lance. Before them Hoding staggered back and dropped his axe. It was not the menacing weapons,—at them alone he would have jeered. The defection of his henchmen—the sudden proof of the Orm power—struck his savage heart with superstitious dread. Then chagrin seized him,—sullen rage and shame that he should thus stand humiliated before servants and outlanders. He gripped his axe and his evil eyes glared upon us with black hatred. But his gaze fell before the Vala's. Utterly cowed, he turned and slunk away, his shaggy head low between the giant shoulders.

"Thord! Thord!" I gasped; "is it not enough that Thyra is with us—that Rolf lies helpless and Frank is borne off to a horrible fate? You have made this brute king our bitter foe."

"Bera will stand with us," answered Thord.

Jofrid turned to him slowly—"You are right. Bera of the Orm will keep guest-troth even against her brother. But though she were with him, you should go unharmed. Yet beware lest yourselves break the guest-peace. As guests, the Orm wards you; as slayers, he will devour you."

"And Frank?" I questioned.

"Odin aid him!—none other can. When the dwerger swarm from Niflheim, they will fetch him for the Orm-blot."

"Sacrifice!" I cried. "But he, too, is a guest—and the Orm-law—"

"This also is the Orm-law, and the dwerger-right—the over-law: Naught may come between the Snake and his chosen victims."

"We shall see," muttered Thord—"we shall see."

And Black turned his anguished face to us with a look of iron resolve—"We'll see!" he echoed hoarsely.

Somehow the firm words, the stern, set features of the two brought me hope. At the worst, we should die with Balderston—and not as victims,

Chapter XVI
The Orm

We did not long delay among the slain dwerger. At a sign from the Vala, Hervard's torn corpse was raised on a litter of lances, and we followed after the gloomy figure of the king. We could see the giant body bend and sway, the great arms outstretch with clenched fists, as the savage spirit within writhed under the goad of shame and impotent anger. But was his anger impotent? Once in the ravine he halted and stared morosely back at us. Then he wheeled and hurried on as though urged by a sudden purpose.

"Thyra!" I cried. My fear pictured Smider, perhaps even Bera, surprised and cut down, Rolf murdered, and my betrothed dragged off into the Ormvol jungles. I thought the brute king capable of any crime, however black. But I failed to allow for the Orm-dread—the grim terror that stalked in his footsteps and chilled his heart with its clammy touch.

As we approached, we heard the king's voice, harsh and angry, and Bera's, no less fierce. Then we came in sight of the two, and Hoding, with a curse, strode off along the mammoth road.

I need hardly tell with what mingled joy and bitterness I ran forward to the group on the ridge slope, and told of Hervard and Balderston.

They buried Hervard on the ridge crest, and heaped above his grave a cairn of heavy boulders. It was a well-deserved monument, for of all Thorlings the gallant herald most fully possessed the nobler qualities of the heathen Northman. Thord himself brought the capstone of the cairn, a boulder that no two others could lift. As he lowered it in place, Varin turned about to Jofrid.

"Vala," he said, "the mound is built. Shall we now brittle the visund?"

Jofrid shuddered. "No!" she cried, "no; they are cursed! Away from this bloody spot!"

"A litter for the Runeman!" commanded Bera, and while two Thorlings fetched Jofrid's litter, the others made a stronger one of crossed branches. Padded with the tiger skins, Rolf could not have wished for a better couch.

It was a sad journey to Hela Gard. We hurried along the mammoth trail with hardly a stop for food or rest, no longer thrilling with the weird pit wonders,—indifferent alike to the white forests, the blood-red jungles, the fire-flowers, the strange insect and bird forms, the grotesque animals. Once only we turned aside, to avoid a mammoth herd. We did not overtake Hoding.

So sunken was I in the thought of Balderston's captivity, even our approach to the Orm scarcely roused me from my apathy. It was otherwise, however, when, turning down a side trail from the "Fire Street," we passed beneath a cyclopean archway hewn ages since through a lofty ridge of obsidian. We had reached our destination.

On the farther side the ridge walled in with its semicircular sweep a terrace of basalt, level as a floor and polished by the age long trample of savage worshippers. Black and smooth and dully shining, it extended without a break to where, three hundred yards away, its brink overhung the gloomy void of Niflheim. Beyond that unguarded edge rolled the vapours of the nether pit,—the exhalations of Hela Pool, whose blue death-glow nickered far below in the uttermost abyss.

The terrace shone with a beautiful light, like the first rosy flush of sunrise. But its source was not the feeble sunrays struggling down through the miles of vapours. Scattered everywhere over the terrace were half-rotted logs, from which sprang great fungi, loathsome in shape and texture, yet aglow with rosy phosphorescence. They were dwerger tribute to the Orm, borne up from the depths of Niflheim. To the left fire-flowers glowed along the crest of the lofty wall which fenced off the castle of the Thorling king. The edifice was a rude unshapely mass, planned, like a Norman _keep_, solely for its strength as a fortress, and was too commonplace to call for a second glance.

Suddenly Thord and Bera stepped from before me. I looked ahead—and gasped. There in the centre of the terrace lay the Orm, vast, menacing, like Fafnir coiled about his treasure. It was the Orm-crown in green obsidian, but immensely magnified; no longer the repellent toy, but a gigantic lifelike monster that might well awe and appal the boldest of heathen. Men who called themselves civilised have trembled before far less imposing idols.

The hideous snaky form swept around in a circle of seventy-five yards or more, and its spiky back, at the highest, loomed twenty feet above the terrace. The rosy light on the semi-translucent obsidian imparted to its polished green surface a glow like the life bloom of a python's skin, while to our startled eyes the monstrous reptilian head reared above its lofty altar of crimson stone, sentient with malignant being. Even Thord faltered as he beheld the black horror of the cavernous maw and the fiery eyes, blazing with opalescent splendour.

110

In dead silence we followed Jofrid across to the crimson altar. Groups of curious Thorlings stood about the terrace, but all made way respectfully for the Vala and her company. I could not help feeling, however, that the people were unfriendly to us, and I laid it to Hoding's influence. The king, I conjectured, had arrived before us and had stated his version of what had happened. I was at least right in part, for soon we perceived the massive figure of the king, leaning morosely on an axe at the foot of the altar. I noticed that Bera looked warily from her brother to the surrounding warriors, as though she half expected an attack. None came, however, and when we reached the base of the altar, Hoding even gave us a sullen greeting.

Rolf's litter was now lowered, and the wounded Runeman, together with his sister and Smider, stared up, half awed, at the great idol. The Thorlings, Bera among the rest, were bowing low in abject worship of the Snake. Jofrid alone stood erect.

She made the sign of Thor' hammer and another sign more complex; then she advanced straight up the blood-red steps.

After the Vala, without moment's hesitancy, followed Thord and I and Black, all thought of sacrilege, all prudence, swept aside by an overwhelming wave of curiosity. Our audacity called forth a murmur from the Thorlings who witnessed it; but the cry was one of astonishment, not menace. Doubtless they looked for the Orm to punish the sacrilege. But, step by step, we followed the Vala, until we stood behind her on the huge bloodstone slab which supported the dragon's lower jaw.

Oblivious of our presence, Jofrid moved forward to the very rim of the green gums, and her short skirt brushed the serrated row of huge gold fangs. Silent and drooping, her white hands clasped to her bosom, the little maiden stood before the Snake like a victim for the sacrifice. She gave no heed to the threatening snout of the Orn which hung poised above her as though on the point of clashing down upon the frail figure. Wide with a nameless horror, the grey eyes were staring fixedly into the black depths of the yawning gullet.

What was the fearful mystery behind those monstrous reptile jaws—what grisly horror lurked in the black hole from which they gaped?—As we stood wondering, a puff of air, warm and musky, exhaled from the Orm throat like escaping breath. It was the last straw to Sergeant Black. All the latent Voodoo instinct in his African blood aroused. The spirit of savage ancestors whose bones had long since mouldered in their native jungles returned to numb his brave heart and cloud his reason with dread of the Snake. Down he fell

111

upon the crimson stone, grovelling as the dwerger had grovelled before the Orm-crown.

In spite of myself, I felt a superstitious terror creeping over me. It was as though the Orm cast a spell on all around. The place seemed accursed. The musky exhalation of the image sickened me. I remembered the berries' scattered by Varin—the alarm of the mammoths and the visund when they scented the odour. Ah, yes; Jofrid had called it the _Orm-scent_! It was the same smell as this of the Orm's breath, strong and musky. Could there be any relation between the two?—was the fright of the great forest kings based on knowledge of the living Orm? There was something uncanny about it all. The mystery perplexed and daunted me. I looked uneasily about at Black's prostrate figure,—at Jofrid, white and impassive as a marble statue. But the sight of Thord, utterly unconscious of fear or awe, braced me up again.

"Ho, doctor," he called from the side of the slab; "step here and look at the thing's eye. It's the biggest show of all. Must be lighted from within."

I sprang to the Icelander's side, and gazed up at the eye flaming in its green socket like a gigantic fire opal. Thord had spoken truly. It _was_ the biggest show of all.

"Give me a lift," I said, and Thord, gripping hold of my knees, raised me arm's-length above his head. I heard a protesting cry from the Thorlings, but gave it no heed. A thunderclap would not have moved me. I was transfixed—fascinated—by the dazzling beauty of the Orm eye. Small wonder! Behind a crystalline lens, two feet across and of the faintest saffron tinge, there sparkled and flashed with blinding irradiance a great hollow disc of jewels, all cut with a skill that brought forth the utmost of their life and colour. Edge to edge, they encrusted the concave surface so thickly that nothing could be seen of the metal beneath. It was not, however, an indiscriminate jumble of precious stones. Around the edge ran an eight-inch band of topaz and yellow diamonds, encircling a gorgeous iris of emeralds and rubies, sapphires, tourmalines and amethysts. The pupil was a nine-inch circle of black diamonds interspersed with carbuncles.

So overpowering was the light which streamed out from this magnificent reflector, I had to shield my eyes. What a collection it was!—and a second as priceless on the other side!—the saffron lenses, too, sealed in place with black adamantine cement.

Surely, only artificers of great intellect and genius could have conceived and graven this dragon idol!—Who were they?—Perhaps the "sons of God" of Genesis, or rather, a people descended from

112

them—the children of some mighty antediluvian race, cut off by the Glacial Epoch from the rest of mankind. Doubtless they had progressed in art and knowledge down through the ages, until their dark civilisation culminated in this masterpiece of evil imagery. And then—had they vanished?—or had their children degenerated under the blight of their Serpent-god into the brutal dwerger of the nether pit?—But that was a fancy too dreadful to harbour. Extinction was a far gentler fate...Yet perhaps the race had fled from its idol; perhaps in some unknown region of the pit, a remnant survived and maintained the better part of their hoary civilisation.

Dazed, bewildered, my brain teeming with strange fancies, I slipped down on the crimson altar, beside the green Orm jaw.

"Well," growled Thord, "what's up?"

His tone brought me back to the practical world with a start.

"Thord," I said, "the Orm's eyes are simply masses of finest gems—worth millions! If only Frank were here."

"Ay; with Rolf on his legs, and your sweetheart at home," answered the giant, his eyes fixed covetously on the blazing crystal overhead—"we'd get away with those jewels, if we had to blast off the whole ugly skull."

"I'd give the last one for a single grip of Frank's hand. To think of him down there, in the power of those ape things—"

"Steady—steady! There's hope yet. We'll pull him out, and cheat this blasted Snake. I'm going to overhaul everything now—after I give Black a tonic. What's the man scared at?"

"You can well ask!—It's Voodoo. Look at Jofrid. She is in a trance. Are you made of cast iron? This idol is enough to upset any one."

"Black is worse, though. Makes me seasick to watch him. Here, you, sergeant; be a man!—get up!"

In two strides Thord reached the prostrate negro, and thrust him aside with a kick in the thigh. Black let out a howl of fear and doubled up convulsively. But then, seeing what had struck him, he scrambled up, shamed from his superstitious worship. The mock-tragic look which Thord assumed in ridicule of his rolling eyes and quivering figure completed the cure. Black stiffened to ramrod stiffness and faced the Orm with Well simulated contempt.

Thord grinned, and proceeded unconcernedly to try his knife on the blackened tips of the huge gold Orm fangs.

"_Um_—hard metal, doctor—these points. Must be platinum or iridium. The fellow who put up this dragon certainly was a daisy—I'm going to take in the rest of the show."

Sublimely indifferent to consequences, the Icelander drew out

113

half a dozen matches, and, before I could protest, stepped over the Orm fangs into the hollow of the monstrous jaw. The taking of such an audacious liberty with their idol might well have been considered by the Thorlings as a sacrilege worthy of death, but Thord laughed at my urgent demand that he turn back. My uneasiness was by no means lessened when a peculiar cry rang over the terrace, and throngs of Thorlings came running from all directions.

Before I could have counted a hundred, the space around the crimson altar was crowded with men and women. In the rose light of the fungi, I could see that all were intensely excited; yet no weapon was brandished, no cry was uttered. Silent and motionless, every Thorling stood with upturned face, watching the outland giant. Nowhere could I perceive an angry glance, but the flushed, excited faces seemed to quiver with an intense expectancy. Perhaps they thought to Orm spue forth this audacious desecrator.

Somewhat reassured, I wheeled about. Thord had walked down into the Orm mouth to the angle of the jaw and we striking a match on his heel. In a moment the tiny flame flared up, only to be whiffed out by a second exhalation of the musky Orm breath.

"Come out, Thord," I called. The answer was a muttered curse. Impatiently the giant took a step forward; then drew the foot back and raised the heel to strike another match. That lucky change of purpose saved Thord from a horrible fate. At the moment when he pressed the weight on his foremost foot, I chanced to glance down. To my utter amazement, I perceived that the Orm jaw was rising from the crimson stone. Then Thord drew back, and the jaw settled down again with a slight jar. In all, it had not lifted three inches; yet that was enough to reveal the diabolical trap. In a flash I understood all—the Orm-dread, Jofrid's trance, the awful expectancy of the Thorling spectators. But the discovery stunned me. I stood speechless, while Thord, all unconscious of the snare, held up his lighted match and stepped forward to his death.

It was Bera who saved him.

"Seize the jaw, skyfarers!" she roared. "Save the hero...Aside, brother! I fear not you nor the Orm...Come forth, Thord `"

Only just in time did Black and I fling ourselves on the upswinging jaw and bear it down again to the red altar. Behind us we heard the noise of a violent struggle, and Thyra and Smider came bounding up the steps; but we could not so much as glance around until Thord stood safe without the hideous trap. Unshaken by his narrow escape, the giant sprang out past Jofrid's rigid figure to confront the Thorling king. At sight of him, Hoding released Bera from his grasp and glared up in sullen disappointment.

"Well done, Hoding Grimeye!" sneered Thord. "Bright is your guest-troth. You sought to quiet your sister, but for whose warning I should even now be fey."

Hoding scowled and gripped his axe helve, but a deep murmur from the crowd of Thorlings checked his intended attack.

"Well spoken, outlander!" he sneerd back. "The dogwise are ever ready to thrust their witless heads into snares and to cast _nid_ on wiser men. The law of Orm-blot overrides even guest-troth, and Bera has broken that law. Ask the Vala why she failed to forewarn you."

"The Vala is not here, nor has she been," I rejoined."

"You see her body, but the spirit wanders."

"Even as Hoding's faith," added Thord. Contemptuous as were the words, the look which accompanied them was far more scathing. Words and look together might well goad such a one as Hoding Grimeye to frenzy; yet Thord climbed fearlessly down from the altar to grasp Bera's hand. The king was purple with rage. I looked to see him swing up his axe and strike the audacious Icelander. Why he did not, I am unable to say. Perhaps he remembered Jofrid's warning. However that might be, he faced about, with a muttered curse, and returned to his ogre castle.

"Ah, thanks be to Frey!" whispered Thyra over my shoulder. "I trembled for you all, Jan."

"Well you might, sweetheart. We owe much to Bera."

"Let us thank her."

But Bera was intent on more good.

"Raise the wounded Runeman!" she commanded the bearers. "The guests shall have hearth-cheer in the Orm-ring."

"But the Vala's will-" protested Varin.

"I answer for her assent; the assembly bear witness. The guests shall not lie in Hoding's hall. The Orm will shelter them, and his Vala shall judge whether Hoding or I have done wrong."

"The judgment is easy to foretell," remarked a man nearby, and few in the crowd failed to join his hearty salute to Bera of the Orm.

Chapter XVII
Waiting

At its rear the crimson altar sloped down along the side of the

Orm's neck, into a narrow passage between the neck and the incurving tail.

To enter the passage, one had first to mount the high altar, either 'n front or on the side. The passage was without door or barrier of any kind. Doubtless the dread of the Orm had always been sufficient to protect the sacred precincts from unwarranted intrusion.

Rolf's bearers now climbed solemnly up the altar with his litter. At the top they placed him on the slab, and descended again with more haste than dignity. They did not appear to fancy the immediate vicinity of their idol's generous mouth. Even Bera, who followed with Thord, betrayed some uneasiness. She walked quickly around the altar and struck half a dozen sharp blow on a bar of metal that hung at the entrance of the passage. Two men and a woman, all dressed in black fur, shortly appeared from within, and advanced to bow gravely before Bera.

"Who calls the Orm?" asked one of the men.

At the name, Bera raised her axe in salute.

"The Vala and her fellow-farers," she answered.

"All seek the Orm shelter. The Vala is _seeing_. I stand warrant for the guests."

The two men promptly turned back into the passage. They reappeared with a chair made of four visund horns, split lengthwise and woven together. The tips had been left whole to form the legs. This curious seat was taken around and placed behind Jofrid, who still stood rigid in her trance. Then, very reverently, the woman attendant knelt by the girl and bent her slender form down into the chair.

"It is well. Follow!" said the woman, and she returned to the passage. After her walked the two men, bearing Jofrid in the chair between them, and Bera came close behind with her hand on Thord's arm. I turned to Rolf; but Smider and Black already had his litter lifted between them.

"Now, sweetheart," I said, and I drew Thyra's arm through mine. Bowing in response to the friendly comments of the Thorlings below, we brought up the rear of our little procession. Thyra shuddered, and I was not far from following suit, when, passing along the side of the Orm head, we peered into the gloomy recess of the great gullet. We hurried on after the others into the passage. Very soon the other end was reached, and then all thought of the Orm horror was forgotten amid the beautiful wonders of the _Ring_.

Most aptly had I compared the Orm to a Fafnir coiled about

his treasure. The likeness was truer than I had fancied. Enclosed within the coil of the monster body was a space forty feet or more in diameter, paved with bloodstone, and roofed over by a single flattened dome of crystalline substance. The translucent panes of the latter were framed in the interstices of a great gold spider-web. In the centre the dome was supported by a circle of columns no less exquisite than unique. The base of each was a gold Orm, in whose coil sat the point of a great bluish-white egg. From the top of the egg sprang a polished shaft of bloodstone, crowned by a flower bud of gold, upon which a huge bluish-white dragonfly lay struggling, its gauzy wings entangled in the gold spider-web of the dome.

Inside the circle of columns lay an Orm whose back-twisted head spued a stream of pure water into the basin formed by its coil. This fountain Orm was made of the same bluish-white metal as the eggs and dragon-flies of the columns,—a substance so extremely hard and durable that the wear of ages had failed to mar or tarnish its polished surface. I set it down as being some amalgam or alloy of metals belonging to the platinum group.

But we had little time at first to examine this splendid Orm court. Three parts around the enclosure extended a bloodstone wall, whose numerous apertures told of rooms behind. The Vala's attendants passed quickly about the fountain and across to a doorway whose lintel was engraved with the ever-present Orm image. In the many-hued rays of the fire-flowers by which the Orm-ring was lighted, we caught a glimpse of a suite of small rooms extending back into the body of the Orm.

Then the skin curtain of the doorway fell back, as the attendants bore Jofrid within, and our party was left to stare about the court. Very soon, however, one of the men reappeared, and bowing, motioned us to follow him to the left. Bera stayed him.

"Hold," she said; "this maiden is a heart-friend of the Vala. May she not abide with her?"

"The Orm does not forbid. Let the maiden enter," answer the man.

"I give you thanks," exclaimed Thyra. "Doubtless I can be of aid to the Vala."

"But see to your own rest, sweetheart," I added hastily.

"That I will, Jan. So farewell for a little—farewell, Rolf."

With a smile and a bow for each of us, the girl darted in to rejoin Jofrid.

"Now lead on," said Thord, and the attendant led us to the guest apartments. On the way Bera paused to grip our hands, and then, with a peculiar glance at Thord, she turned aside to leave the

Orm-ring. A moment later the attendant waved us through an open doorway, and we found ourselves within a suite of rooms chiselled out of the obsidian body of the Orm.

"So," said I; "the builders of the idol took care to provide snug quarters for its priests."

"That's priestcraft, the world over," replied Thord, as he surveyed the bath and furniture of blue-white metal, the crystalline skylights, and the bloodstone panelling, beautifully inlaid in gold with the figures of pit beasts. Aside from the furs scattered about, a stock of food in the first room, and the fire-flower lamps, there was nothing in our quarters that had not been used by the ancient priests of the Snake.

But a groan from Black cut short our selfish enjoyment of these wonders of a vanished race. Sunken in a half stupor, the sergeant had mechanically borne around the rear end of Rolf's litter; but when Smider gave the word to lower the burden on one of the metal couches, Black roused himself to break into lamentation— "Oh, Lawdy, Lawdy!" he groaned. "Whut's all dis gole an' flum'ry? 'Tain't wuth one ob de lut'nunt's lille fingahs."

"You're right, Black," answered Thord. "But we will have the lieutenant, too, fingers and all. Who knows when they will hold their cursed Orm-blot?"

"In about three score _rings_, so Jofrid stated," answered Smider.

"Good!" I cried. "That will give us time to hatch our plans."

"And for you to tinker my leg, Jan, added Rolf.

"True—also Thyra's arm will be in use again. If only Frank comes up alive from amongst the monsters of the lower pit! However, we must do what we can, and trust to the rest."

"That's plain," grunted Thord, and we proceeded, as a first move, to settle ourselves in our ornate quarters.

This was the beginning of two of the bitterest months of my life. In spite of my love for Thyra, and the great joy of being so frequently by her side, the thought of Balderston's terrible captivity and possible sacrifice was ever gnawing at my heart with cruel sharpness. Nor was this all. We had much to encourage us in Rolf's favourable progress towards recovery; but, on the other hand, Jofrid fell ill of a slow fever that all my remedies failed to affect. In her last trance the girl had again seen Balderston thrust within the black gullet of the Orm, and her grief and worry over his fate constantly aggravated and maintained her fever,—if, indeed, such had not been its source.

Between the Vala and Rolf, I found little time to leave the

Orm-ring, while Thyra, keenly mindful of King Hoding's odious admiration, was only too thankful for the seclusion, aside from her desire to be with Jofrid and myself. Black also hung about the court, too despondent to feel interest in anything but the schemes proposed for Balderston's rescue.

Thord and Smider, however, took a leading part in the frequent hunts organised by Bera for their entertainment, and they allowed no Thorling to surpass them in daring. Hoding usually joined the parties, and, spurred on by jealous hate, contended with Thord in a series of foolhardy dares that appalled even Bera. He drew the line very promptly, however, when Thord proposed to descend Niflheim in search of Balderston. Though the lower pit was known to be accessible near the falls of the Giol, neither Hoding nor Bera, nor any other Thorling, would so much as hear of venturing down into the realm of Hel.

With all our scheming, the only other plan of rescue we could devise was Thord's wild proposal to blow up the Orm. In lieu of anything better, this plan was resolved upon, and I proceeded to manufacture a bomb fully capable of accomplishing the purpose. With sulphur and nitre, both abundant in the Ormvol, I obtained nitric acid, the basis of so many high explosives. It was not difficult to distil alcohol, and gold in the Orm-ring was still easier obtained. The result of my labours was a quantity of fulminate of gold, sealed in a slender-necked vase of the blue-white metal, and packed carefully away in a soft nest of feathers.

Yet the longer I considered the desperate nature of Thord's plan,—the all but madness of demolishing the dreaded Orm before a full assembly of its worshippers,—the more anxiously I cast about for some better scheme. The astounding audacity of the deed might overawe both dwerger and Thorlings, but the chances were far greater that they would tear us piecemeal for the sacrilege.

Quickly the time slipped by, and no more hopeful scheme presented itself. Thorlings began to gather from all quarters of the Ormvol, that they might be safe off the trails before the coming of the dwerger. Then, at last, when only a week was left, I thought of a new scheme, and immediately called a council of war. My plan was to appeal to the Runefolk for rescue.

When I had stated in detail how my scheme should work out, Rolf and Thyra gave assurance that the Allthing would respond to the appeal. Smider was not so certain of this, and Thord doubted that the Runemen could withstand the combined forces of the Thorlings and dwerger. Both agreed, however, that it would be as well to see what would come of the appeal, and Smider eagerly undertook the carrying of our petition to Updal.

"I will go, brother," he said gravely, his hand on my shoulder—"I will go, and I will return,—if not with the Rune host, then alone. The Orm devours us both, or neither."

"Put it broader," said Thord. "It is all, or none."

"Well said," replied Rolf, and he stretched his gigantic frame. "The Orm-blot draws near, but I shall stand with you. Already my strength comes back. My leg soon will be sound as ever."

"I'll die for de lut'nunt," muttered Black.

"Ay; none or all, man,—none or all," repeated Thord. And now, if the Runefolk do not come, Bera of the Orm will stand beside us."

"Good!" shouted Smider. "Whatever comes, we will make merry play for the Snake worshippers."

"I, too, can wield a sword," cried Thyra, and she flung herself into my arms.

So, under plea of benefit to the Vala,—for whom, in truth, I needed certain medicines from the balloon,—Thord obtained from Hoding a safe conduct for Smider. Bera offered to send an escort with him, to guard against the dwerger. But in view of our plans, my sturdy foster-brother thought best to travel alone. Many a time he had braved the perils of the Mark and the Ormvol, when the venturesome hunter had to guard against hostile Thorlings as well as the pit beasts and the dwerger. Now, with Hoding's ring on his finger, the danger of the journey was lessened a good third.

Calm and resolute, the big man took leave of us under the lofty archway of the ridge, and swung away into the jungle at a long, slow trot, tireless as the trail pace of the red beasts.

Chapter XVIII
The Secret

Slowly the last week wore away—a week of maddening inaction, of intense, heart-rending anxiety. Had Balderston survived the perils of Niflheim?—would Smider reach Updal?—would the

Allthing grant our petition for aid?—Such were the questions which racked our brains with constantly increasing severity.

As all hunting had ceased, Thord's only diversion was to wander about the terrace with Bera—a gigantic pair, viewed by the gathered host of Thorlings with a depth of respectful admiration such as might have been aroused by jotunkaki and his mate.

The account of the strange swart carl had already spread over the Ormvol, and great was the curiosity of the ingathering hunters to the son of Surt. As a means of winning their friendship, we persuaded Black to leave the seclusion of the Orm-ring and mingle freely with the forestmen The suggestion that this course might result in benefit to Balderston quickly aroused the faithful sergeant from his despondent lethargy.

The rest of our party, however, kept close within the _Ring_. There was no benefit to be gained by showing ourselves. On the other hand, Rolf's pride would not stoop to the exposing of his lameness before Thorling eyes. To hobble on crutches among the assembled foes of Updal was a humiliation he would fain put off till the last moment.

As to Thyra and myself, we had more than enough to occupy us in the care of Jofrid. Already the poor child was wasted away almost to a shadow. She had had scant strength or vitality to start with, and could ill afford the steady drain on both maintained by the slow fire of the fever. Thyra and the woman attendant nursed her with loving care, and I did my utmost to sustain her with stimulating nourishment. Nothing, however, could stay the ravages of her disease, and at last I began to despair of her living through the Orm-blot.

Great, therefore, was our joy and surprise, when, on the third _ring_ before the opening of the _blot_, Jofrid began to rally with astonishing quickness. I ran in at Thyra's delighted summons, to find our dear patient no longer feverish. Though she was excited, her skin was moist, and the flush on her cheeks had a healthy tinge. Even as I entered, she clasped her hands and cried joyfully: "The Father be praised! He comes—he is here!"

Then, with a sigh like a tired child, the girl shut her grey eyes and fell at once into profound slumber.

"Do not waken her, even for food. This sleep will save her," I whispered, and with a thankful heart, I stole silently out into the court.

I was barely in time to hush the shouts of Thord and Black, who came rushing through the entrance like madmen. A glance at their faces was enough to tell me that something momentous had happened.

I waved my hand towards our guest-room, and sprang ahead. In a moment we had entered the inmost chamber, where Rolf lay asleep. Thord and Black could no longer restrain their shouts.

"Frank! Frank!—De lut'nunt!—He's here, doctor!—Yas; I'se seen him! O Lawdy, I'se seen him!"

"What?—how? Where is he?" I demanded with frantic eagerness, while Rolf sprang from his couch bewilderment. My questions checked the wild gestures of the others.

"_Ugh!_" groaned Thord. "That's the point. He's here on the terrace alive and, I believe, fairly well; but in the midst of a horde of cursed dwergers,—tied up—tied up like a sheep! Damn 'em!—ay, and may Hoding be damned with all his Thorlings!"

When the dwerger horde came pouring through the archway, we saw Frank at once, and tried to reach him, but the beastly creatures stood firm. They threatened us with their shark-tooth knives, and we could not face them alone. We ran to Hoding. Bera joined our appeal to seize the passage and rescue Frank. Many of the Thorlings are armed to guard against treachery. A few hundred mailed warriors could have held the archway against the whole dwerger horde. The van, cut off on the terrace, could easily have been made to yield up Frank.

But Hoding,—curse his black soul!—is half a dwerger himself. He pretended to agree at first; then jeered at us. I could have killed the brute—Black did take a shot at him."

"What!" I interrupted.

"Ay; and missed—worse luck. It was while we were running out to rouse the Thorlings, king or no."

At Bera's call, a thousand or more got together...Too late, though. Already the bulk of the horde had wriggled through on their ape paws.

"They have Frank tied up at the lower end of the terrace. But he's 'live—he's 'live, sah!"

"How'd he look?" I demanded.

"White as a ghost—pulled a heap, poor fellow! Gritty as ever, though. He saw us, and put on a cherky look. Lord! he must have been through a tough deal...If the Runemen fail us, damned if I don't blow this Snake into Hela Pool!"—and in his wrath, Thord hurled a metal bench against the end of the room.

"The fulminate!" I yelled, and my hair bristled with terror. But the explosive was too softly packed to feel the jar. The only shock that followed was the crash of the ponderous bench, bursting

122

through the bloodstone panel. I put it advisedly—the bench crashed _through_ the panelling.

"Hello!" said Thord. "I've knocked a hole in the wall of another suite. The Orm attendants won't thank me."

"No," rejoined Rolf. "There is no suite on that side. We occupy the last at this end. See, it is dark through the hole."

"Then it's a hidden chamber!" I cried; "a hidden chamber behind the panel."

"Hidden chamber?—Run and close the curtain, sergeant. We don't want any one spying. There may be something in this hole."

"True; and being of the Orm, it may be devilish," said I. "Rolf can keep watch in an outer room, lest any one enter. We must keep this secret. It may prove of advantage. Thyra, too, might be alarmed, should she come and find all gone."

"Ay," replied Rolf bitterly; "and I am yet fit only for sitting deeds. Yet that is better than back service. I will sit as warder. Who knows?—you may learn something of benefit to Balderston. Go quick!"

Hastily arming ourselves, we each plucked a living lamp from the fireplants in the room, and crawled through the hole in the broken bloodstone panel. The great slab, which was nearly half a foot thick, overlapped a doorway cut into the obsidian. On its inner side we saw the flanges of massive blue-white hinges. It was evident therefore that the slab was intended as a door. On the edge opposite the hinges were bolts of the same blue-white metal. We did not linger, however, to open them, or to search out the secret means by which they might be moved from without.

"Come on," said Thord impatiently, and he entered the room into which the doorway opened.

"Look out for traps! Remember the Orm," I cautioned.

"No traps here. We're fooled," answered Thord in a disappointed tone. Springing after him, we found ourselves in a small chamber, absolutely bare and without other exit than the door through which we had entered. Walls, floor and ceiling, all reflected from unbroken surfaces the glow of our fire-flowers. We could not perceive the slightest crevice in the glassy green rock.

"Poun' de bench," suggested Black.

Thord at once drew in the heavy metal bench, and began striking the walls of the chamber. Everywhere they gave back the dull sound of solid rock.

"Nothing here," growled the giant, and with redoubled energy, he shifted the attack to the floor. Almost immediately the sound of the blow changed. It rang hollow. In an instant Thord was smiting the spot as though he would break through the whole earth's crust. Like a pile-driver, the massive bench rose and fell, and slivers of shattered obsidian flew out from under the sharp metal edge. A razor-like fragment of the glassy rock cut my hand, and I sprang about with averted head to shield my face.

A yell from the sergeant, half drowned in a tremendous crash, brought me around again. Black was staggering back from a hole which yawned across the floor. Had Thord sprung another diabolical trap of the Orm builders, and this time fallen a victim?

Wild with horror, we leaned over the edge of the pit and flung down a fire-flower. It struck on Thord's broad chest, not eight feet below us. The giant lay on a landing, between the metal bench and the fragments of the shattered trap-door. The fall had stunned him for a moment, but before we could cry out, he grasped the fire-flower and peered forward into the darkness.

"Come down. Here are steps and a passage," he called.

"Then you are not hurt?"

"Not a hair. Pass me my axe, and jump down."

Delaying only to tell Rolf what had happened, Black and I swung over the edge of the hole, and followed Thord down the steps which descended beneath the Orm into the black rock of the terrace. At the bottom was an octagonal chamber, from which passages radiated in every direction.

"Looks as if the whole terrace were tunnelled, if not honeycombed," I remarked.

"Nice place to get tangled up in," rejoined Thord. "Which way shall we turn now?"

"Dis way," said Black. "Dah's runnin' watah down dis tunnel."

"Ay," muttered Thord, and, stepping past Black, he led us along the passage. On either side, as we advanced, our fire-flowers shone through the narrow doorways of monkish cells. In one we found a number of iridium chisels and hammer-heads, lying where some ancient mason had flung them, probably thousands of years ago. Others of the rooms were empty and bare; but the greater number were filled to the height of my knee with a greyish calcareous dust. At one doorway Thord trod on a small object, and picked it up for examination. It was a crumbling human tooth. We understood now. The cells were tombs, and the dust decomposed bones. We had found the cemetery of the Orm builders.

"_Ow!_—An' I tole 'em to come dis way," exclaimed Black. "Let's go back, doctah."

"_Bah!_—they're dead as Solomon," broke in Thord, and he stalked on down the passage.

A few steps further it turned abruptly to the left. We heard the gentle gurgle of water near at hand. A whiff of moist, warm air, musky with the Orm-scent, came around the corner. Cautiously we advanced past the angle of black rock; only to halt again, with stifled cries of astonishment.

Before us was a chamber of surpassing magnificence, a veritable Aladdin's cave. The yellow light of our fire-flowers was caught and flashed back to us in rainbow hues from hundreds of jewelled flowers upon the bloodstone walls and from hundreds of jewelled insects entangled in the gold spider-web that stretched across the black domed ceiling. Below gurgled the water of a gold Orm-fountain; gold divans spoke of luxurious ease; to one side a gold table upbore a sparkling burden of crystal service. It was a sight to satiate the greed of a miser.

But as we advanced into the midst of all this amazing splendour, our eyes were drawn irresistibly away from the gold and jewels, to the far end of the chamber. Facing that part was a semicircle of luxurious couches, arranged as a Roman would have placed them for guests at a private spectacle. Before them, however, was no rostrum for the rhetorician or poet, no stage for the dancer or mountebank. The spectacle upon which the ancient priests of the Orm had gazed from the midst of their wealth and splendour was of another character,—a character that would have delighted Caligula or made vain Nero howl with envy. It was the torture of the Orm victims.

At the far end of the room was a steep incline of the blue-white metal, thickly studded with little sickle-edged hooks. We at first failed to comprehend the purpose of this fiendish device; but when we looked up into the shaft at the head of the incline, the hideous truth dawned upon us. The shaft was of green glassy stone—it was the lower part of the Orm gullet. Through it the victims, cast down by the rising of the Orm jaw, fell upon the impaling hooks of the incline. Then, dragged down by their own weight, they slowly descended the awful torture-slope as the keen-edged hooks tore through their flesh. And below was the death-well, where every victim must inevitably drop from the hooked incline into unutterable darkness.

This, then, was the hideous trap into which Thord had all but fallen—the fate destined for Balderston! Sick with horror, we leaned over the blue-white Orm which curbed the death-well, and the fire-flower dropped from the sergeant's shaking fingers into the black shaft. Down, down, down sank the glowing blossom, as though the well were bottomless. Minute after minute passed,—still we saw the light, ever growing fainter with the distance. At last we could discern only a luminous speck, soon to be swallowed up in the blackness of the great depth.

"My soul! That well is bored straight down to Hela Pool!" I gasped.

"Ay; to drop the victims to Nidhug," answered Thord, as a puff of musky air breathed up out of the black shaft. The sergeant and I rolled back on the floor, while Thord staggered up and leaned heavily against the lofty metal frame which rose at the side of the well. We had taken this for a device to prevent victims from leaping from the incline over the well-curb, and such in part may have been its purpose. But it had another use. Under the weight of Thord's shoulders, the trough-like centre of the apparatus swung out away from the well.

"What's that?" he cried, leaping away. The trough at once swung back to the perpendicular, but not before I perceived that it was hinged on a cross-bar, a little above the middle. In fact, it was nothing else than a huge metal teeter, hanging straight in its frame.

"Push again, Thord," I exclaimed. "See if it won't swing up so that the trough runs into that slide."

The giant sprang back, and shoved out again on the teeter. The hinge above, unused for centuries, screeched shrilly, but the trough swung on, out and upwards, until its lower edge rose flush with the edge of a metal slide that ran along the side of the chamber.

"Ho! I puhceives de pupus," cried Black. "Look up dah. Dat end ob de teetah am right out ovah de hook-slide. Ef a man come down now, he'd whoop down de big trof, an' whiz right 'bove Mistah Thod, into dat upshoot."

"You've struck it, sergeant!" I replied, in wild delight—"you've struck it!"

"Ay, doctor. Here's a draw pin to hold the trough up. But what is it all for?"

"What for—what for! To save victims from the hooks and the well, of course. When the old Orm priests wished to save a man, they had only to swing this teeter, and, instead of torture and the well, he landed in the lap of luxury. Perhaps they used to jump into the Orm gullet themselves, and then sneak out the way we came, to pose as immortals. Don't you see?—Frank shall do the same!—Let a man come feet foremost down this slide, and he will suffer nothing worse than a few bruises."

126

"Thank God!—Back to the _Ring_ now. We must tell Rolf and Thyra."

"But not Bera—yet," I replied, as the teeter swung back; "and—hold on a minute. What's that behind you—the doorway in the wall?"

"Where?—Oh! it's a stairway—steps running downwards. _Ugh!_ it breathes the Orm-scent."

"Perhaps it runs down to the well. I thought I saw spiral steps around the shaft when Black's lamp fell."

"'Twould be just like the fiends who planned these devilish traps. No doubt they wished to get a last look at their falling victims. Let's go down, doctor."

"It may be another trap. Here; let me go first, with a grip on your axe-helve, lest I step into a pitfall."

Thord nodded, and slipping off his cloak, he tossed one end of it to Black. Thus strung out in line, we ventured clown the steep stairway in the heart of the black rock. Twenty steps brought us to a broad, low apartment, crowded with tiers of earthenware jars.

"Treasure!" whispered Thord, and his eyes glistened. But when we broke the sealed sherds, we did not even find gold. Many jars were partly fully of powdery substance; others were empty, with only a thin layer of dry mould in the bottom.

"It is the storeroom of the chamber above," said I; "the cellar where the priests kept their food and drink."

"Well, they left plenty behind; but much good it will do us. The wine is dried up; the food gone to dust."

"Ages ago—so come on," said I, and I passed through the room to a doorway whence a second stairway led on down into the black rock. Round and round we followed its spiral winding, until the eighty-seventh step brought us to a small landing, along whose inner side a bench was hewn in the rock. Opposite the seat our fire-flowers shed their glow out into the shaft of the death-well.

We peered warily around, and at once perceived a continuation of the descent,—a spiral stairway which wound around the circumference of the shaft, into the blackness of the well. It was barely three feet wide, very steep, and, on the well side, without rail or guard of any kind. Cool-headed indeed must be the man who would venture to descend such a stairway.

"Golly! Dat am a laddah to the hot place," muttered Black.

"To the well bottom, at least; and that means Hela Pool," asserted Thord.

"I believe you're right, man," said I. "Doubtless the Orm

127

priests climbed down to see the monsters of the lower pit devour their victims."

"That would be like their devilish tricks. Shall we go on down?"

"What! Haven't you had enough? You don't catch me on that fiends' staircase. It's high time to go back and plan for Balderston's escape."

Half reluctantly, Thord gave up his daring intent of descending the well, and we retraced our course, up through the storeroom and the splendid, ghastly treasure chamber, along the cemetery passage safe back to our own rooms and the anxiously waiting Rolf.

Chapter XIX
Orm-Blot

No longer did our little party loiter about the Orm court, heavy with the lethargy of impotent despair. Whether or no the Runefolk responded to our appeal, we felt that Balderston's rescue was now assured. True, there were yet dangers of which we had knowledge, and it might be that others unknown likewise threatened us; but full of hope, we developed our plans with eager energy.

Rolf and Thyra were at once told of the fortunate discovery of the Orm secret, and when Jofrid, after forty hours of unbroken slumber, awoke with renewed life and strength, she too was told the secret and her part in our plans.

Meantime, Black and I had carried fireplants, furs and a stock of food down into the torture chamber, bringing back with us a slab of bloodstone from the walls, together with some of the iridium hammers and chisels. With the tools Rolf squared the hole in the broken bloodstone panel, and chiselled the slab to fit the aperture with the utmost nicety. When the slab was in place, only two or three faint lines showed that the panel differed from the others.

Thord's work was of another sort. Having assured Bera that all would be well with Balderston, he had spent his time on the

128

terrace, gathering information about the sacrifices, and using all means in his power to win the friendship of the Thorlings. There was more in our scheme than the rescue of Balderston.

But though Thord joined in all the wild Thorling games, and won the rude hearts of the forestmen by his skill and strength, not even Bera herself would aid him to communicate with Balderston. If the dwerger chose to seclude their victim, none should interfere. Such was the dwerger-right—the over-law of the Orm. Yet our desire was keen to acquaint Balderston with our plans; not that they depended upon his knowledge of them, but to save him the agony of falling into the Orm gullet ignorant of the safety below.

Finally, at the last moment, I thought of a means of communication. The Vala attendants had come to summon her to the sacrifice, and we stood grouped just within the _Ring_ entrance, armed and ready for the coming contest. Rolf alone was not with us. Suddenly I thought of the metal bar suspended without the entrance, and a happy idea flashed into my mind. In a moment I was out beside the bar, looking about the terrace.

The scene which met my gaze was such a one as Dante might have beheld in his Inferno. No longer did the fungi shed their rosy glow around. A troop of dwerger were bearing the last one with its log, out through the archway into the jungle beyond. But the terrace was not left in darkness. Over the Orm to the northwards—far out across the abyss of Niflheim, towards the fabled Nida Mountains— flared a mighty jet of fire, glaring blood-red through the vapours. My first thought was that I looked upon a volcano in eruption; yet no rumbling earthquake shook the terrace, no thunder of distant explosions rolled across the nether pit, no molten fragments showered back into the depths. It was rather as though light had been struck to the outflow of some vast reservoir of inflammable gases.

Awed and puzzled, I turned to gaze around. The black terrace, bathed in the lurid light of that gigantic far-off flame, spread out before me like a shelf on the brink of hell. And the fiends were not lacking. To my right were the fallen angels—seven thousand blond Thorlings—women fair and fierce; wild forest children; grim warriors, armed as for battle. At sight of that formidable host, I breathed a swift prayer that the Runefolk had not yielded to our appeal. Had the Allthing so done, they could not have sent all their warriors—and what chance would a small host have against these ferocious forestmen?

Then I repeated my prayer with trebled fervency. For my gaze swept around over a sea of devilish faces—the hideous dwerger

129

horde, thirty thousand strong. From the steel-lined ranks of the Thorlings, back to the ridge and far around to the left, every foot of space before the Orm was packed with a brown mass of beastfolk,—squat, foul, naked, staring in mute adoration at the baleful eyes of the Snake. The stench of the horde came up to me like the effluvia of an Oriental city.

Full of loathing, I drew back, and my eyes shrank from the horrible sight. But suddenly, out in the midst of the ape creatures, different figure appeared. Tall and blond and erect, it rose above the uncouth savages and waved to me with bound hands.

"Frank!" I gasped. In a moment I was at the bell-bar, tapping it with quick, light blows—_dash dot—dot dash—out_ over the silent horde rang my Morse code message "All well—walk into Orm mouth—big fall but safety below—Rolf—"

"I stopped short, for a note deep and menacing rolled up from the horde. It was rather the growl of angry beasts than a human murmur. But Balderston waved his hands again and nodded, smiling. He had understood. I waved back. Then footsteps sounded behind me in the passage, and I sprang ahead to the front of the altar. At its right corner I paused and stretched out my hand.

"Hearken, sons of Thor!" I shouted—"hearken, children of Biorn! From the South came farers in a cloud-ship, from Biorn's Land over the Jotun-realm. Now one of the wanderers lies in dwerger bonds; he goes to the Snake, yet Thor's sons stand smiling!—Hearken, forest bairns—hearken, skraelings!—by Var I swear—naught shall stay the Orm-blot, yet shall the victim go unscathed. He shall live, though the Orm devours him...Then shall the Snake close his maw for ever; the outland victim shall choke the dragon, and the sons of Biorn will bow to the Father."

Swiftly with my upraised hand I made the sign of Thor's hammer, and stepped back past the advancing Vala.

Before one of the astonished Thorlings could find a voice, Jofrid stood before them, pale, fragile, yet commanding.

"Sons of the Snake," she cried, "you have heard the defiance. The Orm's might is challenged,—_nid_ lies on Nidhug! Yet stand still and hearken. The Orm Vala speaks, and this is her rede: From Thor's Land come wanderers, foes of the Snake. They shout in the Orm's teeth, and the Orm takes their challenge. His alone is the contest. Thor meets the dragon,—let men stand aside."

Calmly the girl made the Orm sign and the sign of Thor's hammer, and raising the crown from her head, she kneeled to the

Snake. Then she replaced the evil crown, and rose to face the dwerger horde. The time of sacrifice was come.

"Good—good!" muttered Thord, who, with Thyra and Black, had quietly advanced to the rear of the altar. "You both did well, doctor. We have the Thorlings fixed."

"True, Jan," exclaimed Thyra. "You spoke with the tongue of Bragi."

"And the Vala as a—vala," added Thord. "But what's the fuss?"

"_Huh!_" answered Black. "Dat Hod fellah an' yoh gal am climbin' de steps."

"But they are alone," I said. "Jofrid has sent down her attendants. We can manage Hoding. Bera, of course, is with us."

Ay, my head on that. It's the beast-men we must look to."

"Only four will mount the altar with Frank," explained Thyra. "Jofrid said she could turn back all others. Ah, see! they bring him now."

At Thyra's cry we turned from the Thorling quarter, where the king and Bera were mounting the corner of the altar. Below them, on their right, The dwerger horde had opened to form a narrow lane, down which four human monsters were dragging Balderston by thongs.

Our hearts beat fast with eager excitement. The moment of action was close at hand. As Hoding and Bera paused on the far corner of the altar, and the dwerger headmen dragged their victim up the crimson steps to the Vala's feet, we advanced, inch by inch, to group ourselves beneath the gleaming Orm-eye. Black and I held ready our rifles and revolvers, while Thyra, whose arm was fast regaining its strength, carried both sword and lance. But Thord was our trump card. Though his head was bare, he wore beneath his shirt Hoding's best coat of mail, stolen for him by Bera. With his left hand he leaned upon his ponderous battle-axe; a revolver was thrust in his belt, and from his right hand the heavy vase of fulminate, softly packed about with feathers, swung in a leather pouch.

We had not long to wait. Soon one of the dwerger headmen appeared at the top of the steps, and close after him came his fellows, gripping Balderston by the arms. For a moment they stood before the Orm blinking and open-mouthed. Then all four, with beastly howls, flung themselves down on the slab, dragging Balderston to his knees. But Jofrid, with a sign of authority, quietly stooped for one of the shark-tooth knives, and with it cut Balderston's bonds.

"It is time," said Thord.

131

Black raised his rifle and fired directly across the Orm jaw.

Then Jofrid dashed the Orm-crown down the steps of the altar, and clasping Balderston's hand, walked with him straight into the maw of the Snake. Hand in hand, smilingly they walked past us into the black gullet, and the monster jaw swung up and closed. For a moment it hung there, and then, slowly and softly, it swung down again upon the crimson altar. The gullet was empty. The Orm had devoured both victim and priestess.

Astounded by the Vala's self-sacrifice, for a little both Thorlings and dwerger stood dumb. But as the jaw jarred lightly back in place, the whole assembly burst out into wildest tumult. The battle of the Orm had opened,—and it found us hesitating. There was a hitch in our scheme. I had bragged that the Orm maw would stay closed; yet here it swung down again, ready for another victim. The delay came near being fatal. A yell from Hoding brought the four dwerger to their feet. They turned upon us, howling, and charged like mad beasts. The king, tearing himself from Bera's grasp, rushed after with brandished axe.

"Death!" he yelled—"death to the outlanders! Slay the Orm foes!"

With an oath, Thord stepped back to hand Thyra the fulminate. The quick move brought him blundering against Black. The field was mine. My express brought down the two foremost dwerger; a pistol shot caught the third. But the other was upon me. I dodged down, none too quickly. The howling beast-man leaped over me, and his shark tooth shattered on Thord's steel shirt.

Instantly the long arms grappled; but, with a roar, the Icelander wrenched himself free and swung his hairy foe arm's-length overhead. Forward flew the writhing savage, straight against Hoding's axe, and king and dwerger crashed down together.

"Spare, hero!—spare and slay not! He is my blood-kin!" cried Bera.

"Fear nothing. He shall live," answered Thord, and wrenching the axe from the half-stunned king, he raised him up and hurled him into the Orm gullet. As the jaw swung up, Thord snatched the fulminate from Thyra and waved us back.

"Go hold the passage!" he shouted. "Go, Bera, and trust my word. I stay to smite the Snake."

"We go," I answered, and I drew the others with me.

Already the raging dwerger horde trampled about the altar steps. Only our nearness to the Orm saved us from their rude missiles and stayed their rush. Any moment they might surge up and cut off our retreat. So, with Bera beside us, we withdrew to the _Ring_ entrance.

At the mouth of the passage we wheeled about to await our companion. The Icelander had reached the front of the altar. Huge and grim, he stood out in the lurid glare, his back to the frenzied horde, his eyes fixed on the down-swinging Orm jaw. Calmly he waited, bomb in hand, and a sudden quiet fell upon the howling mob below. At the moment of their wild onset, the dwerger halted with upraised weapons, awed by the grand calm of that giant figure.

Over the Thorling host was sweeping a wave of the old Norse spirit. All their wild viking blood was roused. In that red-haired hero, towering high above them on the crimson steps, they no longer saw a man. It was Thor, the great Ake-Thor of their forefathers, come from his Southland home to destroy the Snake. Half-forgotten sagas of the past rose in their memories. With sudden wild joy they waited the dragon's downfall. Jofrid's rede had borne fruit.

Again the Orm jaw jarred upon the altar. The Icelander raised his right hand and bent quickly forward. The blue-white vase, hurled like a stone from the sling, shot straight between the gaping Orm jaws, back into the recess of the gullet.

A thunderous roar stunned our ears. Fragments of glassy stone whizzed about us. The altar rocked as beneath an earthquake. Overthrown by the shock, we fell prostrate as the vast head of the Orm crashed down upon the red altar, grinding the lower jaw to powder. The whole terrace shook with the concussion.

Deafened, blinded, I staggered up. Beside me lay Thyra and Black, senseless. But Bera sat staring wildly at the shattered Orm.

"Thord," she moaned, "Thord—my hero!"

"Up!" I shouted. "To the rescue! He lies stunned. Follow me!"

With a roar, the giantess roused herself. Up we leaped to the Orm's shattered crest and forward over the broad muzzle. Three bounds carried us to the prostrate figure on the edge of the crimson slab. Over it stooped Bera, her massive arms extended. She clasped the inert body and, putting forth all her strength, raised it upon her shoulders. The giantess upheld the giant. At the sight, wild cheers burst from the throats of the Thorlings. Bera turned to descend among her own people. But I sprang quickly before her.

"To the _Ring!_" I cried. "Back to our comrades!"

For answer the giantess wheeled about and staggered with her burden around the edge of the altar. Then the storm burst. From the dwerger horde came a guttural, droning cry—"_Ut-ut-ut_"—more terrible than any roar. The beast faces grinned with tigerish ferocity.

From end to end the great mob swayed as grain before the blast. Foaming, gibbering, drunk with insensate fury, the beastfolk surged forward. A cloud of missiles darkened the air. In a mass the horde struck the Thorling line, and I saw the grim Northmen reel back as before an avalanche.

But my own life hung on a hair. After Bera I leaped, as the wave of beastfolk surged up the altar step. Already clubs and flints and staghorns showered around us in deadly hail. The foremost dwerger sprang up in our path with threatening shark teeth. We were caught on the side steps between the upleaping fiends and a huge fragment of the Orm's head. Against the leaders plunged Bera with her burden, hurling them back down the steps; but the shark teeth struck quick blows upon her mail and gashed her defenceless limbs.-. Hairy arms reached out to drag her down.

In vain I poured my bullets point-blank into their brown mass,—in vain Black's rifle blazed out in deadly cross-fire. Already Bera swayed with the weight of the creatures who gripped her skirt. I felt a clawed hand clutch at my heel. Shuddering, I sprang forward, and stumbled over the great concave disc of the Orm eye, which had shaken from its socket. My hands struck its rounded edge, and as I rose, I swung up the metal bowl to hurl against my assailants. The crystal was gone, shattered by the bomb, but the jewels yet blazed in the hollow of the disc. As I swung it up, their dazzling light flashed in the faces of the dwerger.

A howl of fear rang in my ears, and the beast-men cringed back before me. My disc was a Gorgon shield. I swung it about, and Bera's assailants shrank away like cowed wolves. The blazing eye cleared a path before us. We rushed on into the passage, the missiles whizzing about our heads. Black stood reloading his rifle. Thyra yet lay senseless.

"Black," I yelled, "look to the girl!"

The sergeant sprang about with Thyra upon his shoulder, and ran through the passage before the panting giantess. I wheeled around with the upraised eye, to cover the retreat. But even as the dwerger leaders shrank back, a club struck my arm with numbing force. The great disc whirled from my grasp, down among the howling fiends. Instantly they sprang around it, and came clambering back up the steps on all-fours, like apes. I grasped my empty rifle in the uninjured hand, and fled. Before me stretched a broad wet trail, whose colour matched the crimson stone. It was the blood that streamed from Bera's wounds. Fatal track!—it would lead the pursuers straight to the secret door. Like red beasts, they would break through and follow us down into the tunnels. Yet the door might check their rush for a time. One of us could stand inside the door when they thrust loose the slab, and cut them down as, singly, they sought to crawl through.

Filled with renewed hope at the thought, I sprang out in the court to help Bera across. Black was already darting with Thyra into our quarters. But midway the giantess reeled and fell to her knees, exhausted by the loss of blood and the weight of her burden. A groan burst from the Icelander as he rolled on the pavement. At last he was regaining consciousness. But the droning "_ut-ut_" in the passage told that the dwerger were upon us. In desperation I snatched the gold bowl from the Orm-fountain and dashed water on both giant and giantess.

"Up! up! To the caves!" I yelled.

Bera leaped to her feet, and then Thord staggered up, dazed and groping. A whirling flint struck between his broad shoulders, and the blow brought back his scattered wits. Together we leaped forward, out of the very grasp of the beast-men. Into our quarters we rushed, and Thord, turning, flung up the ponderous metal table against the doorway.

Only for a moment did the barricade resist the assaults of the dwerger, yet it gave us time to dart through the inner rooms and crawl after Black into the hidden chamber. Panting and nearly spent, we fitted the slab in place and looked about us. By the edge of the floor hole kneeled the sergeant. He was hesitating how to lower Thyra to the landing below.

"Wait," I said, and taking the girl into my own arms, lowered her down to him. "Now," I added, "go quickly to Rolf. We will soon follow."

I turned just in time to see the slab crash inwards and a dwerger hurl himself through the hole. He entered only to perish. Bera, with a swift half stroke, brought her axe down upon his skull. Then Thord caught the heavy weapon from her hand, and called to me: "Bind the maid's wounds, doctor. I will hold the door."

With the words, the axe swung down to split a second dwerger skull. I did not wait to see more. With eager fingers I tore strips from my own and Bera's garments to bind up the long gashes that covered her limbs. Serious as were these wounds while open, no large arteries had been severed, and once bound up, the giantess would suffer no further danger from her injuries. Moreover, she would no longer leave a blood trail for the dwerger. I looked to the door. Already four dead beast-men lay within, and three more had been dragged back by their fellows. Yet another was crawling through the hole.

135

"Ready, Thord!" I shouted, and seizing the fire-flower lamp, I balanced on the edge of the hole to follow Bera. Thord slew the eighth dwerger, and stooping quickly, jammed another corpse into the hole above him. Then, while the human fiends without dragged at the obstruction, Thord and I leaped into the hole and down the steps to Bera.

Before us stretched the passage to the torture chamber, lighted with fire-flowers. We ran down it at once, snatching up the glowing blossoms as we passed.

Chapter XX
Nidhug

Though I knew the bloody pit fiends would soon be following on our trail, I turned the corner of the passage with a shout of delight. Well might I. Behind was death—before me Balderston and my betrothed. The jewelled splendours of the chamber, flashing in the light of twenty fireplants, for a little dazzled and blinded us. Then Balderston's arms closed about me in a fervent hug, and over his shoulder I caught sight of Thyra, seated with Jofrid beside the fountain.

"Safe, Frank," I stammered. "Thank God!—safe out of hell."

"Out of hell!" echoed Balderston, and he shuddered in my arms.

But Thord broke in harshly: "Safe!—who says safe, with those fiends on our track?"

"The crossing tunnels may confuse them," I said.

"No," replied Bera; "they trail like the red beasts. Naught but the Orm-scent can stop them."

"Then down into the well," I cried. "We have no time to lose. I hear the _ut_ drone."

"Ay; down the well, and the Orm-scent may check them," answered Rolf's voice. "Yet what shall be done with the king?"

"He goes with us," said Bera, and running to where her brother lay stretched on the floor, she cut the thongs with which Rolf and Balderston had bound him. Black sprang forward with levelled rifle, but a shout from Thord stayed him. For a moment all was confusion. Jofrid darted to Balderston's side, and I ran to meet Thyra. Then every one rushed, pell-mell, down the stairway,—all but Black, who turned at the second step, rifle in hand, to cover our retreat.

Luckily Rolf had kept wit enough to snatch up a fireplant, and Thord still held the blossoms picked up in the passage. By their light we fled downward, across the storeroom and on down to the foot of the second stairway. As we paused on the little landing, Thyra looked back and caught my arm.

"Where is Black?" she cried.

But in a little the sergeant came jogging down out of the darkness. He had lingered at his self-appointed post until the beast-men rushed blinking into the brilliant chamber. One had run blindly across and plunged headlong into the death-well. The others, smelling the Orm-scent, had cowered back from the shaft and stairway, and gathered, howling, among the gold and jewels.

"We are safe!" said Rolf, and he sank on the bench, rubbing his leg.

"True; for a time," answered Thord. "Yet we have neither food nor drink."

"And the _Ut_ will not leave the terrace till we are starved," muttered Balderston.

"Yet we will die together, Frank," whispered Jofrid, almost joyfully. The rest of us stood in coming through such deadly peril— what a fate!

Black's voice broke the silence with a startling proposal—"We mought go down. Dah mought be grub an' watah down dis debbil laddah."

Thord flung a fire-flower out into the well.

"Look," he said; "look at the death-well and Nidhug's stairway. Who dare follow me down to Hela Pool?"

"I, Hoding Grimeye," rolled out a ready answer, and the Thorling king faced his victor with a scowl of hate. His sister stepped out beside him.

"I, too, will go," she said.

"Couse I goes, Mistah Thod," grunted Black.

"And I," added Balderston, his face deathly pale.

Rolf, flushed and uneasy, sat rubbing his leg in silent chagrin. He could not volunteer. Already he had done fat more climbing than he should. To descend that all but endless stairway was far beyond his power, and he knew it. Yet the boldest hunter of Updal found it very bitter to sit still while others dared.

As for myself, with Thyra's arm about my neck, I was slow to speak, but I had to chime in after the others—"There is no need for all to go. I should be one; but Rolf cannot climb that stairway, nor can the maidens. Some one must stay to guard them, for the dwerger may yet venture down here. Frank is out of shape; besides, he has seen his share of the Niflheim show. He must stay; and Bera, with her wounds,—she also."

"No; I go," answered Bera, her eyes fixed on her brother's scowling features.

"Then Black shall stay."

"Dis ain't no cowahd," muttered the sergeant.

"True, man, and there's plenty of danger here. Begin now by trotting up to the storeroom. We will need a jar, if we find water. There's risk enough for you! Afterwards you will be with Frank."

My last argument clinched the matter. Black grunted assent, and darted boldly up the stairway to the storeroom. We waited his return in silence. Balderston stood with Jofrid's head upon his shoulder, and he made no protest against my arrangement of the party. He had had his fill of the lower pit.

Black returned quickly with two large wine jars.

"_Huh!_" he said. "Dah's no 'Paches come down. But day's raisin' blue Cain in the jewel apahtment."

"Ah—those flowers!" cried Thyra.

"Break them, or take them, darling, the brutes are welcome to all—just so they leave me you."

"True, Jan. What can we want if we have each other?—Yet now you go down this fearful well!"

"De doctah can stay. I'se gwin' 'stead."

"No, you're not. Give Thord your rifle, and take our revolvers. They will be as good, or better, in case the dwerger rush you. Bera will want her axe."

"And I," said Hoding scornfully—"would you send me with naked hands into the den of Nid-hug?"

"Take the axe, brother," answered Bera. "Rolf will lend me his lance. He will yet have his sword."

"Ay; take the spear, and welcome. The maidens are weaponless, but, if need be, they can flee down after you. Farewell, and the Father guide your steps."

"Farewell," echoed Jofrid and Balderston. Thyra clung to me trembling.

"Lead on, outlander,—or shall I go first?" jeered Hoding.

Thord stared back at him and laughed.

"Has the Grimeye yet to learn that I always lead? He

138

follows...Now we go. Be wary, Frank. Cover the fireplant, and send Black up to watch in the storeroom."

"Trust us to be careful. And you, at the well bottom, watch both air and water. Keep close to shelter. In Niflheim Death is winged!"

Thord nodded, and passed fire-flowers to the three of us. The fourth flower he thrust in his belt, and, rifle in hand, he led the way down the perilous stairway. Close at his heels followed Hoding, while Bera came softly after, Rolf's lance blade poised between her brother's massive shoulders. I tore myself away from Thyra, and fell in behind, bearing my rifle and one of the wine jars. The other was forgotten.

Thus began that terrible descent of the death-well, the very thought of which yet fills me with a nausea of giddiness. Down, down, down we climbed, round and round the spiral course,— beneath us the narrow black steps, on our right the clammy black wall, on our left the yawning black shaft. A single misstep, a little swaying out from the wall, a thrust one against the other,—and the luckless one plunged down to certain destruction. Once it seemed as though Hoding extended his axe to thrust against Thord's broad back, and Bera shook her lance; yet nothing followed, and I thought my dizzy eyes had deceived me.

Down, down,—round, round,—my legs trembled with exhaustion; the spiral stairway came writhing up to meet me, like some crazy inverted treadmill. Luckily Thord stopped. He had reached a landing similar to the one above. Even the giants were glad to sink on the stone bench. I dropped flat, with outstretched limbs, clutching the rock, which swayed like the deck of a yacht and threatened to roll me over into the well.

Slowly the giddiness left me, and my legs ceased to quiver. When Thord gave the word, I was able to rise and follow. But the Icelander now took the wine jar, and led the way more slowly. Already, he said, we had descended a half-mile sheer. Therefore, we probably had as much still before us. As it would be folly to arrive at the bottom exhausted and dizzy, to face the unknown perils of the lower pit, he called a halt at every few hundred steps, and each time prolonged the rest until all felt relieved.

Yet it was a fearful descent. Our limbs, overstrained by the constant unvarying effort, trembled after a dozen steps, and our throats, already dry from our exertions in the fight, now rasped with intense thirst. Bera, feverish from her loss of blood, suffered most of all. At every stop she sank on the steps, violently panting, and her tongue showed black between the parched lips. Without first quenching her thirst, she could not now have reascended the well. Our only course, therefore, was to creep on downwards. The bottom could not be far off. We heard low rumblings and a sound like the wash of ripples on a soft beach. A glimmer seemed to come and go in the well below us,—dull red, then bluish, then again dull red.

At last the glow of our fire-flowers shone down on a metal framework. We hurried around the last spiral; only to pause and lap with hot tongues the water which trickled from a cleft in the rocks. The first excess of my thirst assuaged, I drew back a little and perceived that the rock here changed. We had reached the granite base underlying the black basalt. The water, warm and strongly mineral, seeped from a fissure that marked the contact of the two stones.

Once and again we returned to the water; but finally even Bera was satisfied, and we advanced warily down the few remaining steps. The last turn landed us upon a level space, fenced about with a massive grating of the blue-white metal. There we halted, staring about us in dread and wonder. The barred space was a shelf on the granite foot of Hela Gard. Above it the basalt arched out in black overhanging ledges. Below us lay the slimy well bottom, a corner of the beach of Hela Pool, which, on the left, ran up in a gentle slope to the front of the metal grating.

But it was neither at the beach nor the grating that we stared. Between the massive wide-set bars we gazed out on the dreadful sea of Niflheim—the sink of the nether pit. Through the black pall of vapours which canopied the abyss, dimly flared the giant torch on the far-off Nida Mountains, streaked and dull red like the distorted sun of a Silurian landscape. And below lay the dead Polar Sea, its stagnant surface aglow with ghastly blue light.

Presently, out in the still water, we saw bright circles forming, as though unseen hands scrolled the surface with fiery pens. Round and round swept the mystic points, now swiftly, now leisurely,— looping, twisting, crossing, in a maze of tangled figures. Behind each bright point trailed a luminous wake that flickered and slowly died out in the blue death-glow.

Then one of the fiery points glided swiftly inshore around a wide circle. Nearer, still nearer, it curved over the waveless surface. Now it was opposite us, skimming along at arrowy speed. But the pointed triangular plane that thrust up from the water like a gigantic fin stood out clearly to view, bathed in a wash of phosphorescent fire.

"A shark!" muttered Thord. "Here, then, the beastfolk find their knives."

Bera nodded, and answered whispering: "True, hero. I have spoken with the dwerger in sign words. Where the Giol plunges into Hela Pool is a great eddy. There the dead monsters of the deep are washed up on the strand, and there the dwerger gather teeth and bones when the Loki-fowl have feasted."

"The Loki-fowl!" cried Hoding—"ay; the Loki-fowl! Look, skraelings, and tremble."

The king stood with upraised arm, pointing to the shadowy form which hovered, like a monstrous bat, high above the blue-lit waters. As we looked, the great shape dove through the heavy air with the swiftness of a falcon. Down it shot, to sweep close in under the precipice. In a moment it wheeled—it was swooping straight towards us. The great pinions suddenly widened and beat violently—hooked talons clashed on the grating.

I looked at the nightmare shape straining against the metal, not ten paces from us—at the hideous crocodile head, thrust forward between the bars on its undulating bird neck; at the malevolent eyes, glowing in their deep sockets like red coals. The creature's dismal croak filled me with frantic terror. Shrieking, I flung up my rifle and fired blindly at the evil apparition. The distance was not twenty feet.

The roar of the shot rolled along the overhanging precipices like a thunderclap, and with the echoes mingled the shrill screech of the wounded monster. Dark blood spurted over the granite ledge, and the reptile gnashed its hooked fangs on the grating, in vain efforts to reach us. We watched its strivings, dumb, motionless, frozen with terror. Had the bars given way, we should have fallen an easy prey.

But nowhere could the horrible thing crawl through, and the blood streamed constantly from its breast. At last the shaking wings drooped in leathery folds; the long neck swayed and bent with weakness. For a little the curved talons held to the cross-bars of the grating; then their clutch relaxed, and the pterodactyl fell writhing upon the slope. The piercing screech died away in a moan. With a last effort, the reptile fluttered down the beach, and sprawled backwards, one outstretched wing splashing the still water.

Utterly unnerved, I drew away towards the stairway.

"Let us return," I whispered.

"Ay; Godfrey says well," murmured Bera. "We have found water. Let us fill the jar and leave this accursed death sea."

"Stay," jeered her brother. "We seek food also. There lies flesh on the strand. We will go fetch it, and Godfrey will fetch the fangs

141

and talons of his quarry. When he boasts of slaying the Loki-fowl, he will have proof of the valiant deed."

But I was far too terrorised to heed the taunt.

"Let us return," I repeated.

Thord faced Hoding, and laughed as he had laughed in the well above.

"Come," he said. "We go to the feast together—a sweet feast of foul flesh. The others stay here."

Silently Bera and I drew back. The soft wash of ripples came up from the beach. The tip of the pterodactyl's wing was undulating in a slow oily swell. Beside us the two giants glared at each other like foes met for mortal combat, Thord, the true Northman, grimly smiling, the king black with malignant ferocity. Then Hoding's eye shifted with a look of crafty triumph to Bera.

"Well said, outlander!" he answered. "We go forth together, you and I—together down the strand of Hela Pool. Nithing is he who first flees to shelter."

"I shall go first, and I shall come last," rejoined Thord. "We each cut flesh from the carcass, and then turn back."

Without waiting for a reply, the Icelander turned on his heel and passed out through the grating. After him followed Hoding like a menacing shadow, down the slope and straight across the shore to the hideous carcass. Their feet sank ankle-deep in the slimy mud. The heavy water crept sullenly up to meet them with the wash of the rising swell. The luminous ripples already flowed half about the dead Loki-fowl. But, undaunted, the giants pressed on to their goal, and together they stooped to cut the flesh from the reptile's breast.

With upraised rifle, I stood against the grating, in fearful watch lest a second winged vampire should swoop down on the venturesome giants. But the peril lay in another quarter. A gasp from Bera drew my gaze from above. She stared out across the flickering waves, her great form rigid, her flaxen hair bristling.

"_Nidhug!—Nidhug!_" she whispered.

Out on the oily blue-lit water undulated a vast form like a fiery serpent. Along its dorsal spines the water rolled in waves of liquid fire; radiant spray spouted beneath the upreared Orm-head; the beautiful Orm-eyes glowed high above the surging water. We beheld the Living Snake Nidhug, Jormangandir, the father of all serpent myths, the fiery dragon whose image was indelibly stamped on the memory of primeval man when he issued forth from the pit to people the earth.

The Orm was advancing with frightful swiftness. Yet Thord and Hoding, engrossed in their work, failed to perceive the danger. I

142

tried to shout, and could not. Half instinctively, I fired my rifle in warning, and sprang back to reload. It seemed as though the cartridges would never enter the barrels. My fingers fumbled with them awkwardly. But at last they pushed home, and the breech snapped to with a welcome _click_.

I raised my head. Hoding and Thord were toiling hurriedly up the beach, knee-deep in the oily breakers which rolled before the Orm. The whole shore flamed with phosphorescent light. A powerful odour was permeating the dense air, musky and overpowering. It was the Orm-scent. But the mosasaur's swift attack was checked. Though his serpent tail yet undulated in deep water, the gigantic forebody wriggled, half submerged, on the shelving bottom. Still, he slid forward over the slimy ooze with perilous rapidity, gaining seven yards to the fugitives' one.

No sound issued from the throat of the monster. In terrible silence, he glided, snake-like, up out of the boiling fiery water. He was now almost upon the bloody carcass of the pterodactyl. Suddenly the mighty jaws gaped, and the upreared head fell in a lightning stroke. We heard the crunch of shattered bones. The Loki-fowl, crushed to a shapeless mass, was flung carelessly aside. The Orm did not pause to devour dead flesh while there was living prey before him.

Vast, pitilesss, silent, the reptile towered up behind the fugitives. Another forward drive of his serpent tail would thrust him upon them. I rested my rifle on a cross-bar of the grating. The mosasaur swung his head about to gain a better view of his prey. It was my opportunity. Taking hasty aim, I fired both barrels into the great opal eye. The smoke rose quickly, and I uttered a frenzied shout. My bullets had penetrated the horny plate of the eye. Already the brilliant opal hues were fading.

Even in his agony, the mosasaur uttered no cry. The huge creature had no voice. Only a hollow rumbling issued with the foul breath from the great throat. Yet so much the more fearful was his fury. No longer did he seek prey; but victims to avenge his hurt. The yawning maw closed, and the flat snake head threshed down upon the beach in swift terrible strokes. The thud of each blow resounded like a cannon-shot. Mud splashed up black showers and deluged the fugitives. In a moment the Orm would be upon them.

Suddenly I perceived that Bera no longer stood beside me. She was bounding down the slope, with brandished lance. I stood fast, so overcome that I forgot the rifle in my hands. Save for the frightful spectacle before me, my mind was a blank.

The fleeing men looked back just as the Orm-head impended

143

above them. Both turned, with the vindictive fury of cornered rats, and Thord fired upwards, three quick shots from the army rifle. Then he flung himself sideways, flat down in the mud. But Hoding stood erect and whirled his axe up against the descending muzzle. As well might he have struck at a falling rock. The blade met the horny snout, only to be dashed back, and the monster head drove down upon the Thorling king with all the ponderous force of a steam-hammer. A scream echoed the thunderous blow, and before the Orm could lift his head, Bera hurled her lance through the showering mud, into the centre of the glowing eye.

At the instant, out over the Orm's head I saw dark objects shoot down from mid-air and plunge violently into the water. Some struck upon the Orm's body. One burst asunder on his spiny crest. To the blinded reptile it was a fresh attack. Instantly he writhed about and sought to vent his dumb anguish and rage upon the dead bodies which hurled down around him.

Close beside where Hoding had perished something moved in the mud. Bera saw it, and sprang forward. I saw her clutch downward and then she toiled up the slope, dragging after her a great slime-covered figure. Was her burden living?—was it Thord, or was it her brother?

Panting, with head turned to glare at the mosasaur, the giantess ran swiftly up the slope. The light of the fire-flower thrust in her hair fell upon an object that trailed beside the prostrate figure. My heart leaped with joy. That object was a rifle—the body was Thord's, and he was alive!

I reached out as Bera rushed up to the grating, and helped her drag the Icelander in through the bars. She sprang through after the muddy form, and dragged it on to the stairs. There she fell exhausted. I ran on up and fetched a jar of water to dash over Thord. Apparently it had no effect. Terrified, I ran for a second jar, but when I returned, Thord was sitting up.

"Wash my head," he muttered. I poured on water until his white face and red hair showed through the black slime.

"Good—where is—Orm?"

"Yonder in the water—blinded—fighting dead bodies. There is a battle on the terrace. Corpses are hurling down Hela Gard. The first of them fell upon the Orm. That is what saved you."

"Hoding—"

"Mashed down in the mud, as though a pile-driver had struck him. You escaped only by a miracle."

"The jaw edge caught my feet. Are they greatly crushed?"

"I see. With proper care I can save them. But how can that be?—how can we get you up the well?"

"We will see. Now wash me off while I rest...while I rest with Bera—my saviour—my Brunhilded."

"Thord—my hero!" cried the giantess, and she burst into a storm of tears.

Chapter XXI
Dwergerbani

Still that awful hail of corpses drove down through the black vapours, and the Orm, with insatiate fury, writhed among the dead, his jaws dripping red. Only the thought of Thord's helplessness kept me from fleeing in mad panic from the horror.

Then fear lest the monster should turn in his blind struggles and burst the grating brought a clammy sweat to my face. I could stand it no longer. The dread was irresistible. I turned to the weeping giantess, and frantically urged her to action. Not until we had borne Thord up by the trickling spring, safe above all possible reach of the mosasaur, could I think of aught else than my fear.

But relief from the horrid sight of the blinded Orm brought with it reason and somewhat of steadiness. We placed Thord on the steps, and washed the slime from his limbs and body. Then I cut off his buskins and bound up his crushed feet as best I could. They must have given him agonising pain, yet he sat throughout smiling calmly at Bera. When I had finished, he turned to me, cool and resolute.

"Thanks, friend," he said. "You have done well. Now for our next move. I shall start crawling up the steps, with Bera to aid me. You will go ahead—"

"No," I interrupted; "I'll not leave you."

Thord smiled, but nodded decisively.

"Yes," he replied; "you will take up the rifles and the jar of water as quickly as you can. The water you will leave at the half-way landing. Then you will hurry on to the top, and send down Black and Frank."

"Go," added Bera. "He will have me with him. Even Hel shall not part us now."

I gripped the woman's hand and then Thord's, and silently slung the rifles on my back. Half sobbing, I lifted the jar to my shoulder, and with a last farewell, started up the black stairway. At the first spiral turn I looked back, to see Thord, in the light of Bera's fire-flower, clambering up after me on his hands and knees. Then I turned resolutely away from the giant couple and faced the steep ascent. The best I could now do for the wounded man was to obey his instructions.

Yet it would have been foolish to climb too hurriedly. My muscles still ached from the strain of the descent, and hunger brought with it an ominous faintness. Moreover, I was burdened with the heavy jar of water. So I restrained my efforts to a pace slow but steady, and paused a moment at every hundred steps to shift the jar and stretch my legs. Round and round, up the black shaft I toiled, counting the steps before me, making my halts and starting on with dogged steadiness. Fortunately, I was not troubled with dizziness, as during the descent. Had I been, I should never have mounted a thousand feet.

At last, almost spent, I reached the mid landing, and, with a sigh of thankfulness, set the jar upon the bench. The wet dripping down its sides tempted me to drink heartily. Then, greatly refreshed, I stretched out on the rock and gazed back down the well to where, far below, Bera's light, like a glowworm, crawled slowly upwards through the darkness. In fancy, I saw the Icelander grimly dragging himself, step by step, up that terrible stairway. The vision soon nerved my limbs to fresh exertions. I took another drink from the jar, and resumed my dogged ascent.

No longer burdened with the jar, I was now able to go faster, and could relieve my strained muscles by stooping forward on my hands as I climbed. Hundred after hundred I checked off, only to repeat the tally with weary monotony. In vain I stared up the well for a sign of the upper landing. Bera's light was now barely visible to me. Surely the watchers above should see mine, and show an answering beacon. Why did they not signal? Could it be the dwerger had attacked them—had slain the men, and borne off the maidens to a fate worse than death?

At the hideous thought, vigour returned to my trembling limbs. Despair gave me back all my strength. I bounded up the narrow steps as though my feet were winged. Once—twice—I dashed up around the spiral ascent, staring wildly above me into the darkness. Suddenly my upraised foot struck empty air. I stumbled

146

and pitched forward headlong. Half stunned, I felt myself roll over on a level surface, and one leg swung out into space. Shuddering, I drew back the limb and sat up. My fire-flower glowed around me upon the upper landing—and it was empty!

"Gone!" I cried. But I should have revenge on the brute fiends. Confused sounds echoed down the storeroom stairway, and I caught the faint glint of reflected light. Hastily I threw down Black's empty rifle, and loaded my own. In another moment I was running madly up the stairway.

Now I was at the storeroom door. Lights flashed before me. With a yell, I sprang forward like a Lascar _amok_. But something struck aside my rifle. My breast met a breast covered with shining ring-mail, and great arms seized me in a bear-like hug. I glared up into the face of Smider.

"Safe!" shouted my smiling captor. His voice sounded rumbling and far away. I looked dully past him to where Balderston and Black stood before a group of armed warriors. They were all swaying strangely the whole room was reeling and whirling about me. I stammered incoherently something about Thord. Thyra's image seemed to flash up in the darkness and disappear. A voice called faintly in the distance: "Air—we will bear him up—the rest go on down."

Then came blackness, full of hideous fiery shapes. The shapes whirled round and round—over and over—it was a cataract of flying Orms—no, it was Hela Pool, roaring in fiery waves against the foot of Hela Gard. The flaming breakers dashed mountains high. In a moment they would overwhelm me with a deluge of eternal fire!

* * *

"Not here, Thyra. He should have quiet."

"Here, I say. Put him down. He was mad with the horrors of the well. The battle will turn his thoughts."

The voices were half drowned in a storm of fierce sounds. It was not the roar of Hela Pool that I heard, but the din of battle—shouts and shrieks, the whir of missiles, steel and stone clashing, and,—under all, pervading all, monotonous and terrible,—the droning "_ut—ut—ut"-_

A gentle clasp drew my head upon a soft, heaving bosom. I opened my eyes. They looked up into the anxious face of my betrothed.

"Jan!" she whispered, as she bent to kiss my forehead. Then— "Look at the battle, dear one."

Jofrid and Rolf drew aside from before me, and the warriors

147

who stood about us with upraised shields opened their ranks. Smider was gone. We were grouped on the shattered head of the stone Orm, and below on the corpse-heaped terrace, not a stone's throw away, raged a deadly battle. From the half-ruined outwall of Hoding's castle across to the altar, from the altar to the brink of Hela Gard, stretched a battleline of steel-clad warriors,—five thousand blond Runemen,—penning the dwerger horde in the outer corner of the terrace.

Behind the broken wall crouched the remnant of the Thorlings, barely able to hold the barrier against the mad assaults of the dwerger. But the beast-folk had paid dearly for the victory that was theirs before the Runemen came. Half the horde lay heaped with the slain forest-folk on the black plain. And now the Rune warriors girt in the rest with a band of steel. Here were no weak children, no unarmed women, but strong men, skilled in arms— viking sons clad in full war gear, wielding blades which shore with ease through wood and stag-horn.

Even Caesar's famous tenth legion never withstood the assaults of the impetuous Gauls with more perfect discipline. Despite my ignorance of tactics I could see that every movement was the detail of a skilful battle plan. I looked for the hersir,—the cool, adroit, captain in the rear, directing the blue-cloaked udallers. But nowhere in the fierce tumult could I distinguish any commander. When, now and again, a udaller raised his horn, only his own fylke responded to the signal. And yet it was evident that each company was but carrying out a part in some general purpose.

"Who is the hersir?" I asked, but no one knew.

Steadily, relentlessly, the Runemen pressed upon the maddened beast-men. The whirring flints dropped harmless from their upraised shields. No stag-horn could penetrate the Runemen's ring-mail, no club beat down their guard. The shark-tooth knives shivered like glass against the steel. The wolf-leaps of the beast-men were met by slashing strokes, each a death-blow. From behind, bowmen poured a stream of war arrows into the thick of the brown mass.

Step by step, the Rune warriors closed in, trampling over the bodies of the slain. Their left wing thrust itself forward along the Thorling wall, until it, too, touched the brink of Hela Gard. The steel line was now a crescent that enclosed the horde in a dense mob between its curve and the edge of the precipice. The fighting raged yet more fiercely.

Steadily the crescent was contracting upon the penned beast-

148

folk and pressing them back. The terrace was paved with brown bodies.

Suddenly skalds ran shouting along the rear of the Runemen. The warriors in the front rank shortened their weapons and raised their shields before their faces. Then, shoulder to shoulder, breast to back, the whole line surged forward. The fore rank struck against the crowded dwerger. The Northmen behind bent forward and pushed heavily upon their comrades. Even the bowmen joined in, every man straining to the utmost of his strength.

There was little more striking. Dwerger and Northmen were crushed together, breast to breast. Beast-men, pierced through by Norse steel, stood dead between the opposing lines. Men, half suffocated by the pressure, reached out upraised arms to clutch foes by the throat. Here and there a Northman of greater stature rained down death into the solid mass before him. But nowhere did the stricken sink from view. All were upheld by the pressure about them. The jam was terrific. All shouting ceased—even the droning "_ut_" died away. The dwerger, with the precipice behind them, strove desperately to resist the fatal thrust. For a little the line stood still, neither gaining nor giving way.

But the weak-loined beast-men could not long withstand the tremendous heaves. Their resistance weakened. The jam swayed a little; slowly the horde began to give back—then more quickly. Shrieks and howls of brute terror broke forth. The dwerger, hurled relentlessly backward, poured in a terrible cataract over the brink of Hela Gard.

* * *

"The hersir!"

All the warriors near us faced about, with saluting weapons. We followed their movement, glad to relieve our eyes of the dwerger destruction.

From the passage the hersir in his gorgeous panoply was advancing alone, with dignity, and yet almost at a run. We soon saw that it was Smider. His glance, alert and commanding, swept the terrace and fixed upon the remnant of the horde, crumbling fast over the edge of the precipice. A grim smile lighted his stern features. He turned quickly in his course and bounded up beside us. At a word from him, the saluting warriors rushed down to join their comrades. We had no further need of a shieldburg.

In an instant I was up to clasp my foster-brother. Flushed and eager with heartfelt joy, he crushed me in a second bear-hug; then, kneeling, he kissed the foreheads of the maidens.

"Good tidings, brother!" he shouted. "I hurried before, to join the battle. The others come after with Bera and the Hammer-drott."

Thyra clasped the hersir's hand.

"We thank the Father," she murmured. "He brought you safe to our rescue."

"It was almost too late," said Jofrid, and she gazed longingly at the passage.

"True, brother," I added; "the maiden speaks true. But for our learning of the Orm secret, we should all have perished."

"That I feared. Yet none can be blamed for loitering. I journeyed with all speed to the Giol, and there I found the bridge strand cast loose by the dwerger. So I must travel far around by Vergelmer. Yet I reached Updal in good time, and the Allthing speedily sent me forth, hersir of the host. We marched at hunters' pace, and should have covered the journey a _ring_ sooner. But in the heart of the forest, mammoth herds blocked the Fire Street. We had to build rafts and pass around through the swamps. Then we rushed on, and all else fled before us. We halted a little way off, while forerunners went forward to spy out the terrace. They brought tidings of the Thorling battle, and we, greatly rejoiced, rushed in to aid the forestmen. But my heart turned to water, when, charging through the archway, we beheld the Thorling slaughter.

"I thought you had perished. A Thorling woman told how the beast-men had followed you into the Orm-ring. We drove the horde back beyond the altar, and, mad for vengeance, I led a chosen band into the Orm-ring. Beast-men streamed up from the Orm-caves. We ran down whence they came, slaying all as we passed, and so chanced upon the maidens and Balderston and Rolf, down below the Fafnir cave. The swart carl had but remounted the stairway to tell that your light was near, when you rushed after."

Chapter XXII
The Pyre

Two _rings_ had passed, and the Rune host yet lingered on the blood-stained terrace. But Fafnir had yielded up his treasure. Hundreds of art-lovers, skilled and strong, had, after careful measurements and numbering, removed all the panes of crystal glass from the dome of the Orm ring. Others removed the supporting columns, and slung their divided sections to poles, ready for transport. Even many of the blood-stone panels, selected for the beauty of their gold-inlaid figures, had been torn from the walls of the Vala's bower. The purpose was to reconstruct the dome in Biornstad, with a bronze frame.

The massive gold spider-web was left in place, for not all the host of Updal could have borne it away. The spider-web of the torture chamber, however, with its wondrous burden of jewelled insects, was cut out in sections and brought up, together with such of the lighter furniture and exquisite jewelled flower panels as had escaped the insensate fury of the dwerger. Even more precious than this were the jewelled bowls of the Orm eyes.

When at last the stream of treasure ceased to flow out from the Orm-ring, another stream poured back in. Thousands of waiting workers crowded through the passage with burdens of white brush and crimson logs. Half up to the gigantic gold web of the dismantled dome they heaped the court with fuel. Then others followed, bearing sorrowfully the bodies of the Thorling dead. Last of all, three hundred slain Runemen were carried to the great pyre.

As the last corpse was born up the red altar, we grouped ourselves about Thord on the shattered Orm-head. Wan and hollow-eyed with suffering, the giant lay stretched upon a litter, one splint-bound ankle extending beyond its footless mate. Henceforth he was to be a cripple. The utmost of my skill had barely saved the other foot. Yet the man's indomitable spirit rose above the loss and the anguish of his injuries. Already he was planning his work Hammer-drott—such time as he had thought to spare from Bera.

His eye strangely softened, were now fixed upon the Thorling princess, who stood bowed with grief, in the midst of her people,—the scant remnant of the once powerful forest-folk. Smider, near by, was addressing the Thorlings, and the pauses in his eloquent speech were filled with the clash of shields from the encircling bands of Runemen. He was urging the forest-folk to become children of the Rune.

A tremendous din of steel and welcoming shouts followed the hersir's speech; but the Thorlings stood silent and gave no sign until Bera had spoken.

"Warriors of the Rune," she said, "in the name of a harried and broken host, I give thanks for this offer. If I know the hearts of my people, I can answer that no Thorling craves to linger in wretched solitude on the bloody plain where his kin and folk fell to the ravening beast-men. It is my wish that they accept your generous offer; yet they are a free people, and now without a chosen leader. Set up the Arch of Odin, and such as are willing will pass under."

"How of yourself, maiden?" questioned Smider.

"That is yet to be seen, replied Bera, and she stared about her with uncertain look. Thord groaned at the answer;—what of her love, if she doubted how to act? I felt Thyra's hand tighten its clasp, as her heart throbbed in sympathy with the Icelander's anxiety. But Jofrid turned from Balderston with a smile of bright promise.

"Have no fear, Smiter of the Snake," she said. "Though despair has seized upon Bera's heart, all will be well with you."

"That I doubt," muttered Thord, and he stared gloomily down upon the terrace, one huge hand tugging at his fiery beard.

From among the Rune warriors, four skalds with headless spears had stepped forward and set up the shafts on the terrace, the pointless tips bound together by a peace-thong. Already the Thorlings were forming in line to pass beneath the Arch of Odin. But Bera did not lead them. For a little she lingered beside a group of maimed warriors who stood, stern and silent, eying their departing fellows with ill-concealed contempt. Soon, however, she turned from these grim watchers, and passed quickly by the Rune host and on across the terrace to her brother's castle. Through the broken gateway of the out-wall, we could see her turn at the entrance of the keep and gaze back at us. Then she disappeared in the gloomy recess of the massive arch.

What might be the woman's purpose? We stared across at the huge pile in silent anxiety. Presently Thord uttered an exclamation and pointed with shaking finger at the castle tower.

"Smoke!" I muttered.

"The castle is afire!" cried Balderston. "She has set fire to her home. Let us hasten to drag her cut!"

"Stay!" commanded Jofrid. "There is no need. She comes of her own will. She has another thought than that."

"She comes!" repeated Thord, and we saw the woman rush out upon the terrace, a blazing torch in her hand. Behind her volumes of black smoke poured from every door and loophole of the castle.

"Now I know!" exclaimed Thyra. "She is minded that none shall linger in this dreadful place. All must now come with us to Updal."

Thord shook his head.

"Yonder are warriors who will not come," he said. "Look; they

152

laugh to see the smoke roll out from the castle; yet none pass through, the spear-arch. All others have gone under—they still stand apart—and Bera joins them!"

"You have read their purpose aright," replied Jofrid. "Now they turn to climb the altar, and Bera follows with her torch."

"Harken!" whispered Thyra, and she drew close to me, shuddering.

Slowly the maimed warriors were mounting the crimson steps, their grim faces alight with wild joy; and as they passed to their doom, they chanted exultingly a fierce song of Ragnarok. One by one, they clambered up the altar, through the passage and up the corpse-strewn pyre, and as each man reached the summit of the ghastly heap, he flung himself upon his sword.

Last of all came Bera, in one hand a sword, in the other the blazing torch. She looked neither to one side nor the other. Her eyes were fixed and staring, her powerful features rigid with stern resolve. Already she was passing us without a sign, when Thord raised himself up on his litter and cried out in bitter despair: "Bera, stay!—Turn to me, Bera!"

The woman faltered, but she did not turn.

"I go to my people," she answered mournfully. "The slain call upon me to join them."

Thord raised his clenched fist overhead.

"Come, then, and bear me to the pyre," he commanded. "Does Bera believe I crave this life—when she goes hence? Come, dear one! You bore me from the dwerger,—bear me now to the pyre."

The giantess panted. Slowly she turned about until her grief-stricken gaze rested upon the Icelander.

"I cannot do your bidding!" she cried. "You have much to live for. Before you is power, and renown greater than yet you have won. But I—I am the last of a broken people. The heroes call me to join their band. Why should I falter?—Where the grey leaders have shown the way, should the queen of the pack shrink to follow? And what is this life, that I should fetter my free spirit with the bonds of the Rune? Can I, Bera of the Orm, stoop to Odin's Arch?"

"Talk not of Rune bonds," answered Thord, his voice full of scornful reproach. "It is another cause that turns Bera from love and life. Rather than wed a maimed man, she seeks death."

Beneath the sting of the cruel taunt, the woman quivered as though Thord had struck her. That he should doubt her love was more than she could bear. With a wild cry, she flung down both torch and sword, and sprang to the side of her hero. Kneeling, she bowed her head beneath his extended hand, and her bosom heaved with bitter sobs. She gave no heed to Jofrid's quick cry—"Take heart, Bera. There is great joy before you."

But then Thord's great arms drew her to him, and she was comforted.

"Bera is fettered, even as another one I know," I whispered, and Thyra hid her face against my shoulder.

"Dis heah coon's mighty 'spicious dat 'gratulashums am in o'dah," observed Sergeant Black. Apt as was the remark, none answered. Our attention 'as fixed on Smider.

The hersir came quickly up the altar steps to the spot where Bera's torch lay flickering.

"Bear up the Hammer-drott," he commanded. Rolf and I grasped the foot of the litter, but Bera herself took the head. As we aised our burden, Smider whirled the torch about his head, and handed it, flaring, to Thord.

"The host forms in marching order," he said. "All now awaits the end. Take the brand, Smiter of the Snake; for yours is the honour of lighting the pyre."

The Icelander hesitated and glanced around at Bera. But at sight of her face, he grasped the torch and drew himself up in the litter. His deep voice rolled out over the terrace, mellow with joy and triumph.

"Behold, Men of the Rune!—behold how I honour the Snake! The hand which has smitten the Orm, now makes him an urn for the heroes!"

With the words, the torch was hurled from the giant's grasp into the brush-strewn passage. Where it fell flames leaped up; then whirled forward as the draught swept them down the passage in under the pyre.

Smider raised his sword overhead, and the host, with a joyful shout, wheeled about for the homeward march. Fylki after fylki, the spoil-laden warriors swept past below us, across the terrace and out through the lofty archway.

From the rearmost company warriors chosen to bear Thord's litter turned aside and mounted the altar. Already they had taken their burden from us—they were wheeling to descend, when, without a moment's warning, blank darkness fell upon the terrace. The great torch on the Nida Mountains was extinguished.

Bewildered by the sudden change, we stared blinking about us. Pale tongues of flame were flickering up from the pyre, and across the terrace the fire shone with a lurid glare through the smoke of the burning castle, but neither lightened the dense night.

154

Half frightened, we sought to grope our way down from the altar, but Bera called upon us to stay.

"Hold!" she cried. "There will soon be light."

Expectantly we turned to the North and peered out into the blackness that rose like a wall from the abyss. We had not long to wait. As suddenly as it had vanished, the far-off torch flared up again through the night with redoubled brilliance, but now its hue was no longer crimson,—it was as vividly blue as the blue coruscations of electricity.

Spellbound by the mystery, we stared in mute wonder until Jofrid broke the silence.

"The _blood-rings_ are ended!" she cried, and as the flames of the pyre roared aloft between us and the blue light, the girl drew herself away from Balderston's arms. Swiftly the flames streamed skyward, a mighty, whirling pillar of fire. We shrank back, but Jofrid faced the roaring pyre with all the calm dignity of her valaship. A glad light shone in the grey eyes as their gaze followed the flames towards the mist-veiled heavens, and her freed spirit voiced its happiness in a chant of solemn joy—

"Behold the doom of the Snake! The power of the dragon is broken. No more shall men bow to the evil— Nidhug has torn his last victim.

"Up from the pit wends the Rune host, Back to the sun and the green-land; Out of the evil and darkness, Up to the land of the Father."

The End

www.ingramcontent.com/pod-product-compliance
Lightning Source LLC
Chambersburg PA
CBHW050952120626
46552CB00001B/496